WICKED PRINCESS

KNIGHT'S RIDGE EMPIRE #2

TRACY LORRAINE

Editing by Pinpoint Editing

Proofreading by Sisters Get Lit.erary

Photography by Wander Aguiar

Models - Joey Lagrua & Kennedy Moran

CHAPTER ONE

Sebastian

As was inevitable, the van rounds a corner and disappears. My chest burns as I try to catch my breath, my legs are not enough to keep up no matter how badly I need to get to Stella.

I'm not enough.

Admitting defeat, I allow my legs to come to a stop. Bending over, I rest my hands on my knees and fight to drag in the air I need.

My eyes burn from the exertion and lack of oxygen, but that's not all of it. And as a giant lump of emotion crawls up my throat, it becomes harder and harder to deny.

A hand landing on my shoulder scares the shit out of me.

In my need to fight, I spin around, pulling my fist

back, ready to attack whomever it is. But the second my eyes land on Theo, all the fight drains out of me.

His chest is also heaving, sweat beading at his temples as he stands before me with his brows pulled together in concern.

Glancing over his shoulder, I find Alex, Nico, and then finally Toby and Galen approaching us.

"Who the hell was that?" Galen pants, desperately trying to catch his breath.

I probably should take notice of the fact that he's struggling more than the rest of us. But I don't. My anger doesn't give a shit about his age.

I surge forward, my body acting on instinct.

"This is all your fucking fault." My fingers curl once more, but this time, I manage to make the hit.

My fist connects with his face. A painful crunch hits my ears a beat before he stumbles back, pain etched into every inch of his face as blood pours from his nose.

It should stop me.

It doesn't even come fucking close.

I go at him again, my fists raining down on his face, as I spew my hatred at him. I don't even know what words fall from my lips. I'm totally lost in my anger, in my past, in my loss and grief.

Knowing how badly I need this, my boys give me a couple of minutes before large hands wrap around my upper arms, hauling me back from a bloody, broken Galen.

The sight of his messed-up face should make me feel something. A sense of vengeance. Relief.

It doesn't.

The only thing that's now flowing through my veins is desperation.

"Okay, Seb. You made your point," Theo barks in my ear as they continue to hold me in fear of me going off again if they release me.

With Toby's help, Galen sits, wiping at his nose and split lip with the back of his hand.

"Who has her?" I spit, taking a warning step toward him, although I have no intention of hitting him again. Not yet, anyway.

"I-I don't know," he stutters as he looks down the street toward where the van disappeared. "Fuck. This is my fault."

"I'm glad we agree on something."

Shaking the hands off that are still holding me, I drag my fingers through my hair and turn my back on the evil cunt on the ground. Not only did he ruin my life, my family, but he's just single-handedly fucked up his own.

"FUCK," I roar, my grip on my hair tightening until it feels like I'm about to rip it out.

"We'll find her," Theo says, stepping up beside me. "We'll fucking find her, okay?"

Turning to look at him, I see a fierce determination in his eyes that settles something inside me.

I nod, unable to do anything else.

"It'll have been the Italians," Alex adds, forcing me to remember the reason I made Theo chase Stella down in the first place.

The image of her walking out of that cinema with his arm around her shoulder.

My knuckles split open once more.

Landing that punch felt almost as good as the one which just broke her father's nose.

"Let's go home. Clean up. And I'll talk to my dad. Get the feelers out for a sign of her. We'll get her, bro. Okay?"

I nod once more and take off back toward Stella's house, only pausing to spit on her father, who's still sitting on the pavement trying to stem the flow of blood from his nose.

"You're going to regret ever being alive by the time I'm done with you."

"Sebastian, please," he begs, as if anything he could say would make this situation any better.

I take a step forward, but Toby steps between us.

"Haven't you got in my way enough recently, Ariti?"

"Fighting isn't going to find her," he hisses, getting right in my face. "And I need her back just as badly as you."

"She's fucking mine and you know it." I stand nose to nose with him, more than happy to prove my point in a more painful way.

"Yeah, that's become abundantly clear," he mutters, making my brow furrow.

Not having the patience for him to get all cryptic on me, I turn my back on him and storm away.

The walk back to Stella's takes longer than I was expecting, showing me just how far I really did chase her in the hope of helping.

You're a fucking idiot, Seb.

4

Even if I did catch that van, there's every chance she'd have rather stayed inside with the hooded guy who's clearly as interested in our princess as I am.

A growl rumbles in my chest as I continue forward, the footfall of my boys slightly behind me filling my ears.

"Why did she run from the house?" Alex asks when we finally get into Theo's car and close the doors behind us.

When neither of us responds, he continues.

"She was inside with Galen and Toby. What could they have possibly said that would make her run like her ass was on fire?"

"The truth."

"Stella's not an idiot, Seb." My teeth grind at his words. "She'd figured us out. It's got to be more than just the Family."

"Just drive," I snap when Theo starts the car but just sits there. I don't want to see either Galen or Toby again for a while.

Without saying a word, Theo backs out of the drive and heads toward his house while my head spins with possibilities and my stomach knots in fear. If someone hurts her then they'll have signed their own death certificate, because I'll happily do whatever it takes to watch the life drain out of their eyes for hurting something that belongs to me.

The silence in the car is almost unbearable as I clench and unclench my fists, watching the skin crack open and revelling in the pain that comes with each movement.

5

I'm out of the car the second Theo pulls up in front of his place, and without so much as glancing at the mansion, I storm into the coach house and run up the stairs, taking them three at a time.

I blow through the place like a tornado. Swiping the fresh bottle of Jack that Theo's housekeeper must have replaced since the other day, I make my way through to my bedroom, swallowing down shot after shot as I go.

I barely taste it. I don't even feel the burn. What I do get, though, is the warmth in my belly, a sign that the numbness I crave is almost in touching distance.

Stripping out of my clothes, I step into the shower and tip my head back, letting the water rain down on me.

Where are you, Hellion?

Who took you?

I stand there until my skin starts to wrinkle, and it's only when my bedroom door flies open and footsteps and voices fill the space that I finally turn the shower off and grab a towel.

I find Theo and Alex lounging in my room as if it's just another normal day. As if the girl I... As if our princess hasn't just been swiped from under our fucking noses.

"Boss hasn't heard anything, but he's putting the feelers out. He's got guys trailing the Italians, so if it's any of them, we'll find out."

"And if it's not? Then what the fuck do we do?"

They both stare at me like I've suddenly sprouted a second head.

"What?" I bark, walking to my bed and grabbing

the discarded bottle of Jack. I twist the top off and take another swig.

"Ready to admit that she's more than just a revenge plan yet?" Theo asks.

"Is this really the fucking time?"

He shrugs.

"You're so fucking gone for her," Alex mutters, irritating me almost as much as the first time he said it.

"What the fuck does it even matter?" I snap, throwing my arms out, successfully sloshing Jack all over Theo's cream carpet. "She's fucking gone. And I hardly doubt that guy was taking her somewhere fucking fun."

"We'll find her," Theo repeats for the millionth time.

"Have faith, bro."

"The only thing I've got right now is this," I say, waving the bottle around in front of them before drinking more.

"That's enough," Theo barks, ripping it from my hand and standing toe to toe with me. "When we find her, she needs you fucking sober. So get a fucking grip."

His palm slaps me across the head and I growl, closing the space between us, my chest bumping against his.

"Back the fuck off, Cirillo," I grit out.

"Seriously?" Alex barks. "Because what the princess needs right now is you two getting into it."

His words have their intended effect and I cool off instantly.

He's right. Dammit.

"Thank you," he mutters when I stand down. "Now put some fucking clothes on and wait, or hell, go out looking for her if you want. But fighting is gonna get you nowhere."

Dragging some clean boxers on, I find some sweats and a hoodie before falling back on my bed and staring up at the ceiling.

"Someone ring Toby and find out what the fuck happened."

"I've tried," Theo confesses. "He's not answering."

"Probably at the hospital with Galen getting his nose fixed."

"Fucker deserved it."

They both fall silent. I'm not sure if that's because they agree or they just don't want to piss me off more than I already am.

Squeezing my eyes closed, I try to focus, to think of anything that might help us.

Italians aside after what went down this afternoon, who would want her? No one knows who she is. Do they?

The guys order some food, and we just sit and wait.

I fucking hate it. I could go out and search. But we're in London; where the fuck would I even start?

I need to be smart. I need to wait for news from Damien. Hell, even Galen, because if that motherfucker knows something and doesn't tell us, I'll make sure he never has the chance to put her in harm's way again.

I don't eat any of the food the guys order. I don't even leave my room. Instead I just lie there with my phone on my chest, waiting.

I've called Toby, but just like Theo, it rang off to voicemail. I've left enough messages for him to know that he really fucking needs to call me back. But he never does.

I have no idea what the fuck he's doing, but there's no fucking way it can be more important than finding our princess.

It's late when my phone finally lights up my dark room.

I jump up so fast the fucking thing goes skidding across the floor and shoots straight under my chest of drawers.

"Motherfucking..."

Dropping to my hands and knees, I reach under for it.

Theo and Alex went out a few hours ago, joining Nico in the search for Italian intel.

I wanted to go with them, to do something to help, but they insisted I stay here in case Toby, Galen or even Stella got in touch.

I felt useless, but I got it.

Once my previous anger had ebbed away a little, I knew I needed to keep a clear head and be ready to move, to get to her.

My heart jumps into my throat as I unlock my phone to find a text from an unknown number.

My hand trembles as I open it. But that's nothing compared to my reaction to the photo that appears before my eyes.

My stomach turns and I have to fight not to vomit over Theo's carpet.

"Hellion," I breathe, staring down at her curled up, lifeless body. Her white shirt is red. Red with... "Fuck. FUCK." I bellow, scrambling to my feet to find my trainers.

One glance at that photo and I knew exactly where she was.

Why was an entirely different question. And I couldn't shake the feeling that maybe this wasn't Galen's fault at all but everything to do with me.

Why else would they leave her in a place only I would recognise instantly?

I don't remember the drive there.

I don't stop to question it any more as I run from my car.

I don't even stop the engine or close the door as I fly through the entrance to the graveyard.

"Stella," I call, despite the fact that she probably can't hear anything I'm saying.

The blood that was so obvious in the photo is even more shocking in reality as I spot her curled up between my father and sister's graves.

"Ambulance," I bark into my phone the second it connects. I rattle off our location and give the guy on the other end as much detail as I have before falling to my knees beside her and dropping my phone to the ground.

I should have made the call on my way over, but all I could think about was getting to her.

"Baby," I breathe, pushing her hair from her face.

My breath catches at how pale she is. I tell myself it's because we're illuminated by only the moonlight, but it's more than that.

Pressing my finger to the pulse point in her neck, I pray to any fucking deity who might listen as the faint sound of sirens builds in the distance.

"It's going to be okay, baby," I whisper. "I've got you. I've got you."

CHAPTER TWO

Stella

My first thought is that someone has filled my veins with concrete and stuffed cotton into my brain.

My second is that the beeping and the voices are loud as fuck.

"I think her eyes flickered."

That voice. I know that voice.

The beeping gets faster.

"Stella?" Warmth spreads from my hand and up my arm.

What is that?

"Stella? Open your eyes, baby."

The voice is closer this time.

"We should call the nurse," someone else says, someone farther away.

"No, just wait," the voice snaps.

My entire body jolts when something touches my face. A soft brush of fingers against my cheek.

"Come on, baby. Come back to me," the voice whispers so quietly I'm certain only I can hear it.

I fight to understand, to get any kind of grasp on reality. It's there. Right fucking there, but I can't quite reach it.

His touch continues, and while it feels nice, comforting, something still feels wrong. There's something deep inside me that wants to pull away.

Sebastian.

Right as that realization hits me, the darkness consumes me once more and everything fades away.

It's not a bad place as I sink into the nothingness the blackness provides. Well, not to start with.

But then images start becoming clear in my mind.

The graveyard. Nico's basement. His bathroom.

Memories of having Seb's hands on me, of him thrusting inside me make my temperature spike before the image of him on his knees before me with my knife in his hand carving his name into me becomes so clear I almost feel like I'm right back there. Pain radiates from my thigh as I watch the blood pool against my pale skin.

The movie in my head continues, taking me back through the next morning when he humiliated me in front of his friends. Him visiting me in my bedroom, the way he played my body, the things he said to me... they all feel so real. The fight with the guys Calli and I went out with is the last thing I remember before the beeping comes back to me.

This time things are clearer, my head cooperating with my body as I come to.

Dragging my eyelids open in that moment is one of the hardest things I've ever done.

I regret even bothering when the bright electric light burns my retinas and makes my head pound.

For a second, all I can see is the white light. I don't even hear the words that are being said to me, or the scrape of the chair legs against the floor as someone rushes over.

"Stella. Stella, baby. It's okay."

I blink a couple of times and my surroundings begin to clear—or more so, the face right in front of mine.

My breath catches as I stare into his dark, exhausted eyes.

A wide smile plays on his lips as he stares down at me, his hand holding mine.

"It's so good to look into your eyes."

I continue to just stare at him as a familiar ball of fury explodes in my belly, poisoning my blood with hate and the need to fight.

"Get out." The words are out of my mouth before I even realize I thought them.

I also don't know why I think them, but something tells me there's a very good reason.

"W-what?"

"Get. Out."

My heart begins to race, the annoying beeping getting louder once more as my chest starts to heave.

"It's okay, Hellion. You're okay. You're in the hospital."

"Just get the hell out," I scream, the words ripping my dry throat to pieces as tears burn my eyes.

I've never felt more hopeless or useless in my entire life.

I fight to move, but my body feels like it weighs a million tons.

Seb's eyes leave mine in favor of whoever the other person is.

"I-I don't—"

"Get. Out. Get out. GET OUT," I try again, wondering if I'm actually talking a different fucking language.

Suddenly, the door bursts open and a harassed looking nurse comes rushing in.

"Stella, you're awake," she says softly, pressing a couple of buttons on the machine beside me. "You need to calm down, sweetie."

"No. I need them to leave."

"You heard her. Off you go," she says, immediately backing me up.

"No, I'm not leaving her alone in here," Seb states.

"She's my patient and you'll do as I say, or I'll have security remove you."

Seb's chest puffs out, ready to argue. "Do you even know who we—"

"That's enough. Let's go."

Someone moves from behind Seb, and when I reluctantly look over, I find Theo with his hand clamped around his upper arm, ready to physically drag him from the room should he need to.

"No, she needs—"

"Space, Seb. She needs some fucking space. Come on."

With one more confused and concerned lingering look at me, Seb allows Theo to drag him out of the room.

The second the door clicks shut behind them, I break down.

"Oh sweetie, it's okay," the nurse soothes as I sob.

She stands beside me and holds my hand as I have a complete meltdown. The only good thing about it is that she's turned the damn machine off and it's no longer irritatingly beeping in time with my heartbeat.

"Here," she says when my sobs finally subside, and when I glance over, she's holding a cup with a straw out for me.

"Thank you," I whisper.

The silence that follows as she begins to check my vitals, something she probably should have done before now, is deafening.

"W-what happened?" I finally ask. "Why am I here?"

Her soft, sympathetic eyes find mine.

The last thing I remember was running from Seb, Theo, and Alex as they beat the shit out of Ant and Enzo.

What went so wrong after that for me to be lying here?

"You don't remember anything?"

I shake my head, swallowing the sarcastic remark that wants to fall from my lips. It seems that even in my state, whatever that might be, I haven't lost my sass.

"You were stabbed, Stella."

All the air rushes out of my lungs as I process her words.

"S-stabbed?"

My eyes drop from hers to take in the state of my body.

"W-where?"

"Your abdomen. You were very, very lucky. You've not sustained any serious damage internally, but you lost a lot of blood."

Lifting my hand, I take in the cannula in the back of it, the weight of the situation suddenly pressing down on me.

"You're going to be okay, Stella."

I nod, but it's all I can do to muster up the energy.

Now I know the truth, it's like my body has just given up.

I stare at my hand for three more seconds before I lose my fight and my eyes finally close.

"Stella, wait," Toby says softly, and my body follows orders, too exhausted to even think about arguing with him. "Are you okay?"

I take a step back, colliding with the wall. My knees almost give out and I think he senses it, because he's in front of me in a flash.

He stares into my eyes and tears fill mine faster than I'm able to comprehend.

"Shit. What's going on? Tell me how to help."

I suck in a ragged breath as his hand lands on my waist, his support, his presence almost enough to send me crashing into the realms of emotional breakdowns.

"I-I don't... I just want to forget it all," I whisper.

His eyes drop from mine and to my lips as I speak, and my heart rate picks up. When they come back up to mine, the blue is significantly darker than a few seconds ago, telling me everything he's thinking about right now.

My chest heaves as I wait for him to win whatever internal battle he's fighting, and when he does, my entire body sags in relief when his lips meet mine.

My eyes fly open, my heart thundering in my chest as I stare around my dark, empty room.

"Oh my God," I whisper.

That was so real.

Too real.

Before I can think better of it, I press my finger to the call button.

The chairs beside my bed are both empty, and I breathe a sigh of relief that Seb might have actually listened to me.

For a moment, I wonder where my dad is. Why did Seb have to be the first person I saw when I woke up?

I would've thought he'd have been right beside me. He might have been absent for a lot of my life, but my safety has always been his highest priority.

It takes a few seconds, but finally the door opens and the bright light from the hallway outside floods my room.

"Hi, how are you doing?" another friendly nurse asks.

"I need to see someone," I state.

"It's three AM. I don't think—"

"Can I have my cell, or can you please call for me? I need him."

Her brows crease, but she nods. "Okay, but don't be disappointed if he's asleep."

"I just need to try."

She rummages around in a cupboard beside my bed before emerging with my cell in her hand.

"The signal is rubbish in here. If you unlock it, I'll connect you to the Wi-Fi so you can make the call."

Resting my head back, I close my eyes and nod after tapping in my code, relief flooding me that she's not going to refuse my request.

The second she passes it back, I hit call and put my cell to my ear. Just like she warned, it rings off and goes to voicemail.

Disappointment floods me, but what did I really expect? He's hardly going to be sitting up, waiting for me.

I leave a pathetic voicemail for when he wakes up and lock my cell again. I don't bother looking at any of the messages I'm sure have come through. I'm too exhausted to even try to read them.

I must drift back off again, because the next thing I'm aware of is shouting out in the hallway.

Glancing at the window beside me, I notice that the sun is just starting to rise. It must still be early. Too early for people to be shouting in a hospital, surely.

Ignoring them, I reach for the cup of water on the table at my side and take a few sips.

I'm staring out of the window once again when my door opens.

Expecting it to be the nurse, my breath catches in my throat when I find someone else in my doorway.

"Stella," he breathes. He looks awful. Like, really fucking awful.

But the second I lift my arms from the bed, he rushes to me and pulls my weak, broken body into his arms.

"Everything is going to be okay," he whispers in my ear. "I promise you, everything is going to be okay."

And for the second time in who knows how many hours, I crumble.

CHAPTER THREE

Sebastian

"This is fucking bullshit," I spit, ripping my arm from Theo's grasp. "She can't be in there alone."

"This whole hospital is teeming with our men. No one is going to touch her here."

"Not fucking good enough. *I* should be in there. I need to be in there."

Theo stares at me as I push my fingers through my hair and pull.

The only other time I've ever felt this useless in my life was that moment ten days ago when I dropped to my knees beside her in the graveyard and pulled her body into my arms.

"She fucking needs me."

"Did you want to tell her that?" Theo mutters.

"You fucking—"

"I will kick both of you out for good if you continue," a scary-ass nurse barks down the hallway.

My jaw tics with frustration as I glare at my best friend.

He doesn't understand.

How could he?

He didn't find her. He didn't have that terrifying moment when I really thought she was dead. That whoever it was who took her ripped something else away from me.

"I fucking need her."

"I know, man."

The nurse's eyes still burn into my side, her warning loud and clear as Theo steps up to me once more, only this time, it's not to fight. His chest crashes against mine as he wraps his arms around me in an unusual show of affection.

Emotion clogs my throat and tears burn my eyes, but I force it all down.

I need to stay alert. I need to fucking focus, because there's no chance in hell that anyone is getting anywhere near her ever again.

After a few seconds and a solid couple of hits to my back, Theo releases me.

His eyes study mine for a beat, clearly seeing everything I'm trying to hide.

"You should come home and get some rest. Or maybe a shower. Mate, I love you, but you fucking stink."

"I'm not leaving," I state, my voice firm. "She just fucking woke up. I'm not leaving. Not now."

Blowing out a frustrated breath, Theo drops onto one of the chairs that line the hallway out here. Also known as my new home.

Following his move, I fall down beside him, resting my elbows on my knees and dropping my head into my hands.

I'm fucking exhausted. But I refuse to do anything about it.

I'm not the one with a fucking stab wound in my stomach. I'm not the one who nearly died from blood loss.

"She hates me," I say, my voice cold and empty. Just like my soul, I guess.

"This isn't your fault, Seb."

It's not the first time he's tried convincing me of that, but all these days on, I'm still not buying it.

"You're right," I say. This isn't all on me. "It's his fault too," I spit, thinking of her father.

He's the reason she ran from the house. He's the reason she ran straight into whoever that motherfucker was who cut her up with her own fucking knife.

The only thing I don't know is why.

The lift dings at the other end of the hall and Alex emerges with a bag of food hanging from his arm.

"Here," he says, passing it straight to me. "Any news?"

"She's awake. Freaked the fuck out and kicked us out," Theo answers for me as I rummage around in the bag for the energy drink I know is going to be in there.

What I really need is a bottle of vodka and a joint, but I'm already on the nurses' shit list so I don't think I'll get away with that.

"Oh shit. Is she okay?"

"As far as we know. The nurse hasn't come out yet."

Cracking open the top of the can, I down the contents in one.

"How was school?" Theo asks.

"Yeah, you know. Same as. You should both have emails with this week's assignments."

"Great," I mutter, ripping open the packaging of a premade sandwich. I could really do with something hot, but the last time Nico turned up with McDonald's, Janice, the scary fucking nurse, almost had a cow about the smell. So unless I leave—which is out of the question—I'm stuck with this shit.

Stuffing it into my mouth, I chew without even tasting it.

I'm running on fucking empty.

I'm refusing to leave so I can protect her, but the fact of it is that if someone turned up here to get her, they could probably squash me like a fucking fly right now.

I need sleep. I need decent food. Hell, I need some fucking real sunlight, not just the tiny bit that comes through the window in her room.

Dropping the empty packet into the bag, I sit back, resting my head against the wall and closing my eyes.

"You really need to—"

"Don't," I snap, halting Alex's attempt to repeat

Theo's earlier concerns. "I know what I need to do. And I'm fucking doing it."

Silence ripples around me when they both thankfully decide not to argue with me. They do this daily, and it hasn't fucking worked yet. You'd think they'd have got the message by now.

Theo sits with us both for thirty minutes, catching up on shit from Alex before he ducks out to get some real food and sleep in an actual bed.

The nurse emerged from Stella's room before he left, saying nothing aside from a very strict warning not to even attempt to go in there.

I fucking hate following orders, but the threat of being kicked out for good is a little too real.

Being out here sucks when I should be sitting beside her bed, but being banished to the car park would be worse.

"Do you need anything?" Alex asks, breaking the unbearable silence.

I've told them that they don't need to sit here with me. They're more than welcome to continue on with their lives. But being loyal to the core, they've organised some kind of schedule between them so that someone's always here.

I appreciate the support more than I could ever express.

"Nah, I'm good."

"Did you manage to get any of that English lit assignment done?"

"Oh yeah. I spent all fucking night on it."

"Seb," he warns.

"I know. I'll do it, okay? My laptop is in her room and..." I trail off, not needing to tell him again how I was dragged out of there by Theo. "You can go if you want. I'm sure you've got something better to do."

He glances over at me, but I don't meet his eyes. It's too painful.

"You heard from Galen?" he asks instead of taking me up on the offer.

"No. Maybe he's not as stupid as he looks."

"I can't believe he listened to you," Alex confesses, stretching his long-ass legs out in front of him.

"Guilt will do that, I guess. How much shit must he have been keeping from her?" I mutter.

That's the only thing that makes any sense in my head.

She had to have discovered something.

My truth, maybe.

I won't know unless she lets me in the fucking room.

My head lolls to the side, waking me up at the same time the lift dings to announce someone's arrival.

Thanks to her connections, Stella's in a private hospital with some of the best staff in the country—scary bitch included. It also means it's pretty quiet.

In only a few days of being here, I'd figured out how things worked, the staff's schedules, and what the correct visiting hours were meant to be.

I also discovered that out of courtesy to their

patients, they tried not to use the lift in the hours of darkness because the thing is noisy as shit. In a hospital full of all the latest technology you'd have thought someone would have fixed it, but apparently not.

I blink against the bright lights. They lower them at night, but it's not enough when you're half asleep.

Although the second the doors open and a familiar body steps out, I'm instantly awake and on my feet.

"What are you doing here?" I bark, my voice echoing down the silent hallway.

"Fuck off, Seb. You're not her keeper." He storms toward me, his shoulders squared and his fists curling, ready for a fight.

His black eye has finally faded, and I'd love nothing more than to give him a new one.

Whatever happened inside Stella's house that day, he knows.

Toby fucking knows, and he won't tell me. He won't tell any of us.

"And you're not welcome here."

A smug grin tugs at the corner of his lips as he holds my stare.

"Well, that's where you're wrong. I'm only here because she wants me to be."

"You're lying," I spit, although I know he's not. When he is, his left eye gets this annoying little tic.

"Am I?" he asks with a shake of his head as he steps to walk around me.

My arm shoots out before he passes, my fingers digging into his upper arm.

"What are you hiding, Tobes?" My voice is damn

near pleading, and I hate it. But fuck, I need to know what he's keeping from me. What Galen is keeping from me despite my best attempts to get it out of him.

"Get the fuck off me. She doesn't want you here, Seb. You should just go home."

Releasing my hold on him, I hang my head as he storms off and slips into the room I so desperately want to be inside.

Knowing that she's not alone, I take off toward the bathroom.

"ARGH," I scream once I'm inside, my fist colliding with the wall, my healing knuckles immediately splitting open the moment they connect. "Fuck. Fuck. Fuck."

Exhausted, I fall forward, pressing my forearms to the bloody wall and resting my head on them.

A sob rips up my throat, the sound echoing around me, tormenting me as burning hot tears fill my eyes.

This wasn't how it was meant to go.

And I wasn't meant to care this fucking much.

CHAPTER FOUR

Stella

I fell back asleep after falling apart on Toby's shoulder and soaking his hoodie with my tears.

But when I come back to and force my eyes open, he's right there in the chair next to my bed, his concerned eyes on me and his hand holding mine protectively.

My heart aches, although not as much as my stomach.

I hadn't really noticed much pain the last couple of times I'd come around, but right now, I have no reason to disbelieve the nurse's words yesterday about me being stabbed. In fact, I feel like I've been cut in half with the burning ache in my belly.

"What's wrong?" he asks, although from the way he frowns, he probably realizes his mistake pretty fast.

What isn't wrong right now?

"It's hurting."

"The nurse said they've been reducing your pain meds."

"Great," I mutter.

"Call them, they can give you more."

"I'll be okay," I say, trying to put on a brave face. I know that the more meds I need, the longer I'm going to be stuck here. And now I'm awake, this is the last place I want to be. I can cope with a bit of pain if it means I can escape soon.

"Stella," he warns.

I stare at him, my eyes flicking over his features. I'm missing something, I know I am. But I have no idea what it is.

A soft smile plays on his lips.

"Do I look different now?" he asks, pouring me a fresh glass of water and passing it over.

"Umm... no. Why?"

"How much do you remember from the day you were attacked?"

My eyes drop to his lips as my dream comes back to me.

That wasn't just a dream, was it?

"I-I remember being at home. I remember you being there. I remember..." I trail off, biting down on my bottom lip as my stomach knots.

Did that really happen? Did Toby really kiss me?

Is that why he came to me so fast last night, because something could be happening here?

"Do you remember what happened after... that? What your dad told us?"

Closing my eyes, I fight with the darkness that clouds those hours before I was stabbed. But I've got nothing.

I remember his body pressed against mine. I remember the relief as our lips touched. The escape, even if it was short-lived.

I shake my head, finally opening my eyes again.

"No. Everything's just not there," I whisper, trying not to show how frustrated I am about not being completely aware of parts of my life. Important parts, if the way he's looking at me is anything to go by.

"Shit," he breathes, nervously rubbing the back of his neck.

"Just tell me, please."

He bites on the inside of his lips for a beat, his eyes dropping before finding some strength from somewhere, because when they come back to mine, there's a determination within them that wasn't there before.

"Stella, you're my sister."

"Fuck off," I laugh, instantly regretting it when shooting pain explodes from my belly. "Oh shit, that hurts. No more jokes please," I beg, pressing my palm gently to my belly.

"I'm not joking."

Any of the humor that was lingering from his statement immediately vanishes when I look into his serious eyes.

"Y-you're not. B-but... you kissed me."

He scrubs his hand over his face and lets out a heavy sigh.

"I had no clue, Stella. If I did... fuck. If I did, I certainly wouldn't have been thinking the things I have over the past few weeks. And I wouldn't have kissed you."

"This is so fucked up."

"Yeah," he says with a laugh. "You can say that again."

"Fucking hell." Lifting my free hand, I push my hair back from my face, trying once again to drag some memories up.

Toby remains silent beside me, giving me the time I need to attempt to get my head around this, if that's even possible.

"That's why I ran," I whisper.

"Yeah," he confirms. "I'm so sorry." His hand squeezes mine, bringing my eyes back to his exhausted ones.

A humorless laugh falls from my lips. "It's hardly your fault."

His brows lift. "No, you've got me there."

"So... is my dad actually my dad or..."

"Yeah, he is."

"Well, that's a relief. Something he hasn't lied to me about."

Empathy oozes from Toby. For possibly the first time ever, someone actually understands how I'm feeling.

How betrayed I feel for being lied to for... well, my entire life.

"I don't know the details. Only what your dad told me after... yeah. He and my mum, they had an affair."

"Holy shit."

"But you're only... a year older than me?"

"Eleven months."

"Jesus."

"Yeah."

"Have you spoken to your mom about this?"

He shakes his head, something dark passing through his eyes.

"What is it?" I ask, dread settling in my belly.

"T-things aren't good. Mum, she's..."

"Just tell me, Toby," I demand. I've already been handed enough shit. A little more will hardly make any difference right now.

"Good morning," a nurse I haven't seen before sings a second after she opens my door. "It's good to see you awake. How are you feeling?"

"Umm..."

"She's in pain," Toby answers for me, and I reward him with a cutting look.

"Okay. Let me see what I can do. I was thinking we could try getting you on your feet today, honey."

"Umm... sure." The thought of getting out of bed fills me with dread. I already know it's going to hurt like hell, but getting to my feet is one step closer to the door, so I'll give it my best shot. "A shower would be fantastic."

"I'm not sure we'll manage that today, but we can definitely freshen you up a little."

"How long have I been out?" I ask.

"Ten days."

"Ten days," I parrot. "I've been asleep for ten freaking days?"

"Your body needed time to heal. You went through something very serious."

"Right," I mutter as she pulls my notes from the bottom of my bed.

I've missed a week and a half of school. But more importantly than that, I missed my freaking birthday. I turned into an adult while unconscious in the hospital.

I glance around the room, wondering if anyone even remembered, or knew.

I've been awake a while now, and I still haven't seen my father.

I doubt anyone else was even aware it was meant to be my big day.

I guess it's just something that's now going to pass by as if it never happened. At least when I get out of here I'll legally be able to drink. I guess that's a bonus.

"I'll give you a little more pain relief now, and then after breakfast, we can try getting up, okay?"

I nod, watching as she checks my vitals. Toby backs up into the corner of the room, allowing her to work.

"If you eat okay today, hopefully you'll be able to get off of this soon," she says, tapping the side of the machine I'm hooked up to.

"Great. When can I leave?"

A soft laugh falls from her lips. "It'll be a few days yet, honey."

Food arrives before she's had a chance to finish her

morning checks. The sight of it turns my stomach, but I need to at least try.

"For hospital food, that looks pretty decent," Toby says, returning to my side the second the nurse is done and has disappeared from the room.

I poke at the porridge with my spoon, willing my body to want to taste it.

"Just have a little. Or I can go and get you something else if you want."

Shaking my head, I look at him.

"What happened, Toby? Who did this to me?"

Regret swamps his features. "I don't know, Princ—"

"Don't," I snap. "Don't call me that."

"Okay," he breathes. "We're trying to find out as much as we can."

"We?" I ask, quirking a brow.

"Yeah, everyone."

I stare at him, needing more.

"The Family. The boss. Everyone."

My eyes widen. I'm not sure if it's the shock of someone other than Calli actually being honest with me about this, or that everyone actually cares that much.

"Wow. So you're really in the mafia then?" I mutter, finally lifting the spoon to my lips.

"I can't believe I hadn't figured out you were connected to us sooner."

"Try living your entire life not having a clue."

"I'm sorry, I—"

"Stop, please," I beg. None of this is your fault. "There's only one person I blame. And where is he, anyway?" Confusion flickers over Toby's face, so I quickly add, "My dad."

"Trying to find the arsehole who did this to you."

"Huh."

While I might appreciate that, why isn't he here?

Toby smiles at me, a weird expression on his face.

"What aren't you telling me?"

"Stella," he sighs.

"No," I hiss. "No. Not you too. I need the truth, Toby. The whole fucking truth."

A soft knock sounds on the door and the nurse slips back inside, apologising when she realizes we're in the middle of something, but she doesn't leave us to it.

"I promise, I'll tell you everything. But—"

A frustrated growl rumbles up my throat. The nurse steps closer, switching the bag of whatever is dripping into the back of my hand.

"We need you healthy, Stella. Focus on getting better and getting out of here, and then we'll talk."

"That's bullshit, Toby."

He shrugs, sitting back in his chair and appearing to not give a single fuck about it. Although the bouncing of his foot tells me something else.

I hold his eyes, shaking my head. I'm not happy about this, but what am I going to do about it? I can't even get out of the fucking bed.

"I'll be back in ten minutes," the nurse tells me, completely ignoring the obvious tension in the room. "Then we'll get you up."

She disappears before I can say anything.

"I guess that's my cue to leave," Toby says, sitting forward once more.

"Toby, I—"

"I'll tell you everything, I promise. Just... get out of here, okay? I hate seeing you like this."

I smile sadly at him. "Trust me, I don't want to be here either."

"If you need me, call me."

He grabs my cell from the table and places it beside me.

"You need anything, I'm right at the other end, okay?"

A ball of emotion clogs my throat as I look into his eyes.

My brother.

"Thank you," I whisper, barely able to talk for fear of bursting into tears all over again.

I hate this. I hate being weak. I hate relying on other people for literally everything.

But more than all that, I hate all the lies. The secrets.

CHAPTER FIVE

Stella

I've never been one to shy away from pain. I usually love it. I push myself as hard as I can with my training sessions with Calvin and in my gym and cheer practice. But getting out of that damn hospital bed is like nothing I've experienced before. And it's not something I want to repeat any time soon.

My legs were like jelly and my muscles, screaming in their attempt to hold me up. My stomach burned like a motherfucker. I might not remember the moment of that knife sliding into my belly, but I can imagine exactly what it felt like, because if it weren't for seeing the baggage attached to my skin then I'd think it was still impaled in me.

I was forced to sit as Carla the nurse cleaned me up. I've never felt more useless in my entire life. I could barely even lift my arms after the journey from the bed to the bathroom mere feet away.

It was pathetic.

I was pathetic, and it only solidified what I already knew.

I'm not getting out of here anytime soon.

The second Carla damn near lifted me back into bed, I almost immediately passed out. The exhaustion from just that small bit of movement was too much to fight.

When I open my eyes once more, the late summer sun is streaming through the windows. The sight makes me feel a little better.

My stomach rumbles loudly, pointing out exactly why I'm awake when I still feel like death. I only managed a couple of spoonfuls this morning, but I take the fact that I'm actually hungry now as a good sign.

I press the button for the nurse before looking back out of the window. There are the first signs that fall is approaching, the leaves just starting to look that little bit old with a hint of orange hitting some of the trees.

A bang from the other side of the room startles me, and I cry out when I twist too quickly, pulling my wound when I try to see what it was.

The door to my bathroom opens in a rush, and a concerned and very wet Seb rushes from the room, straight to my side.

"Are you okay?" he asks, a deep frown forming between his brows as his hair drips, soaking into the sheet covering me.

My eyes hold his for a second, any kind of response

stuck in my throat before they drop to his chest, and then lower.

Water droplets cling to every inch of him, making his skin glisten in the most delicious way under the electric lights.

Something I shouldn't be feeling stirs in my lower belly despite the pain.

It's when I get to the towel that he's barely covering himself up with that I realise I've never actually seen him naked.

"Hellion?" he growls, effectively dragging my eyes back up to his.

Ignoring the fact that my breaths are coming out in short gasps, I force words out of my mouth.

"What are you doing?"

"I just needed to..." He nods his head in the direction of the bathroom.

I guess it was a pretty stupid question.

"Run out of water at home or something?" I snap.

"Or something," he mutters, running his fingers through his dripping hair and pushing it back from his brow.

His stomach and chest muscles ripple with the move, and my mouth waters.

Damn him for looking so good.

He knows it too, if the smirk on his face tells me anything.

"Put some fucking clothes on and get out."

His smirk falls immediately.

Forcing down any kind of feeling the sight of his skin drags up within me, I hold his eyes steady, my own impenetrable mask firmly in place, while the one I'm used to seeing on him seems to have vanished.

"Hellion, I just want—"

A bitter laugh falls from my lips.

"You think I care what you want? You've made my life a living hell since the first time I laid eyes on you. You've lied to me, stalked me, hurt me. I'm lying here because of it all.

"I'm done, Seb. So fucking done. So you can run along and continue with your little games elsewhere. Maybe go and see if Teagan is busy, because you cunts suit each other."

He stares at me, his lips parting as if he's going to argue, but he finally decides against it and takes a step back.

"If you're waiting for me to crack and tell you that I'm joking, you're going to be waiting a while."

Believing me, he spins and storms back into my bathroom, flashing me his perfect ass as he goes.

"Jesus," I mutter to myself as the image of his bare behind lingers in my mind.

This would all be so much easier if he were horrible to look at, or if my body didn't seem quite so addicted to his.

I'm once again focusing on the trees outside when the door opens and his heavy footsteps fill the room.

It takes more effort than it should, but I just about manage to keep my eyes averted from him and ensure my breathing stays steady.

"I get that you're angry, Stella. Trust me, I do. But I'm not the enemy here."

"Pfft," I scoff. "You've been the enemy since you learned my name and failed to tell me what it meant," I say, my voice void of any kind of emotion.

"I didn't think we'd end up here."

My head spins before I have a chance to stop myself.

"No, you just wanted me in a morgue. Now do me a favor. Either finish the job while you can, or fuck off. I do not want you here, Sebastian."

"You're a pain in my ass, Stella," he huffs, marching toward the door.

"I didn't ask to be anything to you, asshole."

"No, and that's the fucking problem."

My brow furrows as the door slams closed, the vibration of it flowing through my body, resonating in my stomach.

"Fucking entitled asshole," I mutter to myself, pushing my hair from my face and trying to calm down.

It's like his mere presence flips some kind of switch inside me.

I get two minutes of peace before the door opens once more and Carla's head appears.

"You called, sweetie."

I did?

"Umm..." I hesitate, not remembering why I pressed the button—until my stomach growls so loudly it makes Carla chuckle.

"Any chance of some lunch or dinner or... what time is it?"

"You slept through lunch, but I'll see what I can find for you. Give me a few minutes."

42

Remembering what Toby said about my cell, I swipe it from the table and stare down at the time.

Two thirty on a Wednesday.

Everyone will be—or should be—in class.

I can't help wondering if anyone's even noticed I've gone.

Who am I kidding? All I did since I arrived was cause drama. They're probably relieved.

Thankfully, Carla returns only a few minutes later with a tray full of all kinds of food.

"I grabbed a bit of everything," she says, lowering it to my table and wheeling it over.

There are sandwiches with different fillings, a sausage roll, a packet of chips, cake, fruit.

My stomach growls once more, and I immediately reach out for one of the sandwiches.

"I don't think I've ever been so hungry," I confess a beat before stuffing almost the whole triangle in my mouth.

"That's a really good sign, Stella. Just try not to over do it. You've had nothing in your stomach for days, so it might be a shock."

I nod, too busy chewing to really pay attention.

"Thank you," I mutter around the mouthful.

"You're welcome. I'll be back in a while with your medication."

She disappears again, leaving me alone.

I've been alone a lot in my life. As an only child and with a mostly absent parent, I learned a long time ago to be happy with my own company. But since moving here, I can't seem to shake the loneliness.

I think of Seb. He's here when he should be at school.

It would have been so easy to allow him to stay here with me. To keep me company.

But can I even do that?

Can I forget everything that's happened between us and pretend we're... friends?

I shake my head, knowing that it's not even worth contemplating.

He's where he needs to be. Far, far away from me.

Reaching for my cell, I open up the messages waiting for me while grabbing another sandwich.

Harley: Call me when you can. We're praying for a quick recovery for you xo

Ruby: Get well soon, girl. We love you x

I stare down at the two messages from my girls in Rosewood and my brows pinch.

Opening my call log, I find that multiple calls to both of them have been made since the day I was stabbed.

Someone's been keeping them in the loop.

But who?

My answer literally bounces through my door less than five minutes later.

"You're awake!" Calli all but squeals, and she flies toward the bed.

Emmie enters a little more demurely behind her.

"It's so good to see you," Calli continues. "How are you feeling?"

"Sore. Confused." *Lonely*. I don't say the last one. I don't need anyone to feel guilty for me being here.

"I can't believe you've been out of it for so long," Emmie says, taking the seat on the opposite side of the bed to Calli.

"Right? I've literally lost a part of my life. How are you? The last time I saw you I was mopping blood from your face."

Emmie waves me off. "I'm good. You should see the other girl."

"Aw man. Tell me she ended up with a shiner."

Emmie smothers a laugh while pulling her cell from her blazer. "How's this?"

"Oh my God," I gasp, my hand coming up to cover my mouth as I stare at the image of Teagan. It's zoomed in from across the room, but her two black eyes from Emmie's solid punch to her nose are clear as day. "Damn, I can't believe I missed seeing it myself."

"I tried getting a better photo, but for some reason she wasn't up for posing for you."

"I wonder why," I joke.

Emmie shrugs. "Beats me."

"Anyway," Calli says, interrupting us. "We come with gifts."

Lifting a bag to her lap that I didn't notice before,

she reaches inside and begins placing everything on my small table.

"You missed your big day, and we've been waiting for you to open your eyes to come celebrate with you."

My eyes scan the items on my table before Calli thrusts a card in front of me.

"I'm not really in the mood for celebrating," I confess, taking it from her.

"Well, that's tough, because we've got all night to try to make you feel better about life.

"The men might be out there trying to catch the arsehole who dared lay a finger on you, but we're not useless."

"Think I'd rather be out there with a gun in my hand," Emmie mutters.

My eyes find hers.

"What? I know about the whole mafia bullshit."

"You do?" I ask, thinking that she's been weirdly chill about it.

"Do you have any idea who my grandaddy is?"

"Literally no clue. Enlighten me."

"I'll take your mafia and raise you an MC."

"MC?" I ask, not totally following. I blame the pain meds.

"Yeah, motorcycle club. You know, *Sons of Anarchy* and all that."

"Fuck off. Your grandad isn't in an MC."

Although saying this, I have seen her dad, and I can totally picture it.

"Oh no, he's not *in* an MC. He *is* the MC. He's prez."

I can't help but laugh, which makes both of them look at me like I'm losing my goddamn mind. To be fair, I could be.

"Wow. Well, aren't we a trio headed right for hell with our heritage? The mafia and the MC princesses. Ohhh... we should totally start our own gang."

"Okay, how strong are your meds?" Calli asks, looking slightly terrified by my suggestion.

"Not strong enough," I mutter.

"Okay, so gangs and killing people aside..." she says, skipping right past any more on that topic, "as you can see, we brought the spa to you."

I look between the two of them, feeling way too emotional at the effort they've gone to. I fight not to let it show on my face, but from the sympathetic looks they give me in return, I don't think I succeed.

They give me a face pack, paint my nails, and brush and braid my hair.

Carla pops her head in a few times to do what she needs to do, and by the time the girls have finished with me, I can't deny that I feel a little better. Well, it could be that or the fact that Carla finally unhooked me from the machine and gave me more pain meds.

The sun has long set, yet Calli and Emmie seem to be more than happy keeping me company.

Calli's put some god-awful reality TV show on that both Emmie and I are trying to ignore while they fill me in on the Knight's Ridge drama from the past ten days.

"I'm hungry," Calli suddenly whines.

I've got a tray full of dinner that I'm picking at, but

they've had nothing. The food here is better than I was expecting, but it's not really what I'm craving.

I want tacos. Tacos like in America.

Oh... or a burger from Aces on Rosewood's beachfront.

Pushing my tray of barely warm food away, I try not to lose myself in thoughts of food I can't have.

"Do you think the coffee shop is still open?"

"There's only one way to find out. If it is, get me a panini," Emmie says.

"Oh, so I'm going, am I?" Calli sasses.

"You brought it up."

"But you're clearly hungry."

I sit there and look between the two of them with an amused grin on my face.

I like this. This is some kind of normal in all this bullshit.

"Ugh, fine," Calli finally concedes, pushing up from the chair and grabbing her purse. "You want anything?" she asks me.

"Nah, I'm good, thanks."

"Okay, be right back."

Emmie waits until she's closed the door behind her to speak.

"She really is the perfect mafia princess, isn't she?"

"Hey," I complain jokingly. "You trying to say it doesn't suit me?"

"Oh no, you're more likely to be standing beside the boys, going in for the kill. I'm not sure that's the kind of princess they expected."

"Yeah, fair enough. I do love the feeling of

wrapping my finger around a hard—" Emmie's eyebrow quirks in amusement. "Gun, Emmie. I'm talking about a gun."

"Of course you are. You're in no fit state to be talking about wrapping your hand around anything else." She winks.

"Don't," I beg. Images of Theo, Alex and Nico with their hardness in their hands that night in the basement come back to me.

Pushing all of that aside, I look at Emmie.

"W-what?" she asks nervously.

"Would you be able to do something for me? Something... big?"

"If you agree to keep my MC secret. Name it."

CHAPTER SIX

Sebastian

I t's been five days since Stella woke up, and other than those two chances I've had to talk to her, the only times I've seen her have been when she's sleeping and I've managed to sneak in unnoticed.

It's fucking killing me, but I know her time here is coming to an end. From what I've heard, she's up on her feet now, and her meds have been reduced to almost nothing.

Any day now, she's going to walk out of here, away from the security we've got set up, and re-enter the world. A world where the man who stabbed her is still at large and potentially waiting.

I wake up Monday morning, a familiar crick in my neck from sleeping on the chairs in the hallway, and stare at the wall in front of me.

I've memorised every mark and indent in the past two weeks. This place is bordering on being more familiar to me than my family home. I swear I've spent more time here than I have in that place in years.

The lift dings, announcing the first arrival of the day, and I push myself up.

"Morning, sunshine," Toby sings, his smile just a little bit too wide for first thing in the morning.

"Shouldn't you be at school?"

"I'm going. Just brought the princess some breakfast." He holds up the takeout bag and coffee cup he's carrying as if he needs to prove a point.

"You bring anything for me?"

"No, you must have forgotten to place your order."

"Wanker," I mutter, less than amused by his attempt at humour.

"Anything new?" he asks.

"Not that I know of. Your end?"

"Nah. The Italians are a dead end. No one's squealing a word."

"Maybe it wasn't them," I say, stating the obvious.

"Yeah, maybe not. That doesn't help with who it was though, does it?"

"She's gonna be out soon," I say, allowing my fear to show on my exhausted face.

"I know. Galen's already increasing security at the house, but she's not going to stay there, let's be honest. We can't wrap her up in cotton wool. It'll only push her away faster."

I scrub my hand over my scruff-covered face. It's

bordering on a full-on beard at this point. It's not my finest look, I'll admit. But it is what it is.

He's right, I know he is. But I need her safe. Protected.

I need to be by her fucking side.

"You still not given her that yet?" he asks, nodding to the box that's been under the chair I've turned into my new home since her birthday.

"No. She's been too busy kicking me out."

The fucker laughs as if he's actually enjoying me getting kicked to the curb while he happily turns up to visit my hellion.

I swear to God, if he's so much as touched her, I'll fucking kill him.

"Right, well, I'd better deliver this."

Pushing to my feet, I watch as he walks toward her room, jealous that he's able to do so, that he's wanted by her, threatening to swallow me whole.

I don't register that he's paused in the doorway until he says my name.

"Y-yeah?"

"Where is she?"

My brows furrow. "Bathroom, maybe?"

Toby rushes into the room, and, without thinking, I quickly follow.

Her bed is empty, the sheets crumpled as if she's been in there recently, but the rest of the room is weirdly quiet.

There's nothing on the table beside the bed or any belongings on the sideboard.

"She's not in here," Toby says, his face twisted in concern.

"Well she can't have just walked out. She—"

"Where's Stella?" Toby asks in a rush when footsteps come to a stop behind us.

Twisting around, I come face to face with one of her nurses.

"Oh, didn't you know? She discharged herself last night."

My stomach falls to my fucking feet.

"She fucking what?" I bark, making the nurse rear back in shock. "You let her discharge herself?"

"I-I'm sorry, but she's eighteen. There's not much we can do to stop it. Plus, she was going to be discharged today or tomorrow anyway."

"Jesus. Fuck."

Threading my fingers through my hair, I pull until I'm on the verge of ripping it clean from my scalp.

"Where has she gone?"

"Home, I guess. I'm sorry, I didn't catch her plans." The nurse's face clearly shows her lack of amusement with this conversation.

"But how did she get out? I was out there all night. I—"

"Was asleep," Toby adds, as if he's asking for a broken nose to match Stella's cunt of a father.

"Fucking hell. Fuck. Toby, let's go. We need to find her."

Walking out of the hospital for the first time in two weeks is fucking weird. Feeling the sun on my skin and breathing fresh, non-sterilised air is even stranger.

We're in Toby's car only minutes later and heading for Stella and Galen's house.

Toby is silent the whole way. His grip on the wheel is tight enough to turn his knuckles white, and his jaw tics in frustration.

Focusing on his reaction to this is easier than trying to decipher my own.

He brings the car to an abrupt stop outside the house and races toward the door, letting himself in, which makes my brow lift.

I run behind him and come to a grinding halt in the doorway to the living room when I find Galen relaxed back on the sofa as if the entire world hasn't just shifted around us.

"Toby, you okay?" he asks, completely ignoring my presence.

I don't blame him. Our last few exchanges haven't exactly been pleasant.

The sling he's currently rocking can attest to that.

I call bullshit on the rumours that he used to be one of Damien's best soldiers, because the motherfucker didn't put up much of a fight either time I've gone at him in the past two weeks.

"Is she here?"

"Who?"

"Stella, you fucking cunt. Who do you think he's talking about?"

Barging Toby out of the way, I stand in front of Galen, glaring unbidden hate down at him.

"She's not here. I haven't seen her. You're the one who's meant to be protecting her. Failed, Sebastian?"

My teeth grind to the point I'm sure I'm about to crack some enamel as my fists curl.

"She can't have just vanished."

Something about Toby's tone makes me turn to look at him.

And fuck, am I glad I do, because his left eye tics.

A bitter laugh rips from my throat.

Motherfucking liar.

CHAPTER SEVEN

Stella

This was probably a really bad idea.

But it's too late to regret it now, because I'm here. And fuck, do I feel better.

For the first time since I woke up, I can actually breathe.

I knew Calli's dad had the hospital surrounded, looking for any kind of threat. And while I was inside, I felt safe because of it.

But the second I walked out, my skin prickled with awareness. It was as if he—whoever he is—was waiting for me.

He couldn't have been.

Emmie, Toby and I slipped out of that place in the dead of night. The only other person who knew what was happening was Carla, who ensured we had a clear run to the back exit.

My heart tumbles as I think of the boy who was curled up on a row of chairs right outside my room, but I refuse to focus on it.

Him being there changes nothing.

I hadn't seen him since the day he emerged from my shower, tempting me with everything I could have.

I assumed he'd just left and stopped trying to see me.

"He's been here since the moment you came out of surgery," Emmie unhelpfully whispered in my ear as we walked away from him.

It had been over two weeks.

That can't be right. There's no way he'd have stayed.

No way.

But part of me knows she's right. Knows that's exactly what he would have done.

Guilt ripped through me as I turned and walked away from him, not once allowing myself to look back.

Both of them helped me into the back of Toby's car and he drove as gently as possible, despite the fact that I told him repeatedly that I was okay.

Every few minutes he would look back at me in the rearview mirror. He thought I was doing the wrong thing. Running away.

I was running. But not for the reasons he thought.

He assumed I was scared. I'm not.

I just... I just need to breathe.

I need to leave the secrets, the lies, the bullshit that my life in London has become behind me.

I'm not stupid. I know that all I'm doing is covering the wound with a Band-Aid. At some point, I'm going to have to deal with it all. Learn everything that everyone seems content on hiding from me.

Even as we drove toward the airport, Toby still refused to give me the information I craved about my reality.

Well, fuck him. Fuck all of them, because I don't need their deceit in my life.

I refuse to be run around in circles by them, by my father.

I never have needed anyone, and I'm not about to start now.

I come to a stop in a doorway, resting my suitcase and purse behind me. I look around the familiar gym, my eyes taking in all the girls before me and landing on the two at the front.

"One, two, three, four. One, two, three, four," Ruby counts, clapping with each number, trying to keep her squad in time as they practice.

No one notices me for a few minutes, allowing me to revel in the feeling of familiarity and safety.

Whoever he is, he's not going to get me here.

Of that I'm almost certain.

Only a second after a couple of the girls clock me, Harley turns to see what's captured their attention

"Holy shit, Stella," she gasps, rushing toward me.

"W-what?" Ruby stutters before turning. "Oh my God."

"Ow, fuck," I groan when they both engulf me.

"Shit. Sorry, sorry," Harley says with a wince.

"What the hell are you doing here?" Ruby asks, her eyes still wide as she stares at me as if she's imagining it.

"I... uh... I needed to get away."

"Aren't you meant to be in the hospital?"

"I discharged myself."

"Stella," they both warn simultaneously. "You should be resting, healing."

"I did. I rested on the whole flight here."

"Jesus," Ruby mutters, twisting her long ponytail in concern before she turns back to her squad. "Practice is cancelled. Go have some fun."

"N-no you don't have to—"

"We're taking you home. No arguments."

Harley takes my suitcase, Ruby my purse, and I follow them through to the locker rooms so they can grab their things, familiarity washing through me at the sights and smells of the only place I ever felt like I belonged, before I'm ushered into Harley's car.

"Mom's away on a business trip this week. We'll go there. You'll get some peace."

"Okay," I breathe as she closes the door on me and has a discussion with Ruby before putting my stuff in the trunk.

I hate being shut out, but I appreciate that I've just turned up in the middle of their lives.

"I'm sorry, I know I've kinda dropped myself on you," I say the second Harley falls into the driver's seat and Ruby slides into the back.

Harley looks at me, sympathy written all over her face. Reaching out, she takes my hand in hers.

"You don't need to apologize, Stel. You're always welcome here. I mean, a little heads up would've been nice, but..."

"It was all a bit of a whirlwind. I just needed to be... here, with you."

"Aw, you going soft on us, girl?" Ruby asks.

"Almost dying will do that to a person."

"Oh shit, I didn't—"

"It's fine. If we can't joke about it, what can we do?"

"Let's get you home, you crazy bitch," Harley jokes.

All three of us ignore the elephant in the room as Harley drives us toward her house. They focus on catching me up on school, cheer and the dumbass things the football team have done already this year.

It's all so easy, so natural to insert myself back into life here.

This place really was my home, and it makes me appreciate why I missed it quite so much when I moved across the pond.

I let out a contented sigh when I walk into Harley's house.

"Oh my God," Poppy cries from the kitchen, spotting me as I enter. "What the hell?"

"Surprise," Harley sings.

"What are you doing here?"

I look between the three of them, the only girls ever to properly smash down my walls and force themselves into my life.

"It's kind of a long story. Shall we go sit down?" I

ask, aware that I'm starting to feel spent. "Any chance of some water? I need to take some pills."

"Yes, yes. Hang on," Harley says, rushing forward. "Go and make her rest," she shoots over her shoulder before disappearing into the kitchen.

"Come on, she's right."

I gently drop down in the middle seat of Harley's sectional and attempt to cover the lingering pain and discomfort that wants to show on my face.

I'll be the first to admit that getting myself here after what I've just been through is utterly insane.

But I just couldn't stay there.

I was going to have to go home and deal with Dad. I loved the security the nurses provided in keeping Seb away when I asked them to. But without them...

I just... I don't need any of it.

I need peace. I need... I don't know what I need.

But when the Uber drove alongside the ocean, I felt a hell of a lot better about life.

I know that running isn't the answer.

I can't hide out here forever. At some point, I'm going to have to go back to London and deal with all the shit I've left behind.

I'm just not ready yet. I'm not strong enough, and that's not something I want to confess to anyone who's trying to ruin or control my life.

I want to face it head on. And right now, I can't do that.

Both Ruby and Poppy's concerned eyes burn into me as I sit there with my head spinning, listening to Harley crash around in the kitchen.

"Here you go," she announces, joining us.

She passes Ruby and Poppy cans of soda before placing a huge bowl of chips on the coffee table between us all.

"And for the patient," she says, handing me a bottle of water and my own bowl of chips.

"Don't, please. I was being discharged today anyway. I only missed a few hours of lying in that uncomfortable bed."

"I'm pretty sure they weren't going to let you out if they knew you were going to get straight on an airplane," Ruby chastises.

"So go on," Poppy starts. "Tell us everything."

The three of them stare at me, concern and intrigue filling their eyes and covering their features.

When I don't immediately start talking, Harley breaks it down a little.

"Who stabbed you?"

Shaking my head, I look down at my nails, picking at the skin that's received a bit of a battering over the past few days as I run all this shit through my head over and over.

"I don't know. It seems no one knows."

"How is that even possible?" Ruby barks. "Someone must have seen something?"

"Whoever it is, it's got something to do with my father, I'd put money on it."

"Your dad? Why?" Ruby asks, her brows pulling together.

Blowing out a long, slow breath, I prepare to fill

them in on everything I learned in the days leading up to finding myself in the hospital.

"You know how you laughed about my dad being a part of the mafia?" I ask Harley, remembering the jokes we had about it after I helped save her from some psycho from her past earlier in the year.

"He's not?" she asks, her eyes wide.

"Apparently so."

"But you're not Italian," Poppy points out, much like I had.

"Nope. Greek. My dad moved us back to London and right into the middle of the Greek mafia."

"Riiight," Ruby says, rubbing at her brow.

"Trust me, I know. But wait, it's about to get worse."

"Christ, Stel. You really know how to bring the drama."

"One of the guys I've told you about. The nice one."

"Toby?" Harley confirms.

"Yeah. He's my brother."

Ruby starts laughing—until her eyes land on me once more and she gets a look at my serious expression.

"You're not kidding, are you?"

I shake my head.

"Weren't you lusting after him?" Harley asks, amusement in her own tone.

"I sent you pictures. Can you blame me?"

"Well, no, but..."

"Okay, so how's this working then? One of you was adopted at birth or..."

"I don't really know. Just like everything else, it seems to all be secrets and lies, even now I know some of the truth." I look between the three of them, irritated at Toby for keeping everything close to his chest. He assured me it was for my own good, but I call bullshit.

How is lying to me about where I come from, about my own mother, for my own good?

"We've got the same mom, I know that much. She and my dad had an affair, and I arrived only eleven months after Toby."

Harley's mouth opens as if she wants to say something, but no words come out. In fact, the only sound that filters around the room is tires crunching on gravel as the weight of everything I've told them, or been unable to tell them, weighs down on all of us.

We remain silent as the front door opens and two sets of footsteps enter the house.

"Nah, I'm telling you, man. He's gonna do it. You've seen his stats," a familiar deep voice says.

"In the living room," Harley calls.

"You're wrong. He's not all that. He's—" Ash and Kyle appear in the doorway, Kyle's words halting the second his eyes land on me. "Shouldn't you be in England? And like, in a hospital?" His brows pull together, his head tilting to the side slightly like some kind of cute puppy.

"Long story," Ruby mutters.

"Well, it would be if I knew all the details," I add.

"I'm gonna order pizza. We'll call you when it's here," Harley tells the boys.

"Oh, it's like that?" Ash jokes. "We know when we're not wanted. Come on, bro."

"Uh... yeah," Kyle mutters, still looking a bit shell-shocked by my presence. "I'm glad to see you're okay, Stel," he says before they both disappear.

"So what's the plan then, Stella?" Harley asks after placing our order. "I'm assuming you're not actually moving back with just one suitcase."

Resting my head back on the cushion, I stare up at the ceiling.

"No. I'm going to go back... sometime. I can keep up with school work online. There are only a few weeks until the holiday. So I guess I could go back after that. I don't know."

"Do you think they're going to let you stay away that long?" Harley asks, a look I don't like in her eyes.

"What aren't you telling me?" I ask.

"You told us that Seb spent every minute either at your bedside or outside your room at the hospital. Do you really think he'll let you just hang out here?"

"He doesn't know where I am," I argue, although I know it's weak.

"Really?"

"He's hardly going to get on a plane and drag me back. Is he?" I ask, hating that I sound anything but confident as the image of him doing exactly that plays out in my mind.

All three of them stare at me with the answer I don't want.

A thought hits me, and it's out of my mouth before I can think better of it.

"He was the one who called you, wasn't he?"

Sympathetic smiles play on their lips.

CHAPTER EIGHT

Sebastian

"**M**otherfucker," I boom, flying at Toby and taking him with me until his back hits the wall.

Pressing my forearm against his throat, I glare right into his blue eyes.

"Where is she?"

"Fuck you, Seb. I'm not telling you anything," he snarls.

"I need to know where she is. I need to—"

"To what? Hurt her some more? All of this is your fucking fault."

My fist collides with his cheekbone, forcing his head to the side as I battle with the monster inside me who wants more than anything to continue until he's physically incapable of answering me.

"And you wonder why he doesn't want to tell you," a deep voice rumbles from behind him. "We're trying to protect her."

"No," I shout. "You're letting her run. *I* was protecting her."

"Who are you kidding, Sebastian? You've lied to her just as much as the rest of us."

"Are you fucking kidding me?" I release Toby in favour of turning toward Galen. "You've been lying to her since the day she was born."

"She's not the only one," Toby scoffs from my side.

"So what, I didn't tell her what her name really meant. So what, I didn't tell her what *you* did? Those are your secrets. Not mine. You have no right to have a say in how we protect our own. How I protect what's mine."

"She's not yours," Toby states.

A humourless laugh falls from my lips.

"Oh, so that makes her yours, does it?"

"No. She's never going to be mine."

"Finally," I announce to the room, throwing my arms out to my sides. "He finally gets it."

"No, *you're* the one who doesn't fucking get it. She's never going to be mine in the way you want her."

"Why? It's what you want," I spit.

"Because she's my sister."

Silence ripples through the room at his words. I swear all three of us actually stop breathing.

Sister?

His sister?

"No. No you're not. You're an only child."

"Yeah," he scoffs. "I fucking thought so, too."

I stare at Toby, my eyes narrowing in confusion before I twist back to Galen once more.

"You're a lying fucking cunt. You know that? You don't deserve a daughter like her. She's too fucking good for a scumbag like you."

I'm out of the house before I even know I've moved.

My chest heaves as I stand in the middle of the driveway, staring at Stella's Porsche.

It's not until footsteps hit the gravel behind me that I drag myself out of my daze.

"Where is she, arsehole?" I growl when I find Toby staring at me, his cheek glowing red from my hit.

"Safe. Away from you, away from him. Away from all this shit."

"I need her," I confess in a moment of weakness.

"That may be true, but she doesn't need you. She's better off where she is. She's safe."

"Whatever," I mutter, taking off across the driveway.

My body aches with every step I take. Barely sleeping on a fucking row of chairs for two weeks is starting to take its toll.

"Do you want a lift home?" Toby calls out. Always the fucking good guy.

Flipping him off over my shoulder, I keep moving, feeling more and more hopeless as each second passes.

I walk home.

Well, to Theo's. It's been more of a home to me in the past few years than my own has.

Walking inside and seeing that almost everything

was exactly as it was before we left that morning makes my chest ache.

While everything in my life has been turned upside down, the rest of the world is still spinning like it always does.

Raiding the cupboard, I find a bottle of vodka and take it to my room with me, grateful there's something here other than that bottle of Jack.

I wince as I drag my hoodie over my head and throw it in the direction of the laundry basket— although based on the smell radiating from it, I should probably take it outside and burn it.

I strip down to nothing and twist the top of the bottle as I walk through to the bathroom.

I can't remember the last time I ate anything decent, so the second the liquid hits my belly, I swear I start to feel the effects.

I crave it. The numbness, the nothingness.

I need to forget.

Her.

Us.

All of it.

The hot water rains down on my head, yet I don't release the bottle. I just stand there, letting the scent of the sterile hospital wash off me as I prepare for the darkness the vodka is going to provide me with.

I don't get out until the bottle is done, and only then do I put it down, abandoning it on the counter beside the basin.

Absently, I drag some clean clothes on and I'm out

of the house long before Theo might return from school and training.

My head is already starting to swim, my limbs feeling heavy as I make my way down the street and to the closest shop to get another bottle.

My surroundings spin and my stomach clenches with its need for food, not just alcohol, as I sit, resting my head back and staring up at the dark sky.

The sun set a little over an hour ago.

I left my phone in my room to ensure no one would be able to track me here. Stella isn't the only one who can ditch and run.

I tried tracking her phone with the app we've all got, the one I connected hers to when she was drunk at Nico's birthday party, but its last location was at the hospital last night.

Smart bitch has either left it behind or turned it off.

Toby might not have told me where she's gone, but that doesn't mean I haven't got a good suspicion.

She knows no one here, and I can't imagine her going somewhere alone. Toby is here, and according to the app, Calli was at home. Surely, if she wanted to take anyone with her, it would be those two?

That only leaves one option.

She's gone home.

It didn't take a lot of research to figure out all the places she's lived over the past few years.

Her Instagram account helped me figure out where

Galen had dragged her. Some places only had a handful of images. But the last place—Rosewood, Florida—had loads. Friends, parties, cheerleading, at the beach, in different houses. One glance and it was clear that she had a real life there.

That was only confirmed when I called her two friends from her bedside.

They cared for her, that much was obvious.

My grip on the bottle tightens. My need to get an Uber to Gatwick and book myself on the next flight is almost too tempting to ignore.

Blowing out a long, steady breath, I try to get a grip on what I need to be doing.

I need to find the motherfucker who thought stabbing our princess with her own knife was a good idea.

I need to figure out how he even had her knife in the first place. The last time I saw it, I'd placed it in her bag after her fight with Teagan.

Scrubbing my hand down my face, I try to get my thoughts in order, but the alcohol in my veins is making it harder and harder.

I don't realise that I've passed out until the crack of a twig in the distance startles me, making me sit up straight and turn toward the entrance.

Images of her walking through the darkness, her curves being illuminated by the moonlight as she comes to find me flicker through my mind like a film.

But it's a fantasy. A dream.

She's not here, and she's not coming for me.

The second the figure does appear, a lump so huge

appears in my throat that I have no chance of saying a word to her.

Silently, she walks in front of me and lowers her body so she's resting half on the same gravestone as me.

Reaching out, she takes my hand in hers, squeezing tightly in support.

"I brought you this," she says, dragging another small bottle of vodka from her bag, followed by the most incredible sight of a freshly rolled joint. "I stole it from Jason. I'm sure he won't mind."

Reaching out, I take it, placing it between my lips as she digs out a lighter and flips it open, illuminating her face with the soft orange glow as she lights the end.

"Thank you," I force out before taking my first hit.

Resting my head back once more, I revel in the high, holding the smoke in until my lungs burn for air.

"This isn't very responsible of you, Sis."

"It wasn't that long ago that I was eighteen."

Eighteen.

The realisation that Stella wasn't the only one to miss their big day over the past two weeks slams into me.

Everyone tried to make me leave the hospital for the day to at least attempt to celebrate, even just to shower and shave, but I refused.

Stella didn't even have a say in celebrating hers, so why should I get to enjoy myself? Why should I get to put our reality behind me and pretend that everything was normal?

"You were a good girl."

Sophia scoffs. "I only let you see what I wanted you

to see, Seb. You had enough bad influences in your life. You didn't need me being another."

Appreciation for my sister swells within me. Despite our drastic situation, she always, *always*, tried to do what was best for me.

She's a fucking angel.

"I miss her," I whisper, glancing back at the headstone behind us.

"Me too. Every day."

Silence stretches out between us but her support surrounds me, making things feel just that little bit better.

"Talk to me, Seb."

"She's gone." Sophia doesn't say anything, but I catch her nod out of the corner of my eye. "She's run from me. From this."

"Can you blame her?"

"No," I answer honestly without missing a beat. "Doukas never should have brought her back here."

"Why? What's your issue with him?"

Taking another hit, I rest my forearm on my bent knee.

"H-he... he killed Dad."

"That's what you think?"

"That's what I know," I confirm, ensuring my voice doesn't show any sign of hesitation.

"Seb," she sighs, pain lacing her tone. "This world we live in, it's... dangerous. Every single day we're risking our lives, those of the ones we love. And unfortunately, death is a part of it. It's inevitable. We were at war back then. Fighting is messy, and sometimes the wrong guys get hurt by the wrong men. But that's kinda the way it goes."

Her calmness, her rationale shocks me.

"So you're okay with one of our own killing our father?"

"There's no evidence of that, and even if there was... it just... is what it is. Nothing can change the past, Seb. Nothing can bring him back."

"But I heard it. I heard Damien say it. Galen killed our father."

She lets out a sigh.

"Tell me the truth here, Seb. This is deeper than some past beef between our fathers."

My head swims with vodka as I try to formulate an answer. An honest one. But the thought of even confessing to the things that Stella makes me feel, what her absence makes me feel, terrifies me.

"She's one of us. We should have protected her."

"So it's guilt that kept you outside her hospital room all this time?"

"Something like that," I mutter.

"It's okay to admit it, you know. That you feel something. It doesn't make you weak."

"Doesn't it?"

"No. Not if you don't let it."

Her words repeat in my head for a couple of long seconds and she allows me the time to try to process everything.

"I don't know anything about her, Seb, so I might be way off the mark here, but... she's not weak. She might not have had a choice in moving here, but it seems to me like she fits right in. From the rumours I've heard, she's given you a run for your money."

"What do you know?" I ask, exasperated.

She chuckles. "I know all the things you're too chicken shit to admit. You want her, and it's killing you. You're terrified, so you lash out. You think you hate her, you blame her for all this shit that has nothing to do with her, but really, all you want is her."

"Wow, that's quite a big opinion, considering you've never met her."

"I don't need to meet her. I know you, Seb. I know how your mind works."

"Great," I mutter.

"I know you're trying to do the right thing by protecting her. Staying outside her room all that time. Hell, that's the thing of fucking fairy tales, Seb. But she's hurting, and not just from her injuries.

"I have no idea what's really gone down between you, but something tells me both of you need this time, this distance.

"You've known each other, what? Six weeks at the most. Take a step back, take a breath, and try to figure out what you really want here. And trust that Damien and everyone is doing their best to find this asshole and keep her safe. You don't have to take all of this on. Trust the people around you."

"I just... I want her here. I need to know she's okay."

"Trust her to know what she needs and just hope that involves coming back to you."

"And what if she doesn't?"

"Then, and only once you've figured out what you really want, you show your hand."

"How long will that take?"

"Only you know that, Seb." She sighs. "If in, I don't know, two weeks, she hasn't reappeared and you're still feeling like this, then maybe it's time to do something about it."

"Two weeks?" I ask. That feels like a million years right now.

"There are no rules here. You've just gotta trust your instincts."

"Because they're so trustworthy."

"You're a good person, Seb. Maybe you just need to show her a little more of the person we see, the uncle Phoebe sees."

"Yeah, maybe," I mumble.

Stubbing out the end of my blunt on the ground, I stare up at the twinkling stars above.

"You want a lift home?"

"Umm..."

"You need a good night's sleep. Maybe after that, everything will be a little clearer."

With her arm around my waist, Sophia manages to get me to her car without me face-planting the damp ground. My life is already in ruins; I don't need to add a busted-up face into the mix as well.

I remember falling into her passenger seat, but the next thing I know, strong hands are clamped around my upper arms and I'm being hauled into the air.

"What the fuck?" I slur, the world spinning around me.

"Shut up, you drunken buffoon," a familiar voice grunts as another says, "At least try to make your legs work."

I blink, trying to come to my senses and figure out where the fuck I am.

The cool air of the night is replaced by something warmer, and then the scent of home hits me.

"Stella?" Her name tumbles from my mouth without any thought from my brain.

"She'll come back, man. Have faith," Theo says, sounding much more confident than I feel. Not that I can really feel anything right now. My face is numb, and I'm sure my legs aren't actually attached to my body.

Everything flickers from darkness to colour as I'm hauled through the flat, but before long, the softness of my bed hits my back and I immediately allow myself to sink into it.

"I'm not getting him undressed," Alex mutters. "Stupid fuck can stay like that."

"I've got it," Sophia says. "Thanks for your help."

CHAPTER NINE

Stella

By the time I roll over and open my eyes, the school day at Rosewood High has long started.

I lie there, staring up at the ceiling, listening to the nothingness around me. The only thing that would be better were if the windows were open and I could hear the ocean in the distance.

The dull throb I'm becoming used to radiates from my stomach, but I can't deny that a night's sleep away from the noise of a hospital—even if a bizarrely quiet one—has done me a world of good.

Finding my morning pills and a bottle of water beside the bed, I take them and then climb out, walking straight over to the windows.

I swear my entire body sighs with relief at the view.

I'm here. I'm safe.

The feeling is one of pure bliss, until another thought hits me.

What did Seb do when he discovered I'd left?

Reaching out, I rest my hand on the wall beside the window, really not wanting to acknowledge the pain that slices through my chest at the thought of him waking up from his makeshift bed to find me gone.

It's what he deserves. He might not have been the one wielding the knife that afternoon, but he had a hand in it.

Had he been the one to organize it?

No. Surely not.

If he actually wanted me dead like he'd threatened in the past, he'd have done it himself.

I've seen him fight. He doesn't hold back. He jumps right in the middle and ensures he gets the first punch in.

But even knowing all that, something isn't sitting right with me.

My stomach grumbles, forcing me to move from my spot at the window, and I go about freshening up for the day.

As expected, the house is deserted, and the only thing I find to show that there was life here at some point this morning is a note on the kitchen counter.

Stella,

Help yourself to anything. Poppy will be home right after school and I'll be back after practice.

Please rest.

Kisses,
H x

A smile pulls at my lips as I read Harley's words. Next to the note is a set of house keys, telling me that I'm safely locked inside, and attached is her car key. When I look out the window, I find it sitting out there in case I need it.

I've no intention of going anywhere, but I appreciate that she knew I wouldn't like being stuck. My plan is to do exactly what she's suggested. Rest.

I make myself a quick breakfast and a coffee, grab a blanket from the box in the summer room, and take it out to the pool with me.

The sun is shining, but the heat from the summer I left behind has started to edge away.

Laying the blanket out on one of the loungers, I wrap myself up like a burrito and grab my bowl of fruit and granola.

The peace is incredible, but when I glance at the time on the cell phone I bought when I landed, I know that I needed to do something.

While I might be glad that I skipped town, leaving everyone in my new life behind, I know there are going to be people who are going out of their minds right now.

Guilt washes through me.

Not so much for my dad. He never bothered to even visit me in the days after I woke up. But Calli... she has every right to hate me.

Finding her number that I stored in my phone on

the Uber drive toward Rosewood High, I hit dial and lift it to my ear, hoping like hell she takes a chance on an unknown number.

Relief floods me when the line crackles and connects.

"H-hello?"

"Calli, it's Stella."

"Oh my God," she gasps, a rush of air passing over the microphone. "Where the hell are you? What the hell is going on?"

"I just… I needed to get away."

"And you didn't trust me enough to tell me?" Hurt laces her voice and my chest constricts. "I could have helped. Emmie said—" Her voice cracks with emotion, and I instantly feel like the worst kind of friend in the world.

"I know. That's not why I didn't tell you." *I was trying to protect you.* I swallow the words she won't want to hear.

Maybe I made the wrong decision in keeping this from her. But I was doing it with her best interests at heart.

"Those guys are ruthless. I didn't want them coming after you for information."

"I'd have kept any secret you wanted from them."

"I know. I never once questioned your loyalty. I just didn't want you to deal with their wrath." Silence descends over the line. "I'm sorry. I just—"

"It's okay. I don't like it, but I get it."

"Have they come to you?" I ask with a wince.

"Yes."

I knew it. I fucking knew they'd go straight to her thinking that they'd get everything they need.

"I haven't seen Seb, though. He didn't show up for school today."

I hate that my heart aches at her words.

"What did you tell them?"

"The truth. They wanted a phone number for you. Anything." I blow out a long breath and rest back. "I won't give it to them, I promise."

"I know you won't." But honestly, what's him calling going to do? I can just not answer.

"How are you? Where are you? I've been so worried."

"I'm fine. I'm... You've probably already guessed," I say, still questioning giving her any kind of information. She might be their princess, but I don't trust Seb not to do whatever is necessary to get information out of her.

"Yeah, I pretty much had. Is it nice to be back?"

"Like coming home," I say honestly.

"Y-you're not going to come back, are you?" The emotion in her voice shocks me.

We've only been friends for weeks, but her reaction tells me that she recognized our connection as much as I did.

"What? Don't be crazy. Of course I'm coming back. I just... I need some time, some peace. The last few weeks have been..."

"Insane."

"Yeah, that'll do." I laugh, although it lacks any kind of amusement.

The last few weeks have been painful, torturous.

Thrilling.

I lock that thought down.

"Okay, good. That's good. I miss you," she whispers.

"So aside from all this, what's happened since I last saw you?" I ask, trying to get her to talk about something else, anything else that's not going to involve me hearing his name.

She chats away about classes and gym practice, and I lose myself in the nonsense drama from Knight's Ridge.

That place is so different to here. To everywhere I've ever been before.

Not only is everyone insanely wealthy, but it's like an entirely different world that I'm not sure I'll ever be a part of.

I'm used to Friday night football games and beer pong, not the rowing club and listening to every other person speak like they're related to the queen. Hell, most of them think they're important enough to be freaking royalty.

It would be so easy to put my foot down and try to re-enrol here. I'm sure I could easily rent a place with the tuition fees Dad would save alone. I could get a job, I could...

"Are you okay?" Calli asks, hearing my loud sigh.

"Yeah. I've just got thoughts running at a million miles an hour around my head. It's hard to keep up."

"I can imagine. Any idea when you might come back?"

Soon, I think. But that's not what falls from my

mouth, because I feel like I've lost my ever-loving mind even considering returning right now.

I shouldn't miss that place. I should hate it and be glad I escaped.

The bullying, the stalking, the torment. All of it should be enough to keep me away.

But I can't deny that I crave that kind of drama, that excitement, that risk.

I've never been one to take the easy route in anything, and running here means I've run away. And despite knowing I did the right thing, being here, resting, healing... I'm always going to feel like I chose the coward's option.

"When it feels right." *When I've got the strength to look him in the eyes and stand my ground.*

"Okay, well... I'm here. Whatever you need. Please, just call me," she says, obviously sensing that I'm ready to hang up.

Talking to her is amazing, but it's just a reminder of the new life I was building that I left behind.

"I will. I'm sorry I kept this from you, I—"

"I know you were just trying to protect me." There's an edge to her tone that I totally expect.

"I'm not them, Calli. I'll always tell you everything, I promise. You're the first person I've called. You're the first person I wanted to talk to."

"It's fine. Honestly. I get it. Call me tomorrow, yeah?"

"I will. Have a good evening."

"You too. Bye."

I sit there for the longest time with my cell still in my hand and resting on my chest.

Did I make a mistake keeping this from her?

Shaking my head, I drag myself from the maybes and what-ifs. It's too late now. The damage is done.

I start tapping in numbers and hit call before I change my mind. I didn't need to save this number; I've known it like the back of my hand for years.

"Doukas," Dad's deep voice booms down the line.

"Daddy."

His loud gasp fills the line. "Stella," he breathes. "I'm so sorry."

Swallowing the emotion that threatens to bubble up at the torment in his voice, I square my shoulders and forge on, desperate for some answers.

"Why? Why didn't you come and see me after I woke up?"

"Sweetheart, things aren't that simple."

I scoff. I almost died and things weren't simple enough for him to be there and support me?

"I was alone, Dad."

"I can assure you, you weren't."

Realization hits me. "Oh my God, it's because of him, isn't it? Do not tell me you stayed away because you were told to by a fucking kid." My anger begins to get the better of me and I'm unable to stay seated.

Hauling my sore body up from the lounger, I begin pacing back and forth in front of the pool.

"It's complicated. I've been busy trying to find who did this to you, and yes, Sebastian and I had… words, of sorts."

"I can't believe this," I mutter, wondering how Seb suddenly managed to find the power to call all the shots. "He doesn't have a say in all this. In who gets to visit me. He's no one. Insignificant."

Dad sighs, shifting around as if he's unable to stay still too.

"He cares about you, sweetheart."

"He's an asshole," I hiss.

"Yeah, well. We all make some less than stellar choices in life from time to time," he confesses.

I stop dead on the spot. "You don't say," I mutter. "The mafia. The fact that I've got a brother. The fact that my mother isn't actually dead. Where would you like me to start with your screwed-up choices, Dad?"

"Everything I've done is to try to protect you."

"And how's that working out for you?" I spit, my legs moving me forward once again.

"Why did you run? We could have looked after you here."

"We? Who's we, Dad? Because from what I can see, you haven't done all that much since I was stabbed."

An exhausted groan rips from my father as soon as I say that final word, and I can't stop the guilt that threatens to wash through me.

Despite all his lies, his deceit, I know that deep down, he's not a bad person. He's not. I'm a better judge of character than that. I think... I hope.

"We just want you to be safe."

"And you decided that the best way to do that was to lie to me my entire life. You let me walk into that school, not having a clue who I was. Who *they* were."

86

"I had measures in place to protect you."

"To protect me, or to protect your lies?" I spit.

His silence says it all.

"Why's it so bad knowing who I am? Who you are?"

I start to think that he's not going to respond with how long it takes him to formulate words.

"Things in London before we left... They were... messy."

"Having a baby with another man's wife? Yeah that'll cause some mess, Dad."

"It's way more complicated than that, sweetheart."

"Well, I've got all the time in the world right now. How about you spell it out for me?" I say, gently lowering myself back to the lounger.

"How about you come home and we'll do it in person?"

"Wow, that's a real cop out for someone who hasn't seen me since I woke up."

"I couldn't, Stella. Trust me, it wasn't through choice."

"What did he do to you?"

"He's protecting you."

"I'm sick of men thinking I need protecting. I'm more than capable of looking after myself." Dad's returning silence says it all. "Yeah, well if you hadn't lied, I wouldn't have been running."

"Please, Stella. Just come home."

"I suggest you forget this number unless you have something important to say." I hang up before he has a chance to respond and throw the cell down on the lounger.

I knew he wasn't going to be forthcoming with the truth, but I had hoped for a little more than that.

Although, I can't deny that I'm frustrated. Right now, I'm more curious about what Seb did to keep him away from me. He had to have pulled out the big guns... maybe literally.

My fingers curl as my need to find out begins to get the better of me. But I didn't come here to call him on day one. My plan when I left was to never talk to him again if at all possible.

CHAPTER TEN

Sebastian

I slump down in my chair as our teacher prattles on about something I'm not listening to. Just like every moment since Stella decided to give me the slip and leave the fucking country, my mind is firmly on her.

It's been almost two weeks since my lying cunt of a so-called brother tried to pull a fast one on me and convince me that he was as shocked as I was at her sudden disappearance.

I haven't spoken to her. I haven't tried to reach out, despite the fact that her phone number is currently sitting in my phone, courtesy of Nico, who swiped it from Calli last week.

I told myself I wouldn't call, that I'd give her the time she quite obviously wanted, but my patience is running thinner and thinner with every day. So is my temper.

"Are you going to be able to hold it together for tonight's game?" Theo asks, clearly paying minimal attention to what's going on as well.

I glance over at him, my face blank.

"I'm just saying, if you're gonna cause us shit then maybe don't bother."

"Wow, your faith in my ability to focus astounds me."

"We're playing Westminster. You know they'll sniff out any weakness before we even get on the pitch."

"I've got this, and we're gonna fucking win. Okay?"

He's pissed. I get it. We lost our last two games, and he's put that down to my absence. I mean, I'm good, but I'm not that fucking good. The rest of the team still needs to be on form, and it seems that everything that went down with Stella didn't just affect me, because they were walked all over for both the ninety minutes.

I refuse to feel guilty. I refuse to take responsibility, no matter how badly Theo seems to want to land it on me.

"Okay, fine," he snaps. But it's completely insincere.

He wants a trophy this year. Hell, so do I. But possibly not as much as he does. Not now, anyway. Finding Stella in that graveyard might have put a few things into perspective for me.

None of us are going to be hitting the Premier League anytime soon, so whether we win or lose, it doesn't matter all that much in the grand scheme of things.

"Are you doing this or not?" Theo barks a few hours later, his anxiety over the outcome of this game even higher than it was earlier.

There's bad blood between our two schools. Not to mention that they've beat us for five years in a row. Theo wants to prove himself.

Closing down the webpage I was looking at, I shove my phone into my bag and push to stand.

"I'm good. I've got this." Theo's brows lift. Glancing behind him, I find Alex and Nico looking at me with matching concerned expressions on their faces.

Blowing past all of them, I make my way to where Coach is ready to give us his speech before we attempt to hand these motherfuckers their arses.

"Letting you play today, huh?" the Westminster player standing behind me mutters as we wait for the whistle.

Sucking in a deep breath, I fight to keep my cool and not react to him.

All eyes turned on me the second we walked out. They know something is up. They know there's a very good reason I missed the last couple of games, and I already know they've come up with more than a few dirty tactics to make it work to their advantage.

"What's wrong, number ten? Cat got your tongue?"

My fists curl in my need to ignore him. Theo would never forgive me if I swing a punch before the whistle has even blown.

The guy, their number nine, has clearly been set a

task, because at every opportunity he makes a dig at me.

I've got a rep at being more than a little hot-headed. Last year, I had more than my fair share of red cards waved in my face, something I told myself would change this season. But if the first half of this game is anything to go by, I might not be able to make it happen.

"What's wrong, ten?" he taunts seconds before the whistle blows. "Your whore not putting out?"

"Fuck you," I hiss. I regret responding immediately as I watch an accomplished smirk pull at his lips.

"I'm good. My girl sucked me dry last night. I'd offer her up, but she doesn't blow scum."

My nostrils flare as I suck in a deep, calming breath.

It works for a second. Until the stupid motherfucker opens his mouth again.

"I thought your new American would be right at home on her knees with your tiny coc—" His words are cut off when my fist collides with his mouth.

"You motherfucker," he barks as I swing another punch.

"If I ever hear you say anything about her again, a broken fucking nose will be the least of your worries," I growl, getting him to the ground before hands wrap around my upper arms.

"You stupid fuck," Theo barks in my ear. "Couldn't have just kept your fucking cool, could you?"

"Not when he mentioned her, no." I spit down at him, showing him what I really think of him.

"You need to sort your-fucking-self out, Seb," Theo barks pushing me away from the arsehole and going chest to chest with me. "Either forget about her, or go and fucking get her. You can't keep this shit up. If you're not off-your-face drunk then you're busting up your fists. Get your fucking head on straight."

His palms slam into my chest as he pushes me back.

"Coach is going to rip you a new one for this, and I'll be right behind him to do it all over again. You're a fucking liability."

"Fuck you," I hiss. He might be my best friend, but right now he needs to get his fucking opinions out of my face.

"Sebastian," Coach booms from the side of the pitch. "Get your arse in the dressing room."

Spinning on my heels, I don't even register the ref waving what is inevitably my first red card of the season around.

"We'll be talking about thi—"

"Yeah, yeah," I mutter, leaving Theo behind and storming past Coach and the rest of his training staff and subs who are at the sidelines.

The sound of the door slamming back against the wall echoes through the empty dressing room.

"Motherfucker," I roar, finishing up the few more punches that fuck deserved on the wall instead.

Pain shoots up my arm with the first hit, but it's not enough to stop me. My anger and frustration have taken on a life of their own.

I don't bother hanging around for the arse ripping I've been promised. Instead, I drag my bag from the bench, throw it over my shoulder, and storm out of the locker room, still covered in sweat and a blend of mine and that stupid prick's blood.

My bag flies across my car, hitting the passenger window before crashing to the seat and tumbling into the footwell. I fall down into the driver's seat and jam my finger into the start button, bringing the engine to life.

My grip on the wheel is so tight it makes blood pool at my busted knuckles, and by the time I pull up outside Theo's place, it's running down the backs of my hands.

I don't remember a second of the drive home. My head was firmly on her, wondering what she's doing right now. It's early afternoon where she is. Is she out having fun, or is she wallowing in her bad decisions?

Knowing that I need to be out again before Theo comes storming in, ready to go postal on me for my behaviour, I have the quickest shower of my life, drag on a clean set of clothes, shove some others in a bag and grab my wallet, phone, and most importantly, my passport.

This is fucking ending. Right fucking now.

It was obviously too much to ask to turn up at Gatwick and walk straight onto a flight to Florida. I knew it wasn't going to happen; I'd been studying the flight times for a couple of days as I debated booking myself onto one and going to get her.

I'd tried to do the right thing.

But time was up. I couldn't wait any longer.

After shelling out more than I was expecting for the last seat on the next flight—which was still hours away from departure—I find myself resting back on a sofa in the lounge.

I'm the youngest person in here by at least fifteen years, something that most people around me have clocked onto. Well, it's either that or the state of my hands. They don't exactly scream wealth and first class. But fuck them all. I paid good money for this. I've worked my arse off for years for the money I've got.

Images of the things I've done since I was just shy of fourteen to pay my way flicker through my mind.

Demi hated what I was doing. Sophia and Zoe, too. But they were both old enough to understand, to know that me working for the Family was inevitable. Even more so with the situation we were in. We needed money, we needed to keep a roof over our heads, and while Sophia and Zoe did what they could, I knew that to really help, I needed to step up. And I did. I gave up my childhood and became a man that first day Damien handed me my father's old gun and switchblade and pointed me in the right direction.

My cell vibrating in my pocket drags me from my thoughts. I already know who it's going to be, and all I do is smirk when I pull it out and find that I'm right.

I could ignore him, but there's no point.

Swiping the screen, I lift it to my ear.

"Taking my advice at last then," Theo mutters.

"I'm doing what needs to be done."

"Too fucking right it does. Have you figured out how you're gonna make her talk to you yet?"

"Nope. Not a fucking clue."

"Good luck with that, bro."

"Thanks," I mutter, tipping the beer that was resting on the table beside me to my lips.

"What time's your flight?"

"Couple hours. It'll get me in first thing in the morning."

"She's gonna be thrilled to see you, man," he jokes.

"If I don't make it back, can you ensure everything I have gets put into a trust fund for Phoebe?"

"Sure thing," he laughs.

"Was Coach pissed?"

"Pissed doesn't even cover it. His face was damn near purple when he realised you'd fucked off. He's going to lose his mind when he discovers you're not even in the country."

"I might be back by Monday."

"You're more likely to be dead by Monday, mate."

"Fair point."

"I gotta go. We're heading to Nico's to celebrate our win."

Guilt swamps me that I didn't even ask how the rest of the match went, although I did tell them they didn't need me.

"Yeah, okay."

"Let me know you're still breathing when you find her, yeah?"

"You got it. Bye."

I hang up but don't immediately put my phone away. Instead, I take a risk and send a message to someone who might just be on my side when I get to the other side of the pond.

I need a plan. A really fucking good one.

CHAPTER ELEVEN

Stella

"You ready?" Poppy calls through my bedroom door at Harley's house.

She usually spends her weekends up in Maddison County with her boyfriend—Harley's older brother—but he's got an away game this weekend so she's staying in Rosewood.

"Yeah," I shout from the bathroom. "You can come in."

I continue straightening my hair and then finish off my makeup as she perches on the edge of my bed.

"You look good," she says, taking in my skirt and oversized sweater.

"I feel good, too," I admit.

The pain is much more bearable now, mostly just

an ache if I haven't rested enough or a twinge if I move too fast. I'm not going to be doing gym or cheer anytime soon, but at least I can pretty much function like a normal human again. And go the day without desperately needing a nap.

"Any plans to go back yet?" she asks, just like one of them does almost every day now.

I need to make a decision. School isn't going to wait forever. I can only attempt to keep up to date online for so long, but now I'm here, living my old life that's void of drama and assholes who want to hurt me, the desire to return is getting less and less. Even if the thought of not seeing a certain someone I shouldn't give a shit about makes my chest ache.

"I need to look at flights," I say. It's the truth. Reality isn't going to wait forever.

Calli is desperate for me to come back. Toby and Dad, too. And I'm more than ready for answers from everyone.

"As much as I'm going to miss you, you know you've gotta just do it."

"I know. I think I've maxed out on my moping."

"I'm not sure recovering from what you went through can be classed as moping, Stel."

"Well, whatever. It's been fun. I've loved being back with you three."

"Maybe next time we could come to you."

"Yes," I squeal. "That has to happen. Next summer, before you all start college."

"I'd better start saving," she mutters, her own reality hitting her.

"S'all good. You've got plenty of time," I say, not wanting to tell her that I've got her covered, because I know how much she hates feeling like a charity case, even though that's far from the truth.

"Come on. I'm starving, and Bill's waffles and bacon are calling me," I say, marching toward her and dropping my gloss into my purse.

"Let's go." She hops up and we head for the door.

Poppy swipes Harley's key from the dresser in the hallway, and after saying goodbye to Jada, who returned from her business trip last weekend, we head out to meet the others at Aces.

Just like every other time I've been down here since I came back, I walk through the doors to the old-fashioned American diner with a smile on my face.

We're the first here, and after waving at Bill, the owner, we slide into our usual booth. Both Harley and Ruby had cheer practice this morning, and their boys were at training.

"Morning, ladies," Bill says with a huge smile on his friendly face. "What can I get for you?"

We both order milkshakes, telling him that we'll order food once the others arrive.

"Oh shit," Poppy hisses a few minutes later, frantically searching through her purse.

"What's wrong?"

"I can't find my cell. Zayn said he'd call. Shit."

"You put it in there before you left," I say, remembering her doing it.

"It must have slid out in the car. Scoot out and I'll go look."

"Give me the keys, I'll go," I say, holding my hand out. I need all the excuses I can get to do some exercise right now.

I've eaten like a pig since landing here, and I'm feeling it. It's not going to stop me ordering waffles within the hour, though.

"Are you sure?"

"Of course."

With the keys in hand, I head out to the parking lot, breathing in the fresh ocean air as I go.

I'm going to miss this the second I walk into departures ready to head back to England. There might be a lot I like about London, but there's also a lot to miss about this place.

I search the car but find nothing.

Assuming it's just disappeared in Poppy's giant purse, I swing the door closed and make my way back toward the diner.

I'm almost there when movement out of the corner of my eye startles me a second before a strong pair of arms wraps around me from behind, stopping me from fighting.

"Don't even think about it, Hellion," a familiar deep voice rumbles in my ear as I lift my foot from the floor, ready to slam the heel of my boot into his foot.

"Seb?" I breathe, my body immediately relaxing, although I'm not sure why. He's probably more dangerous to me than some random mugger.

"Who else is stupid enough to jump you in broad daylight?"

"You've got a point there," I mutter as he keeps the length of his body pressed against my back and walks me toward the side wall of the diner.

Releasing his grip on me, he grasps my upper arms and spins me so my back is against the wall.

I keep my head downcast, afraid of what might happen the moment I look into his dark eyes.

"Stella," he growls, one of his hands risking releasing me so he can tuck his fingers under my chin and force my head up.

If he's expecting my anger to have weakened in our time apart, he's about to get a shock.

"What are you doing here?" I spit the second I take in his face.

He looks awful. Well, no. That's not true at all. He's still as breathtaking as ever. Asshole. But he looks wrecked. Like he hasn't slept in a month.

His hair is longer and a total mess, and the scruff on his jaw could almost be classed as a beard, but it's his eyes that concern me. They're so dark. Exhausted.

But I refuse to allow any of that to dampen my frustration at him.

"I've come to take you home, Princess. You don't belong here."

He takes a step closer until there's only an inch between us.

His scent, his warmth seeps into me, making it hard to hold firm.

"I am where I belong, asshole. With people who actually care about me."

He swallows harshly, his Adam's apple bobbing.

"You need to come the fuck home," he growls.

"And what are you going to do about it? Throw me over your shoulder and force me on a plane?"

"If it's what it takes."

"Why? You hate me. You've made it clear time and time again that you don't want me there. Isn't this exactly what you wanted the second you found out my name?"

"Calli wants you back. T-Toby... he needs you back."

My eyes narrow.

"Toby? You expect me to believe that you're doing this for him?"

"He's your brother."

My breath still catches, hearing that.

"He told you?" I whisper.

His jaw tics as he stares at me.

"I think it's time we banished the secrets, don't you?"

I can't help myself, I throw my head back and laugh. Although it stops abruptly when Seb's fingers close around my throat and he moves so close our noses brush.

"Fuck you, Seb. You're a fucking hypocrite and the biggest liar of the lot."

His eyes bounce between mine. "That's a pretty big accusation when we both know that title belongs to your father."

There's some commotion behind him, but with his huge body crowding me, I can't see what's happening.

Although I soon discover that I've been totally played when four familiar faces appear beside us.

"Glad you could make it," Kyle says to Seb as if they're best fucking friends.

"You're right, Stel. He's hotter in real life," Harley announces, much to Kyle's annoyance.

"You knew about this," I seethe, looking between the four of them, "and you didn't think to warn me?"

"You're a big girl, Stella. We all know you can fight your own battles," Ash says, a smirk playing on his lips.

"Now, are you two going to kiss and make up, and are you coming for breakfast?" Ruby asks.

Pressing my palms to Seb's solid chest, I push him away from me. For some reason, he takes pity on me and actually releases my throat and backs up.

"I'm having breakfast. He can fuck off, though," I shoot over my shoulder as I walk away from him, ensuring I have plenty of swing to my hips.

His groan makes me smile as I march toward my friends.

"We all need to have words," I tell them, but I can tell by their smiles that they don't take it very seriously.

"You'd have done the same for us. Actually, come to think of it, you might have already meddled," Harley said, quirking a brow. "A photograph of me in a red bikini ring any bells?"

"I have no idea what you're talking about, sweetie," I purr innocently.

Turning toward Ace's, I head for the door, knowing they're all going to follow me.

"You're a lying little shit, Poppy Thorn," I

announce, sitting down opposite her this time and sliding my milkshake to me, taking a long sip as I beg my heart to stop racing from his touch.

"I'm sorry, they said I had to—"

"It's fine. I can't believe it's taken him two weeks, if I'm honest."

Her eyes leave mine as I continue talking. I know why. It was like all the air was sucked out of the diner the second he walked inside.

"Whoa, he looks pissed."

When doesn't he?

"Nice work, Pops," Harley says with a laugh as she stops at the table, the others slowing behind her— everyone except Seb, who marches around our small audience and drops down beside me, sliding right over until I'm almost pinned to the wall.

"Is this necessary?" I snap, everyone's eyes boring into the two of us.

"It's been weeks since I had a chance to get this close to you," he whispers, tucking a lock of my hair behind my ear.

His hot breath races over my skin and down my neck. My nipples immediately harden, and I internally curse myself for my reaction to him when I should be hating him.

It was easier to do that when I was doped up on painkillers in the hospital. But here, without the constant reminder of what he and that life did to me, it's easier to forget.

"Yeah," I hiss. "There's been a very good reason."

His large, hot hand lands on my thigh. It burns, the

heat shooting up my leg and settling in the form of an ache in my core, but I try to shove him off, pushing that aside.

"Seb," Ruby says, rescuing me from his over eagerness. "Here's the menu."

He reaches out and takes it when she hands it over but doesn't remove his attention from me.

"I already know what I want to eat," he growls, his rough voice full of promises I should have zero interest in.

"You can eat with us. And then you can get back on an airplane and fuck off back to London. Deal?" I ask, everyone else silent as they wait for his response.

Ripping his eyes from mine, he looks around at our group.

"So, what's good here?"

Shifting forward so he can read the menu, he slides his hand higher on my thigh, his fingers slipping just beneath the hem of my skirt. But once again, I fail at attempting to move it.

Bill comes over only a few minutes later to take our orders. I'm not sure if it's his need to feed us that gets him over so fast or his need to know who the newbie is. Bill takes pride in knowing everything there is to know about Rosewood. So in his unique and slightly rude manner, he demanded to know who Seb was before even considering taking our orders.

"So you play soccer?" Kyle starts once Bill has gone, content with mine and Seb's conflicting opinions about who he is.

Seb seemed to think he has something to do with

me. I, on the other hand, just informed Bill that it would be the one and only time he'd ever get the displeasure of meeting him.

"Soccer? Puh-lease. F-O-O-T-B-A-L-L," Seb enunciates. "You know, where you actually kick a ball with your foot, as the name eludes to."

Kyle and Ash stare at him for a beat before the three of them embark on an argument about which game is the real football while the four of us just stare in amazement.

They've literally just met, yet they're as comfortable with each other as if they've been friends for years.

It's weird.

Too weird.

He shouldn't have the ability to insert himself in my life like this. Not in London, and certainly not here.

"I might have issues with your opinion on football, but this I can get on board with," Seb says, cutting a piece of pancake with his fork and placing it into his mouth.

He's insisting on eating one-handed while the other remains clamped on my thigh.

But while he's more than happy to eat his weight in syrup, my stomach is in knots.

He's different. The aura of hatred and anger he's usually surrounded by seems to have dissipated, and I have no idea how to handle him as he laughs and jokes with my friends.

It's clear from their faces that he's got them well and truly under his spell.

Traitorous assholes.

"What are your plans for the rest of the day?" I ask the girls, hoping like hell that whatever it is involves leaving the boys behind.

"Heading home to watch the game, remember?" Harley reminds me. It's not just Zayn who's now playing for the Maddison Kings Panthers, but Kyle's brother is too, and he's first string in his freshman year.

"Oh yeah," I mutter.

"Sounds like fun," Seb announces.

"You've had a long journey. You should probably go to wherever you're staying and get some rest before you go home again," I say, once again trying to remove his hand.

"Not happening," he growls, pushing his hand higher—so high that his fingers brush my panties.

I gasp, but while everyone around the table might miss it, Seb doesn't.

Leaning closer, he whispers in my ear, "I know you're wet for me, Hellion. You might as well stop pretending you don't want it."

"I don't," I whisper-hiss, but I have to quickly smother a moan when his little finger brushes the damp lace.

"Sure," he purrs, his voice deep and rough, sending thrills through me.

"The game doesn't start for a few hours. Maybe you two should... talk," Harley suggests, clearly aware of what's happening at this side of the table.

"No."

"Sounds like a great idea," Seb says, continuing the movement of his finger.

"No," I repeat. "I'm coming with you guys. We've nothing to talk about."

"I think we both know that's not true, Hellion."

"Oh God," I whimper when the lace of my panties grazes my clit.

"I think we should definitely *talk*. Maybe on the beach."

"You can have the keys to Kyle's place if you want. It'll be empty. You can have some privacy," Harley offers.

Narrowing my eyes at her, I silently threaten to end our friendship right here and now, but all she does is smile at me.

"Just remember she's still healing," she tells Seb. "So keep the talking... gentle."

"He wouldn't know gentle if it smacked him in the face," I scoff, earning me another graze on my clit.

"Oh, I don't know," he murmurs, somehow managing to slip his finger under the edge of my panties. "I'm all about surprising you."

My fingers wrap around his forearm beneath the table, my nails digging into his skin with enough force he's likely to end up with bloody little crescents when I remove them.

"Take all the time you want," Kyle offers.

I'm just about to reply when Seb pushes his finger inside me.

"I'm going to hurt you for this," I warn quietly.

"Oh, I'm banking on it, Hellion. What do you think I've been fantasizing about for the past few weeks?"

"I hate you," I hiss.

"Yeah, that's why you're dripping down my hand right now."

CHAPTER TWELVE

Sebastian

My lips curl as we follow Stella's friends out of the diner not long later. I can still taste her on my tongue from where I sucked my finger into my mouth—while she watched, her eyes betraying her true feelings despite her words—seconds before I slid out of the booth to let her up.

The temptation to make her come right there at the table was strong. There was no way everyone didn't know what I was doing, but for once, my need to do the right thing and keep her pleasure all to myself was stronger. The second someone suggested leaving, I ripped my finger from her, much to her displeasure if her squeak of protest said anything.

The second we're out in the warm sun, she spins

toward me and without batting an eyelid, slams her tiny, curled fist into my stomach.

"Holy fuck," I grunt, bending over as I try to catch my breath. Pride for my girl washes through me, making my cock even harder for her than it was before.

"Oh my God," Ruby gasps with a laugh. "You hit him."

"It's the least the fucker deserves."

"Bro, you should have just finished her off," Ash states, as if it's a fucking normal thing to say.

A smirk curls at my lips as I look from him to Stella.

"Oh, I don't know. Making her wait only makes it more fun."

"Your funeral, man," Kyle adds, throwing his arm around his girl and moving away with the others.

"My car and Kyle's place are yours as long as you need them."

"Just make sure any blood or body parts are fully cleaned up before you leave."

Clearly, Stella's friends really do know her well.

"We'll see what we can do," I murmur, never taking my eyes from Stella's angry ones.

In a flash, her friends are gone and it's just the two of us and the crackling chemistry between us.

"Shall we?" I gesture toward the car park, but she doesn't so much as move.

"Why would I go anywhere with you?" she spits, her voice full of venom.

"Because we have things we need to talk about."

An evil laugh rips from her lips. "When have you ever wanted to talk?"

"Since you nearly got killed by some random guy who somehow had your knife."

Her lips part as if she wants to continue fighting, but her intrigue wins out.

"Fine. But if I don't like what you've got to say, then I will hurt you."

"I'm counting on it, Hellion," I say, happily following her toward the car she was searching inside before I announced my arrival earlier.

No words are said as I join her in the passenger side, feeling all kinds of weird being on the wrong side of the fucking car.

She angrily jabs her finger at the start button and backs out of the space.

"Are you healed enough to be—"

"Shut up," she snaps. "You don't get to be concerned about me. Not after all the shit you've pulled."

"Fair enough," I mutter, my eyes taking her in as she drives with ease.

She looks sexy as hell with her skirt riding high on her thighs, her grip on the wheel turning her knuckles white, and the hard set of her jaw as if she's stockpiling a bunch of insults ready for when she will inevitably need them.

"Oh, this is... different," I say as the kind of houses change around us.

"It's Kyle's brother's place. It's what he could afford."

She pulls up in front of what I can only describe as an old person's bungalow before killing the engine and climbing out of the car, as if merely breathing the same air as me is annoying her.

"You need to stop running from me, Hellion," I call as she jogs up the few steps to the wrap-around deck.

"I know. It seems you always fucking find me."

Pushing the key into the front door, she disappears inside, leaving me to either stand out here like a loser or follow.

By the time I close the door behind me, I find her bent over, searching inside the fridge for something.

Grabbing what she wants, she stands tall again and knocks the top off the bottle of Bud Light she found.

"I'm okay, thanks."

"I wasn't offering."

She tips the bottle to her lips and swallows down a generous amount, the muscles in her neck rippling in the most delicious way. My mouth waters for a taste, and not for the beer.

"Anyone would think you're nervous, Princess."

"Me? Nervous?" she asks, pointing at herself. "I don't think so."

"Oh that's right," I murmur, taking a step toward her. "Nothing ever fazes Estella Doukas."

Her eyes narrow on mine before she holds up her hand in a futile attempt to keep some distance between us.

It doesn't work.

Batting it aside, I step right up to her, knowing that my closeness makes her brain misfire.

"I-I thought you wanted to tell me some things. Get on with it so I can leave and you can fuck off."

"Baby," I whisper, my voice rough with need as my hand slides up her neck, cupping her jaw and forcing her to look at me.

Something flickers through her eyes, something that makes excited tingles spread through my body and my cock swell in my jeans.

"I missed you."

She chuckles. "Smooth, Seb. Really. Anyone else would probably fall for it."

"It's the truth. When I found you... fuck, Stella. I thought you were fucking dead."

Her gasp clues me in to the fact that everyone has done as I asked and not told her the details of that night. I wanted her to hear it from me. I wanted her to know just how fucking wrecked I felt in those few minutes as I held her limp, lifeless body in my arms, waiting for help to come.

"That cunt... he left you at the graveyard." All the air rushes out of her lungs. "He sent me a photo. I have no idea if he intended for me to find you dead or what. But he left you there."

"Why?"

I shake my head, wishing I had some kind of answer for her. "I have no idea."

"So whoever it is has something to do with you?"

I shrug, wishing I could tell her it didn't. But while I might believe this is all to do with Galen, I'm not naïve enough to think I'm not racking up my own epic enemy list.

"We thought it was the Italians. Retaliation for what we did—"

"The Italians? Who— Oh my God," she breathes. "Ant and Enzo. They're—"

"Part of the Mariano Family."

She works her jaw as she thinks, dipping her head and breaking our contact.

Sensing that she's about to try to slip away from me, I reach out, take her hand and lead her over to one of the sofas. Dropping down, I pull her right beside me. Now I'm here, with her, I need her close. I'm like a fucking junkie.

"But they were at Nico's party. Why did you let them—"

His brow quirks.

"Okay, fine, so you didn't exactly let them do anything."

My heart sinks for Calli.

"Does Calli know?"

"She does now, yeah."

"See?" she spits, trying and failing at jumping up.

"Stop running," I growl.

"This is why you need to stop keeping Calli in the dark. If she knew the truth, then..."

I stare at her.

"She wouldn't have met him if she knew, Seb. She's not an idiot."

"You're right."

"I-I'm sorry, what?"

I can't help but laugh at the incredulous look on her face.

With a smile, I repeat my previous words. "You're right."

"Wow," she breathes, resting back into the sofa. "Hell really did freeze over."

"So that means you forgive me?" I ask, turning to her and sliding my hand up her bare thigh.

"Oh yeah," she laughs, her eyes crinkling with her faux amusement. "That's *not* happening."

"But I've got all these ways in mind to help convince you."

"I'm sure you have." Her fingers curl around the edge of the sofa and she hauls herself up. "Well, this has been fun and all..."

She's not quick enough and I move with her. My hand on her throat stops her movement, although she doesn't look at me. She keeps her eyes locked on the door, ready to run.

"We're not done yet, Hellion. Not by a long shot."

I run my nose along her jawline forcing a shudder to rip through her body.

"And I think you're more than ready for it."

Her face hardens, her eyes narrowing as my fingers tighten on her throat.

"I've thought about nothing but this since the moment I found you," I confess quietly in her ear. "I'm fucking dying for you here, baby."

I sense her resolve cracking, but she still stands firm.

"I've done everything I can think of to protect you, but all you did was run."

The movement of her chest increases as her breathing turns ragged.

"I spent two weeks in the hospital with you. In the fucking corridor when you forced my hand."

"I didn't ask you to—"

"You didn't need to," I growl, gripping her chin and turning her to face me. I hold her eyes so she can see how deadly serious I am. "You didn't need to ask me because it's my fucking job."

Her small gasp pierces the air and I use her shock to my advantage, crashing my mouth to hers and pushing my tongue past her lips.

I move against her, my tongue teasing hers into action, but still the stubborn bitch holds out on me.

"Stella," I warn, my fingers in her hair, holding her still as my head presses against hers, my eyes boring into her angry, horny blue ones. "Kiss. Me."

Her body tenses, her eyes narrowing once more.

"Kiss me like you hate me, and I'll fuck you the same way."

A clock somewhere in the room ticks, taunting me as she makes me wait.

But then she shifts. It's the tiniest tilt of her head, but I see it, and I finally make my move.

This time, her lips meet mine in a violent kiss full of hate, passion and need. Our teeth clash, our tongues duel as her fingers curl around my shoulders in a painful hold.

"Fuck yeah," I murmur into her kiss. "This is what I fucking needed."

"Seb," she moans when I bend down a little and lift her into my body, wrapping her legs around my waist.

"B-bedroom?" I ask, more than happy to fuck her on her friend's sofa but knowing she deserves more than that.

"Umm…"

"Don't go shy on me now, Hellion. They all know exactly what we're gonna do here."

My lips connect with the long column of her throat and I lick up the length, her sweetness exploding on my tongue.

"Decide, or I'll take you right here."

"O-okay. Down the hall on the left."

"Good girl."

Pushing the door open with her back, I kick it shut behind us, not bothering to look around. Everything I need is right here in my arms. I couldn't give a shit where we are right now.

Her feet hit the floor a second before I drag her jumper up her body, my hands skimming up her sides, delighting in the feeling of her curves that I've missed so damn much.

I've run this moment around in my head over and over during the past few weeks. I had all these ideas for how it would go. Turns out my planning was useless, because all the things I thought I wanted to say to her just shrivelled up and died the second I looked into her eyes. The second I truly discovered just how her presence, her touch, affects me.

Her head falls back on a moan when I cup her lace-covered breasts and squeeze enough to hurt.

"Yes, Seb. Please."

"Knew you were desperate for me, Hellion. You were fucking soaked in the diner."

"It… It's been a while."

A smile curls at my lips. "You waiting for me, baby?"

Her eyes open and she stares at me as realisation hits her.

"What are you going to do about it if I was?"

I can't help but shake my head and laugh. Even now, she can't admit it. Can't accept whatever this thing is between us.

"Prove to you just how good a fucking decision that was." My fingers find their home around her throat once more and she tilts her chin up, defiance covering every inch of her face. "I told you, baby. I fucking own you. This body..." My free hand moves to cup her. "This pussy. It's mine. You got that?" I squeeze tighter and her eyes flare with heat, her already soaked panties only getting wetter. "Yeah, you fucking love it too, don't you? Filthy slut."

Releasing her, my hands go for the button on her skirt, but something else catches my attention before I get it open.

"Seb?" she whispers as I drop to my knees before her, my hands holding her waist as my eyes land on her wound.

My heart thunders in my chest, my need for vengeance on the man who hurt her like this, who left his mark on her body, burns through me like wildfire.

"I'll find him, Hellion. I'll find him and I'll fucking kill him for doing this to you."

She sucks in a shaky breath, hearing the resolve in my voice as I gently brush the pad of my thumb just beneath the healing skin.

"Does it still hurt?" I ask, suddenly feeling like an asshole for manhandling her and not thinking about this in my need to get inside her.

Her body moves as I assume she shakes her head, but I don't lift my eyes from her belly to confirm my suspicions.

"No, not really. I had a check-up here the other day. Everything is healing nicely."

Leaning forward, I press my lips to the very top of the incision, the image of her knife cutting through her skin the only thing in my mind, making my grip on her waist tighten.

"I'm sorry, baby. I'm so fucking sorry."

CHAPTER THIRTEEN

Stella

A lump crawls up my throat and hot tears burn the backs of my eyes as I stare down at him on his knees before me, his lips pressed to the top of the scar left behind from that day.

The sight does something to me, threatens to crack my chest wide open. But I can't allow that to happen.

This, him, us. Everything he's saying. It's all just a fantasy.

Everything between us always has been.

It's been this exorcism of hate and burning chemistry. It's not real. Not really.

And while he might be saying all the right words to make me melt, it's all an act.

For whatever reason, he's here with an ulterior motive. He wants me home for something he's yet to confess to, but I'm certain he's not just concerned about my education.

"If you're just going to kneel there and stare, how about you take a photo and let me get on with my life?" I sass.

He sucks in a sharp breath before his eyes roll up my body, finding my own. They're dark, dangerously so, and for a second, that iron cladding I've erected around my heart almost fractures at the sincerity staring back at me.

"Do something," I whisper. "Please." *Before I end up bleeding out all over Kyle's bedroom floor.*

Thankfully, for once, he does as he's told, and a heartbeat later he returns his lips to my belly, kissing along my scar, making those damn tears burn once more before he pops open the button on my skirt, pushing it from my hips.

"Fuck, baby. It's like you knew I was coming for you," he growls, sitting back on his haunches and running his eyes over my body.

My skin prickles wherever his gaze touches, my breasts swelling, my nipples hardening in my need for him.

"If I'd have known you were coming, I'd have put a gun in my purse this morning," I say darkly.

"I love it when you talk dirty to me." His eyes flare with heat, his fingers twitching where they're resting on his thighs.

With his eyes still locked on me, he pushes to his feet, reaching behind him and pulling his shirt from his body.

Swallowing, I run my eyes over the inches of taut, tanned skin he reveals. Not content with just removing his shirt, he immediately drops his hands to his waistband, and after toeing off his sneakers, he pushes both his pants and boxers down his legs, allowing his cock to spring free.

My eyes zero in on it as he takes a step toward me.

Noticing where my attention is, he growls. "I knew you'd missed me."

Ripping my eyes from his cock, I stare into his dark and dangerous ones, not missing the mirth within.

"N-no, I've just never seen..."

"Anything so impressive?" he finishes for me, closing the final space between us and wrapping his hand around the side of my neck as our fronts collide.

"You naked. It's... yeah," I sigh, not wanting to tell him just how fucking impressive it is. His muscles, his ink, his power. All of it talks to me in a way it really shouldn't. It makes me want things I shouldn't, things that are ultimately going to hurt in the not-too-distant future.

I'm not sure I can do it all again.

"I-I can't do this, Seb," I whisper, hating that I sound so vulnerable.

"Shh," he says, running the pad of his thumb along my bottom lip. "Let me show you all the reasons why it's the only thing we should be doing."

Leaning forward, he brushes his lips against mine. The move is testing, hesitant. The total opposite of what I'm used to from him.

His hand slides from my waist, up to my ribs and then around to my back.

"Let me show you how serious I am about missing you. Let me prove that the person you think I am isn't the only part of me."

"So you're not a complete cunt, then?" I ask, trying to keep my head on straight. I can't fall straight into this... this bullshit. I can't.

My head knows it's wrong, but my heart... that wants to dive headfirst into what Seb's offering, and I can't allow that to happen.

"Just don't tell anyone else. There's usually only one girl who gets to see another side of me."

"Another girl?" I ask as the fabric around my hips falls loose.

"My niece. Come home and you can meet her. She used to be the only one who could wrap me around her little finger."

"Used to be?" I whisper as his fingers drag my straps from my shoulders, baring me to him.

"Yeah. Fuck, baby."

Before I even know he's lifted me, my back hits the mattress and he crawls over me, caging my body to the bed with his and dipping his head to capture my lips in a searing kiss.

Silently, he tells me everything I'm too terrified to acknowledge in his words. And as he brings his hands to my body, he touches me as if I'm the most delicate, precious thing in the world.

It makes every inch of me sing in a way I've never experienced.

And I fucking hate it.

I need the old Seb. The vicious, brutal lover who ensured I knew that the only thing between us was pleasure, if he allowed it.

This... this is too much.

"I-I need you to stop," I tell him, my voice firm as I plant my hand in the middle of his chest and try to push him from me.

Taking pity on me, he lifts up.

A deep frown mars his brow as he stares down at me.

He looks like a confused puppy. It's almost cute. Or it would be, if I didn't know the brutality he was capable of.

Pushing a little harder, I force him to roll off me and quickly scramble from the bed before swiping his shirt from the floor and fleeing from the bedroom.

My chest heaves as I fight to drag in the air I need, the walls continuing to close in around me.

"Fuck," I breathe, pushing my hair back from my face as I race for freedom.

I'm at the front door, ready to rip it open and drag in lungfuls of fresh air, when his booming voice stops me.

"What the fuck are you doing?"

The anger in his tone stops me in my tracks.

"You need to stop with the act, Sebastian. Stop pretending that you're here for me because you care when we both know you don't."

He gasps, sucking all the air from the room as if I'd just hit him.

Spinning on my heel, I almost smile at the sight of the fury on his face.

"You don't get to keep running from me, Stella."

"Says who? You?" I ask, throwing my arms out. "Newsflash, asshole. I don't, and never will, answer to you."

His jaw tics as his teeth grind.

Thankfully, he dragged on his underwear before storming out here after me. I'm not sure I could cope having this argument with him still naked, tempting me.

"Tell me why you're really here," I demand. "And don't give me the 'I missed you' bullshit. The only thing you could have missed is humiliating me in front of anyone who cared to watch."

His lips part to argue and a warning growl rumbles up my throat.

"The truth, Seb. For fucking once in your life."

His lips purse, but something flashes in his eyes. Guilt.

I fucking knew this wasn't as simple as him missing me.

"Fine," he spits. "The boss wants you back to lure out the attacker."

"Finally," I cry. "The fucking truth." I hold his eyes, hoping like hell that he can't see the pain that lashes at my insides when he doesn't continue to plead his case for missing me.

I knew I was right. I knew he was spinning me a line.

"So what, he told you to do whatever necessary to get me back where I belonged?"

"Something like that," he mutters, clearly pissed.

"And my friends?"

"What about your fucking friends?"

"When did you decide to make them yours and insert yourself into every part of my life?"

"And here I was thinking you'd be grateful that I called them to explain why you wouldn't be in touch for a while."

"You expect me to believe you did that for me?"

"Believe what the fuck you want, Princess. Clearly it doesn't matter what I say. I could tell you the fucking sky was blue and you'd go outside and check."

"Can you blame me?" I shout back, the anger that's making my body tremble starting to get the better of me. "All you've done since the day we met is lie to me."

His lips part to argue, but I beat him to it.

"Why do you hate me, Seb? We're here now. Tell me everything."

"Your dad," he spits. "He killed mine."

Disbelief floods me and forces a laugh to erupt from my throat.

"Fucking hell," I mutter. "All of this is some fucked-up revenge tactic on my dad? Humiliating me, leaving me creepy fucking messages, generally being a fucking cunt... all of it's because of him?"

I shake my head. Unable to stand still any longer, I start pacing.

"And your plan was what, exactly?"

He doesn't respond immediately, and when I look at him, he swallows nervously.

"A bit fucking late to be shy, don't you think? What were you planning, Seb?"

"I wanted to break you, hurt you, and then deliver you back to him in the same kind of mess he left my family in."

"Wow," I breathe, everything suddenly making sense.

"He killed my father, took you, and ran like a fucking pussy. He was never meant to come back."

"So why did he?" I blurt out in my desperation to know everything.

He blows out a long breath. "I don't know. Clearly it wasn't for you to get to know Toby. But he wanted you protected."

"Protected?" I ask, my brows pulling together.

"Yeah, your dad had things put in place when you arrived to keep you safe."

I can't help but laugh. "What a joke, when it was *you* I needed protection from."

"He's smarter than he looks. He clearly knew I wasn't your worst threat."

The reminder that someone out there wants me dead sends a wave of fear through me, but I lock it down fast. He shouldn't have that kind of power over me.

"So now what? I come back, you use me as bait and what... hope he kills me this time as revenge for my father's pa—"

I don't get my final word out because my back collides with the wall, all the air rushing from my lungs as Seb's lips slam down on mine in a bruising kiss. It's a move that I'm much more used to, and as his fingers dig into my ass and he squeezes harshly, I forget all about my freak out and finally let myself drown in him.

Gone are the soft and gentle caresses from before, and in their place are his brutal touches that burn me from the inside out.

"I hate you," I seethe when he finally releases my mouth, but not before sinking his teeth into my bottom lip until the familiar taste of copper coats my tongue.

"Fuck, yeah," he grunts, ripping my panties from my body and throwing them somewhere behind him before his fingers find my core. "You love me hating you, don't you, Hellion?"

"Seb," I cry, my head falling back against the wall with a loud thud as he spears two fingers inside me. "Fuck."

"So wet," he murmurs against my neck. "So tight."

A wanton moan rips from my lips when he bends his fingers, finding my G-spot right as he sucks on a patch of skin, grazing it with his teeth.

"I'm going to fuck your cunt raw, Princess. It's been too long. Way too fucking long."

With his hand holding my hip, he sinks to his knees once more, but any tender kisses or comforting words are long gone as he throws my leg—the one with his initials still cut into my skin—over his shoulder and dives for my pussy.

"Missed this. Been fucking starving for it." The vibration of his voice against my sensitive skin is almost too much to take as his fingers and tongue work me toward what I know will be an earth-shattering release.

He's right about one thing. It's been too fucking long.

His tongue laps at my clit, his teeth biting and grazing as his fingers rub at the exact spot that makes me see stars.

"Come for me, Hellion," he growls darkly. "Come all over my face."

My fingers twist in his hair as my release approaches, but the pain only spurs him on and he eats at me like a man possessed as the one leg that's holding me up trembles, my knee threatening to give out.

"Princess." His eyes lift to mine and I lose all my fight to defy his orders.

"Seb," I scream, my eyes slamming closed as pleasure barrels into me, making the world, everything other than the two of us, disappear.

This... this is what I fucking needed.

"Fuck, I need inside you, Hellion."

I don't realize we're moving until a door slams and I'm thrown onto the bed. Any concern about my healing seems to have been forgotten as he falls on top of me, crushing me to the bed.

"This what you wanted, baby?"

He kisses down my spine, sucking my skin into his mouth and biting until I swear he's going to break my skin.

"Please," I whimper, my previous orgasm already forgotten as another begins to build.

This is how we work. The hateful barbs. The painful touches. Anything else is just—

"Oh my... fuck," I moan when he lifts my hips, licking at me from behind.

His tongue dips into me before gliding up to my ass.

"Oh God. Oh God," I chant as he circles my puckered hole, making my body crave more.

"Anyone been here before, Hellion?"

"N-no," I answer honestly. A few have promised, but no one's ever followed through.

"One day soon, I'm going to slide balls deep inside your ass, baby. Make every inch of you mine."

A violent shudder rips through me. Unlike all the other times I've heard similar words, I know that he'll act on it. He'll be the one to take me there. Be my first.

"Fuck, you're desperate for it, aren't you?" he asks, his lips trailing over my ass cheek before he sinks his teeth into the soft flesh, making me howl like a whore.

Crack.

His palm connects with the same patch of skin he bit, but his hold on my hip on the other side stops me from crashing back to the mattress.

He shifts, sliding his hand up until he's gripping the back of my neck, pinning me to the bed.

"Seb," I whimper when the tip of his cock drags through my wetness. "Please, I need—"

"I know what you need, Hellion. I always know what you need."

You didn't earlier when you tried all the nicey nicey bullshit.

"Yesss," I cry, forgetting my previous thought when he slams inside me.

He doesn't give me a chance to adjust to his

invasion. Instead he pulls out, his cock dragging against my walls and sending sparks shooting around my body before thrusting back inside me so hard I'd shoot up the bed if he weren't holding me in place with his bruising touch.

He does exactly as he promised and pounds into my pussy, fucking it raw until we're both gasping for breath, our skin glistening with sweat.

"Come for me, Hellion. Milk my cock."

"Seb," I cry, my release approaching even faster at his lust-filled voice.

Crack.

"Fuuuuck," I cry, my orgasm crashing into me, my entire body exploding with pleasure until everything goes black.

When I come back to myself, I'm lying on my side, my body pinned in place with a heavy arm and leg wrapped around me like a fucking koala.

"W-what are you doing?" I ask, fighting and failing to get away.

"Holding tighter than last time. You're done running from me, Stella."

Stella.

He must really mean business.

"What now?" I half moan, half sigh.

"Everything I said earlier." I groan, still not wanting to hear any of it. "I meant everything, every single word."

"You still lied to me."

"The boss might have suggested you need to come back, but I can assure you, I'm not here on his orders. *I* want you back, Princess. Calli, Toby, even your fucking father want you back."

I can't help tensing at the mention of my dad. At everything Seb told me out in the living room not so long ago.

"You've spoken to him?"

"We've... uh... had words."

I try to sit up so I can look at him, but he doesn't release his hold on me.

"What the hell does that mean?"

"I've had a chance to settle a few grievances I had with your father," he says cryptically.

I've spoken to him, so I know he's alive, but...

"What have you done to him?"

He pauses, his body shifting as if he's suddenly uncomfortable with this level of sharing.

"I might have hit him... a few times."

"Seb," I warn.

"What? He deserved it. Fucker's been lying to you for your entire life, the result of which landed you in the fucking hospital."

"So that's how you kept him away from me," I muse. "You put him in his own hospital bed, didn't you?"

"Briefly. But that wasn't why he didn't come to you."

"No?"

"He knew I was right, Princess. I might have said the words, but it was his guilt that kept him away."

"This is such a fucking mess."

He chuckles. "Welcome to the Family, Hellion."

I sigh, feeling the weight of that press down on me.

There are so many questions spinning around in my head, yet as my lips part to ask the most pressing, all that comes out is a yawn.

"You need to rest," he breathes, his hot breath tickling down my neck and making me shudder.

Despite my better judgement, my body gets heavier as I begin to lose my fight to the exhaustion.

I might pretend that all is well, that I'm healed. But the truth is, I'm not. I don't need the ache in my belly from our activities to tell me that.

"Relax. I've got you."

As I drift off, his weight lifts off me before his head disappears.

I want to complain, to demand he comes back, but I'm too far gone.

I do, however, sense when he returns and moves me so that he can clean me up.

The warmth of a washcloth seeps into my sensitive skin before sheets cover me.

"Seb," I whisper, my hand reaching out.

"Princess," he whispers back, crawling beside me and pulling me into his body. "I meant it. I missed you so fucking much, baby."

CHAPTER FOURTEEN

Sebastian

I didn't intend on falling asleep with her in my arms, but the second her breathing evened out, my jet lag seemed to slam into me like a truck, and it was all I could do to keep my eyes open and watch her.

Squeezing her a little tighter, I dropped my lips to the top of her head and kissed her hair.

The next thing I know, the hot body that's wrapped around me tries to discreetly slip from my arms.

A chuckle rumbles up my throat as my arms tighten around her.

"I don't think so, Hellion."

"I need to pee."

Dragging my eyes open, I stare up at her, my breath catching in my throat.

Fuck, she's beautiful.

"If you run, I'll chase you."

Sitting on the edge of the bed, she releases a sigh and glances back over her shoulder at me. Disbelief floods her face as she chews on her bottom lip, deep in thought.

All the things I want to say to her get stuck on the tip of my tongue as I remember how she reacted to me earlier.

The past few weeks, seeing her lying beside my dad's grave was something of a wakeup call for me. It's allowed me to reevaluate how I feel about this thing between us, about her. It seems she's not had similar reflections where I'm concerned.

Ripping her eyes away from mine, she shakes her head as she pushes from the bed and makes her way to the door.

My eyes track down her body that's covered in my shirt, and then to her bare, shapely legs sticking out of the bottom.

"I can feel you staring," she mutters before disappearing from the room.

"That's because I am. You look good in my clothes, Princess."

I swear I hear her murmur, "Not as good as you look in none."

I lie there, listening to her moving around, and the toilet flushes before the water runs.

My need to march in there and drag her into the shower with me is strong, but I manage to push it aside. It's helped when the door opens and her footsteps get closer once more.

Only, she doesn't come back. She walks straight past.

Afraid she's going to try to give me the slip, I throw the sheets back and pull my boxers up my legs once more.

"What are you—oh," I breathe when I find her leaning back against the counter beside the coffee machine, her bare legs still on show, my shirt sitting high on her thighs and her arms crossed under her breasts.

"Coffee?" she asks, her eyes tracking down my naked chest.

"Please."

Despite the fact that she's giving off 'don't come anywhere near me' vibes, I do the complete opposite and step right up to her, sliding my hand around the side of her neck.

Her pulse thunders beneath my fingers, showing me just how much my presence affects her.

"Helli—"

"Don't," she breathes. "Please don't."

My eyes hold hers as my thumb brushes her jawline.

"Talk to me, Princess. What's going on in your head?"

She remains silent, the rise and fall of her chest increasing.

"I don't... I don't trust you, Seb," she states coldly. "I can't believe anything that comes out of your mouth."

"That's fair," I say, despite the pain that radiates from my chest.

Yes, I've hurt her. Yes, I've lied to her. But I've sure as hell put more effort into protecting her than I did any of that.

Silence falls around the house as we continue to stare at each other, the coffee machine long finished, the smell of the beans mixing with her mouth-watering scent.

"Did you have any plans for the rest of the day?" I ask, swallowing down my need to say anything about what she told me earlier. There's no point in me trying to convince her that she can trust me when all I've done is prove otherwise. That's something she's going to have to figure out on her own, even if it kills me.

She shakes her head. "I think we're just hanging out at Harley's later. They haven't let me do anything fun since I arrived." She rolls her eyes at their overprotectiveness.

"You've got good friends, Princess."

"Yeah," she agrees, finally moving herself from my hold and putting another mug in the machine. "Here."

"Thanks," I mutter, taking it from her and stealing her place at the counter.

Silence once again falls between us, but it's not uncomfortable.

"Will you do something for me?" I ask once she's got her own coffee and pulled out one of the seats at the table.

She glances over, hesitation filling her eyes.

"Take me to your favourite place here."

Her lips part, but no words find their way out for the longest time.

"My favourite place?" she asks, a deep frown forming on her brows.

"Yeah, the place you'd go when shit got too much."

"Like the graveyard?"

"Y-yeah, but maybe somewhere a little less depressing."

"Only you could have a happy place full of dead people."

"Hellion, that place is anything but happy for me."

Regret passes over her face. "Right. Sorry," she says on a wince.

She sips on her coffee, and my need to be closer to her gets the better of me. I pull out the chair next to her and drop down, ensuring my leg brushes hers under the table.

"Seb," she breathes.

My heart slams in my chest as I stare at her, waiting for the other shoe to drop. She's too calm after her nap.

"I'm... I'm sorry about whatever went down between our fathers. I'm sorry you lost yours so early. That's not fair. But none of that is my fault."

I nod, knowing that she's right.

"There is so much bullshit surrounding my life. I just... I really need this—" she gestures between the two of us, "to stop."

"This?" I ask, sliding my hand over the table and capturing hers.

Her breath catches at the contact, her eyes jumping to mine.

"I hate to tell you, Princess, but *this*," I twist our

fingers together, "isn't stopping. I need this, and I think you do too."

"I m-meant the revenge. The pain."

A wicked smile curls at my lips. "You love the pain."

Her cheeks pink, a smirk appearing on her lips.

"That might have been the wrong word," she jokes. "Drink up," she instructs, draining the contents of her mug and pushing away from the table.

"Where are you going?" I ask, watching as she washes it up and heads back toward the bathroom.

"You wanted me to take you somewhere, didn't you?"

"Yeah," I breathe, a smile twitching at my lips. Maybe we're already making headway on the trust thing.

An hour later, she pulls back up to the car park beside the diner we had breakfast in earlier, only now, the sun is starting to drop lower in the sky and the families that were enjoying an early autumn day on the beach have left, leaving the sand almost deserted aside from a couple of groups of kids still playing volleyball.

"The beach is your happy place?"

"Not all of the beach. Only a certain part of it."

"Lead the way."

She takes off ahead of me and heads for the sand. The second she's descended the few steps, she stops and pulls her boots off.

"You might want to roll your pants up," she tells me when I come to a stop beside her.

"Okay."

With my jeans rolled up to my mid-calves, we walk side by side, down to where the sea is lapping at the beach.

The warmth of the water surrounds my feet, reminding me that we're a long way from home right now.

"I could get used to this," I mutter, thinking how nice it must be to live somewhere you can swim in a sea that's as warm as stepping into a bath.

"It's pretty incredible."

Silence falls between us as we walk, and although we're shoulder to shoulder, I can't help myself... when our hands brush, I grab hers, twisting our fingers together.

Keeping my eyes focused on where we're going, I sense her glance up at me.

"We're not fighting, Hellion. Not here. Not in your happy place."

She sucks in a breath that I swear steals all the air from my lungs, but she decides against whatever it is she was going to say, instead nodding her head subtly.

"I can't believe I'm bringing you out here."

"Is allowing me to get to know you really that terrifying?"

"It gives you power."

"How'd you figure that, Princess?"

"The more you know, the closer you get, the more pain you can cause."

"Baby, I'm not—"

"I need more than your words, Seb. I've heard enough bad ones. If you're serious, then I'm going to need more solid evidence."

Lifting her hand, in a move very, very, unlike me, I bring the back of it to my lips and press a kiss there.

"I'll see what I can do."

The warm sea water laps at our feet and ankles as we continue walking hand in hand, the sun sinking in the sky making our shadows stretch ahead of us.

"Do you really think the person who stabbed me will try again?" she asks after the longest time.

"Yes," I state firmly.

"It could have just been a random attack."

"Don't be naïve, Stella. You're smarter than that. He stabbed you with your own knife. Unless there's something you're not telling me..."

She tenses and immediately tries to rip her hand from mine.

"What the hell, Seb?" she barks when I refuse to let her go.

"I was just asking. If there's anything you haven't told us about the lead up to that day, then..."

"There isn't. I ran because my dad just dropped the bomb that the guy trying to fucking kiss me was my brother."

"He kissed you?"

"Really?" she snaps. "You're really going to get jealous now?"

"He wanted what was mine."

"Firstly," she spits, turning to me and forcing me to

stop walking, "I'm not yours. I'm not a thing that belongs to anyone, especially not you." I nod, although I fully intend to prove her wrong. She's mine. End of. "And two—"

"Secondly, you mean."

"W-what?"

"You said firstly, and then said two for your second point."

"Fucking hell. Are you always this fucking— No, don't answer that, I already know. *Secondly*," she rolls her eyes at me, although from the hard set of her jaw, I wouldn't put it past her to give me a matching scar, "he's my fucking brother. We share the same DNA. If I'm going to be running away with any of your friends, it won't be Toby. Theo, though... he's ho—"

My hand clamps over her mouth.

"Do not finish that sentence. You're mine, Stella. I might love my boys, but they've already had enough of you."

I don't need to pull my hand away to know she's smiling. I fucking know why, too.

"Yeah, all right. You hit your target every fucking time that night, Princess."

Dragging my hand away from her face, I find the exact smug grin I was expecting.

"He was the best kisser, you know. Although Daemon did this thing with his tongue that—"

This time I cut her words off with my own lips, plunging my tongue into her mouth to find hers and prove that the only person she needs to be kissing is me.

Looping our joined hands around her back, I drag

her closer, pressing the front of her body against mine, allowing her to feel exactly what one kiss from her does to me.

Ripping my lips from hers, I lick a line to her ear.

"The only person who's going to be kissing these lips from here on out, is me, Hellion. You got that?"

She nods, it's subtle, but I feel every bit of it.

"Good. I don't care if it's one of my brothers. I will end anyone who touches you, Princess."

"Seb," she whimpers, my promise of violence doing things to her, just like it does me. It's the reason that we're a match made in hell.

"Okay, now we've cleared that up... Shall we?" I gesture to the beach before us, and after a beat, she returns to my side and we continue walking until we come to a stop by some huge rocks that end our path.

"The water's higher than I was hoping for. You're probably going to get wet pants." She looks to the end of the last rock, clueing me in to where we're going.

With a shrug, I release her hand, drop my shoes and pop open my jeans, dragging them off my legs and throwing them over my shoulder.

"Better?"

"Uh..." She takes a couple of steps back into the water, but her eyes remain glued to my boxers, which do a really shit job at hiding my semi. "This could be either a really stupid idea or the best I've ever had."

Her eyes sparkle with evil intent.

"You're meant to be resting, Princess. I'm not sure those ideas would be good for your wound."

"Huh... and here I was thinking you didn't want me to go seeking comfort from anyone else."

"Comfort? I thought you just wanted my cock."

I wade into the water, following her as she spins around and walks out until the waves lap up over her knees, rounding the huge rock and disappearing around the other side.

There weren't many people back on the beach, but it becomes immediately obvious that we're totally secluded around here.

The small cove is surrounded by towering rocks on each side. It's the last thing I was expecting to see after all the perfect white sand we've walked over.

"Wow, this is—"

"Paradise?" she finishes for me. "It's almost like you're the only person on the planet around here."

"Two people."

"Huh?"

"The only two people," I say, catching her hand once more and pulling her into my body for a burning kiss.

The second it ends, she slips out of my hold and walks out of the water.

"So you really think this guy is going to try again?"

"Where was the last place you saw your knife, Hellion?" I ask, lowering myself to the patch of dry sand beside her.

"You brought it back to me the day Teagan trashed my car. It was in my cheer bag."

"Did you ever take it out?"

"Uh..." She thinks, resting back on her palms. "I

might have put it on my nightstand. I don't remember putting it into my purse."

"So it was still in your bedroom?"

She looks over at me with a knowing smirk playing on her lips.

"Are you sure you didn't take it? You seem to have a thing for sneaking into my room and stealing my things."

"Your knickers, Princess. I like to steal your knickers, not your knife."

"Well, you were giving it back because you stole it," she points out.

"Yeah, okay. Guilty." I lie back, resting on my elbow and staring down at her as she fully reclines. "I was hoping for a little tit for tat. I return yours, I might get mine."

"Ah, there's always an ulterior motive. And to think, I just thought you wanted me to stab Teagan in the leg for even daring to go near my baby."

"Your baby?" I ask with amusement.

"Yeah, and I miss her. What of it?"

"You're something else, you know that?"

"Takes one to know one." Twisting onto her side, we lie facing each other while the waves continue to lap at our feet and the sky around us turns orange with the sunset. "So you didn't take my knife back again, and the Italians apparently didn't stab me. So who did, Sherlock?"

"That's the million-dollar question, baby. Right after how he got your fucking knife if it was safely in your room."

"You're suggesting there's some other sick fuck out there who likes sneaking into my room and leaving little love notes on my mirror?"

"I'm sorry. That was petty." She quirks a brow. "I thought you were there. I was pissed when I didn't find you covered in soap and naked in the shower."

"Nope. I was getting my rocks off with an Italian stallion at Nico's party."

A growl rumbles low in my throat, making her chuckle.

"You really are quite possessive, aren't you, Sebastian?"

"I thought you realised that the second I carved my name into your thigh. And for the record, I'm not sorry about that."

CHAPTER FIFTEEN

Stella

Seb stares down into my eyes with a look that makes my heart race too quickly.

It's too much, and I can feel myself closing down again.

I want the truth. I want to know how he really feels, but hearing that he doesn't actually hate me doesn't make me feel anything like I expected. I thought I'd be relieved. Relieved that this thing I feel isn't just one-sided. But, along with all the others, he's obliterated my trust, and I just can't find it in myself to believe a word that rolls off his tongue.

My heart desperately wants to, but my head is set on being sensible and protecting my fickle heart.

"I thought that was more of a 'no one else can have you' move."

"Partly," he admits, lowering his face to mine until our noses brush, "but mostly, it was a 'you're mine' move."

He captures my lips before I can respond and kisses me so deeply it makes my thighs clench, and all my arguments about his caveman ways fall from my head.

When he finally pulls back, his eyes are dark and full of wicked intent, and his chest is heaving. Seeing that his mask is long gone, I dive into the honesty thing with both feet, risking asking something he's not going to want to talk about.

"Tell me about Demi," I whisper.

All the air rushes from his lungs and he rolls onto his back.

I knew that demand would hit him hard, but I wanted to push him. If I'm ever going to trust him, I need to know the hard and ugly shit that makes him tick.

Sensing that he needs it, I tuck myself into his side and place my hand on his abs. His muscles jump at the contact, and I have to smother a smile, knowing that my touch alone affects him.

"She was..." he blows out a long breath. "The most incredible person. Genuine. Kind. Caring. Pretty much everything I'm not."

I'm not sure if he wants me to argue with him, but I don't.

"She kept me grounded. Especially after our older sisters, Sophia and Zoe, embarked on their own lives. Things were easier when it was the four of us fighting for survival. But they grew up and left us behind."

"Fighting for survival?" I ask.

"One disaster at a time, yeah?" His eyes find mine and my breath catches at the dark pools of nothingness that stare back at me.

I nod, allowing him to continue.

"She'd just started working her first job. I'd been making money since I was fourteen, thanks to Damien, but Demi didn't like it. She was older and wanted me to be a kid like I should have been. But that was never a possibility for me. We needed money, and I could make a hell of a lot more than she could at our local corner shop."

I nod, my eyes holding his, urging him to continue.

"On a Thursday night, she worked until closing. I'd always bike to meet her so she didn't have to go home alone. We might live in one of the nicest areas of London, but knowing she was alone when it was dark terrified me."

"You're a good brother, Seb."

He scoffs at my praise. "You might change your mind in a minute."

He blows out a shaky breath, and I shift that little bit closer.

"I was hanging out at Theo's with Alex and Nico that night. They knew it was the anniversary of my dad's death, and they were trying to distract me. We were lost in the new PlayStation game that had just come out, and I completely lost track of time."

My stomach twists, a million and one things beginning to run around my head about what could have happened.

"By the time I realised, I threw the controller down and raced from the house. The guys felt as guilty as I did. I don't need to tell you how protective Nico is over Calli, and Theo is the oldest of four, so he always understood my need to keep an eye on Demi.

"They followed me out of the house, and the three of us jumped on our bikes and raced toward the shop she'd have left about ten minutes earlier."

Reaching up, he wraps his hand around mine as his heart thunders beneath my palm.

"I remember the panic, which I knew was ridiculous. She'd have just biked home, and she'd be fine. But something in my gut told me that wasn't right. My legs burned as I cycled as fast as I could, and the second I heard a siren in the distance, I knew.

"The rest of the journey is a blur. All I remember is turning the corner and finding all the flashing lights. The police cars, the ambulances, the fire engines. It was carnage, and I swear to God my heart actually stopped.

"There were three cars completely mangled, and as I approached, pushing officers aside so I could find Demi, my eyes landed on her crippled bike in the center of it all."

"Oh my God," I sob, needing to lift my hand to my mouth in shock but unable to with the force of Seb's grip on me.

I stare down at him, my vision blurred with tears. Seeing his own pooling at the corners of his eyes does nothing to help me keep the emotion down.

"The driver who caused it was off-his-face drunk. He collided with another car at the junction with such speed that they spun out of control, hitting another car, and Demi on her bike as they skidded across the road."

"Seb..."

"She looked so perfect, lying in the middle of the road. I expected her to just get up, shake it off and ask me to take her home. But she never did."

My entire body trembles as I fight to stay strong for him.

"They think she died on impact. Her body stood no chance against the speed of the hit.

"S-she—"

Cutting off his words, I lean down and capture his quivering lips in an all-consuming kiss as my hand cups his face, my thumb brushing away the tear that finally drops.

I kiss him until we're both breathless, but when it comes to an end, I barely move, just pressing my brow to his.

"Fuck. You've got a great way of making me feel better, Princess."

I can't help but laugh at his attempt at a joke.

"I'm so sorry you had to go through that. I can't even imagine."

"I wish you could have met her," he whispers.

"Me too."

"Although, the more I think about it, the two of you would have given me hell between you."

"Are you still close with your older sisters?" although from his confession about his niece earlier, I assume he must be.

"Yeah. When you've grown up with lives like ours, you've got to stick together."

The fact that he hasn't mentioned his mom at all kind of terrifies me. To the point that I swallow down the question about her that's on the tip of my tongue. I'm not sure I want to put him through anything else after reliving the horror of that story.

"You can meet them when you come home."

"When?" I ask with a smirk.

"Yeah, baby. *When.* There's no *if* here. You're mine now, remember?"

My jaw flexes, but when I see the corner of his mouth curl up in amusement, I know he's just baiting me.

Asshole.

"Anyone would think you don't want to get laid again."

Throwing my legs over his waist, I roll my hips over his cock.

"Hellion," he growls.

Leaning forward, I brush my lips over his ear.

"I thought you liked my distraction techniques."

"Did you bring me to your happy place to have your wicked way with me, Princess?"

"Why? Aren't you up for it?" I ask, rolling my hips over his hard length to prove my point.

He chuckles.

"I'm always up for sinking inside your tight cunt, Hellion."

"Prove it," I growl as his hand slips between us, his

fingers hooking my panties aside so they can sink into my wet heat.

"Mine," he moans, curling two digits inside me, making me cry out.

"Yes," I scream but regret it the second I see his wide smirk. "Just fuck me, asshole."

"And they say romance is dead," he mutters, ripping his fingers from me and tugging his boxers down to release his hard length.

"Fuck romance, take me to heaven."

When we finally make it back to Harley's a couple of hours later, I've got sand in places there should never be sand, and my body is aching in the most delicious way.

"Hey, look," Ruby calls from the kitchen as we close the front door behind us. "They haven't killed each other. Oh my God," she adds when she gets a proper look at us, "on second thought, you both look thoroughly fucked up."

"I should think so," Seb mutters happily, running his fingers through his hair and pushing it back from his brow. "Sex on the beach really is all it's cracked up to be."

My chin drops at his serious lack of filter as the others all barrel into the kitchen to find out the latest drama.

"Nice one, bro," Ash says, holding his hand up.

"Oh my God, Ashton," Ruby snaps. "You did not just high-five him for that."

Ash shrugs before sweeping his girl into his arms. "You gonna try to convince everyone that sex on the beach isn't fucking epic, little one?"

Her cheeks burn bright red before he captures her lips in a kiss that is way too erotic for an audience.

"Right well, as fun as this little porno is, I could really do with a shower."

Seb's words make realization hit me.

"Where are you staying?" I ask, looking up at him, ignoring the lip smacking on the other side of the island.

A smug grin pulls at his lips.

"Seb?"

"Top of the stairs, second on the right," Harley tells him.

"Wait, what?"

"Come on, Hellion." He slips his hand into mine and all but drags me from the room and up the stairs.

"What the hell, Seb? You can't just—" He crashes through the door of the guest room I've been staying in, pulling me along for the ride. "Why is there a suitcase on my bed?"

"Thought you might have been lonely."

"How? What? I can't believe—" My protests are cut off when he wraps his fingers around the hem of my sweater and drags it up my body.

"Did you want to get the sand off, or what?"

My bra is gone a few seconds later, quickly followed by my skirt falling down my legs and my panties being ripped from my body.

Balling them up in his hand, he lifts them to his face and sniffs.

Gross.

"Fuck, I missed this."

Throwing them to the side, he drags his own clothes from his body and then resumes pulling me around like I'm nothing more than a rag doll.

"Wait," I cry a second before he turns the dial in the shower. "It's going to be—argh—cold."

"I've got you covered, Princess," he groans, pulling my body up against his warm one as his hands slide down my back until he's cupping my ass.

Lifting me, he presses me back against the tiles, but this time, I don't feel the cold. I'm too lost in his dark eyes.

"Can't get enough, Hellion."

"Kiss me," I demand, my breaths coming out in gasps as he stares at me with something akin to awe.

Unlike the last time I said those words, he doesn't refuse. Instead, he wraps his hand around the side of my neck, allowing him to tilt me exactly as he wants me, and he claims my lips in a kiss that only solidifies everything he's said to me since jumping me in the parking lot earlier.

I might not be about to admit it anytime soon, but he's right.

I'm his.

CHAPTER SIXTEEN

Sebastian

"Come on," Ash screams at the TV when the Panthers fail to score a touchdown. "Fucking hell, Dunn," he barks, throwing his hands around for effect.

"Chill the fuck out, man," Kyle says. "They've got this."

"Are we even watching the same game?"

Ripping my eyes away from their bickering, I look back at the screen briefly before continuing around the room to where the girls are chatting, not the slightest bit interested in the football game.

I thought Poppy might have wanted to watch, but I've since discovered that Harley's brother, her boyfriend, is on the bench, so she's happily ignoring the TV with the others.

My eyes run down the length of Stella's body, my cock stirring once more. After weeks of nothing, it's more than ready to make up for lost time.

Her black dress wraps around her curves like it's a second skin. Her hair is piled on top of her head, leaving her neck exposed.

My tongue licks along my bottom lip right as she looks over her shoulder at me, obviously sensing my attention.

Her eyes drop to my lips, darkening in desire.

"For someone who hates you, she's good at the come-fuck-me eyes," Kyle mutters beside me.

"She loves hating me. It's half the fun."

"Remember it well, man. Another beer?" he asks, nodding toward my almost empty bottle.

"Thanks."

"Oh for fuck's sake," Ash barks once more, making Kyle pause at the door to see what's gone wrong this time.

"Something is up with that bunch. I know the team is new this year, but it's like they're all on a different fucking field," he mutters before disappearing from the room.

"This is bullshit. Poppy," he calls, earning himself the attention of all the girls. "Have a fucking word with your boy. This is a joke."

"Oh yeah, because the new recruit holds all the power," she snaps back.

"Well, these motherfuckers don't seem to have any," he sulks, falling back onto the sofa.

"Aw, baby. Do you need cheering up?" Ruby asks, walking over and crawling onto his lap.

For a second, he tries to look around her, but when the Panthers fumble another pass he gives up and turns his full attention to his girl.

His hands slide up her thighs, his fingers vanishing under the fabric of her skirt.

"What have you got in mind, little one?"

She brushes her lips against his, and he forgets all about the game and dives in.

"You really are all about the voyeurism, huh?" Stella asks, dropping down onto my lap with an easy smile playing on her lips thanks to the vodka shots I saw her and the girls necking an hour or so ago.

"What?" I ask innocently. "I'm doing nothing."

"Suuure. Watching those two with desire filling your eyes is nothing."

"I don't want Ruby, if that's where you're going."

"I'm not. I know you don't. Although, I must admit," she says, her eyes lighting up with excitement, "if my girls did want you, I could turn the tables and mark my territory." Her fingers walk down my stomach toward my waistband.

"Oh yeah. And how exactly would that look?" I ask, playing along with her.

"Well first, I think you'd need my mark on your skin."

"That's kind of permanent."

"Didn't bother you when you marked me," she points out with a raised brow.

"Fair point. Then what, Hellion?"

"Then..." Lifting my shirt, she finds the button on my jeans, toying with it and me. "I'd show them exactly what they can't have." Finally, she opens my waistband, tucking her fingers underneath.

"Baby," I warn, knowing that if she touches me, all bets are going to be off, her friends be damned.

"What?" she asks, innocently batting her eyes at me. "So it was good enough for you to expose me in front of all your friends, but I can't do the same to you?"

"Hellion, if you wanna suck me off right here, there's no chance I'd fucking stop you. I couldn't give a fuck who's watching."

"You're wicked."

"Just like you, Princess. Match made in hell, remember?"

"Ashton!" Ruby's cry pierces the air, but neither of us looks over. We don't need to. We know exactly what's happening on that sofa.

"So what's it gonna be, Hellion? You gonna make me yours right here?"

Her hand dips lower, her fingers just brushing my dick before music fills the room and Harley shouts, "Let's dance."

"Aw, sorry, babe. Looks like our time is up." She winks before jumping from my lap, leaving the very obvious bulge in my jeans open for everyone in the room to witness.

"You're gonna pay for that," I warn, running my eyes down her body.

"I'm counting on it."

Reaching over, she helps Ruby off Ashton's lap and

drags her over to where Harley has decided the dancefloor is.

"Fucking tease," Ash barks, tugging at his jeans in a very familiar way.

"What did I miss?" Kyle shouts over the music as he throws beers at both of us.

"Just them playing their usual tricks," Ash snaps, shooting a heated look at Ruby as she dances with her front to Stella's back.

"Fucking hell."

Harley passes them both another shot that they both immediately throw back.

Kyle mutes the TV, both of them mostly giving up with watching the Panthers get thrashed as the three of us watch our girls let loose and drive us fucking crazy, dancing together.

And they know exactly what they're doing.

"I need some of that vodka if I've gotta watch this," I announce, pushing to the edge of the sofa.

"Got you covered, man," Kyle says, passing a bottle over that I didn't notice him carry in. "Let's get fucked up. Show the Brit how it's really done."

I can't help but laugh. "I could drink both of you under the table," I say with confidence.

"Okay," Kyle says, deep in thought. "Willing to bet tomorrow's workout on it?"

"I go to training most days with a hangover. I'm all in, motherfucker." Just to prove my point, I tip the bottle to my lips and chug a good quarter of it, the vodka burning down my throat and making me wince.

"We start at seven, so make sure you're ready," Ash

smirks, swiping the bottle from my hand when I offer it over.

"I'm always fucking ready. Excuse me."

Finally pushing up from the sofa, I walk right up to my girl, drag her from Ruby, and pull her into my body.

"Dance with me."

"Demanding asshole."

"You love it," I growl in her ear, gripping her ass and holding her against me.

"Seb," she cries when I drop my face into the crook of her neck, sucking on her soft skin before biting down until it hurts.

A loud pounding on the door startles me, and my first reaction is to throw myself over Stella's sleeping body.

"What the fuck, asshole?" she hisses, her voice all rough and sexy with sleep.

"S-sorry," I say, my surroundings coming back to me.

"Get the hell up, motherfucker," a deep voice booms through the door.

"Aw, fuck."

"Fuck off, Kyle," Stella calls. "It's too fucking early for this shit."

"No can do, girl. Your boy told us he'd be ready for a session this morning."

"Really?" she hisses at me. "You agreed to work out with those assholes first thing on a Sunday morning?"

I shrug. "Sorry, baby," I say, rolling over her with a

very different intention this time. "Gotta show them how it's really done."

"And to think, I was expecting you to stay here and show *me* how it's done." Her voice is pure sex, and I instantly regret ever agreeing to this plan.

"Go back to sleep. I'll wake you when I'm back." Dipping my head to her ear, I growl, "With my tongue."

"You're full of shit, Seb."

"And you should be full of me."

I climb from the bed and walk naked to the bathroom.

"Big words for someone who's about to leave me in favor of hanging out with *my* friends."

I can't help but laugh as I take a piss, trying to ignore the rhythmic banging that's taken up residence in my head.

Fucking vodka.

By the time I emerge from the bathroom to find something to work out in, Stella is asleep again.

Walking over, I gently brush a strand of hair out of her face and tuck it behind her ear.

"Sweet dreams, Princess," I whisper, dropping a kiss to her brow.

"Ah, he is alive," Kyle booms the second I round the corner into the kitchen. I'm about to bark back when the sight of a woman sitting at the counter with a coffee stops me.

"Um... hey, I'm Seb."

"Stella's guy?" she asks, assessing me.

"Um... yeah. Harley's mum, I assume."

"Jada," she says, finally breaking a smile. "It's nice

to meet you. I've heard... a lot about you, and not all good."

"Well," I say, holding my hands up in surrender. "I can't really argue with that."

"He's cool, J," Kyle adds, helping me out. "I don't think you've got anything to worry about."

"Not true. I worry about all my kids." She smiles at him, but when her eyes return to mine, there's a darker edge to them. "You're not the only one with connections to some dangerous men, Sebastian. Hurt one of ours, and we'll make sure justice is served. With blood."

My chin drops as Kyle barks out a laugh beside me.

"Okay, that's our cue to go."

I follow Kyle out of the kitchen, looking back briefly before we leave the house, Ashton is jogging down the stairs to catch up with us.

"She's joking. Right?" I ask, her words still on repeat in my head.

"What did Momma Hunter say?" Ash asks.

"Threatened Seb with blood spill."

"Damn, she must really not like you."

"She is joking, right?"

We come to a stop at Kyle's car, and he turns to me before we climb inside. Ash doesn't bother waiting and slides into the passenger seat.

"Yes and no. Stella and her dad probably didn't end up here by coincidence."

"What the hell does that mean?"

"Have you ever heard of the Harrow Creek Hawks?"

"Umm... no. Should I?"

"I have no idea. It hasn't been my life for a while."

Before I can respond, he ducks into the car, leaving me standing there with my head spinning.

"You were in a gang?" I ask after a few minutes of silence as he drives us to wherever we're going.

"I was never really *in* it. But my brother is more than connected, and some others I know. This motherfucker ain't all that innocent either," he says, nodding to what I now realise is a very green looking Ash.

I guess that explains why we all hit it off so well. We're all cut from the same cloth.

"She's right, though. Stella's one of us as much as she is one of you. Our girls see her as a sister. You hurt her, you hurt us. And I'm sure you don't need me to spell out what that means."

Kyle's eyes meet mine in the rearview mirror.

"And I thought we were just working out. I wasn't expecting the death threats," I mutter, looking out at the passing houses.

"Then you'd better look after our girl."

We meet a couple of the guys' teammates down at the beach, and one guy who graduated last year but hasn't left town for college takes charge of their insane morning workout.

And when I say insane, I really fucking mean it. These guys do not mess about, and by the time we're done, my legs are like jelly, every muscle in my body quivering with exhaustion, and I can't catch my breath.

"Regretting it yet?" Kyle asks, sounding almost as

out of breath as me as he collapses at my side in the sand.

"That was fucking brutal."

"Don't say we didn't warn you."

I lie there, staring up at the cloudless blue sky above me as sweat drips from my body, but damn, do I feel good. I lost count of the number of orgasms I've had since reconnecting with Stella yesterday, and now this. It's the most alive I've felt in a long time.

"Come on," he says after a few silent moments. "The girls are prepping food for us."

Everything aches and pulls as I climb to my feet and follow Kyle and Ash back to the car.

The drive home is pretty quiet, all of us shell-shocked.

There's another car in the Hunters' driveway when we pull up, but I pay it little mind.

I've put everything in place to ensure Stella's been safe every second she's been here, so I have no reason to think she's in any danger—and I quickly discover I'm right when we all pile out and find the girls in the kitchen.

"Holy fuck," I breathe, coming to an abrupt halt when my eyes land on Stella and what's in her arms.

The guys on either side of me bark out laughs, as if they totally understand.

"Did your future just flash before your eyes?" Ash asks, slapping me on the shoulder. "Been there, bro. Freaky shit, right? Be careful of the mother, raging bitch," he says a little too loudly.

"I heard that, Ashton Fury," a curvy brunette snaps

from her seat at the island. "Ignore him. I'm lovely, really."

Both Ash and Kyle snort a laugh.

"Whatever," she scoffs. "I'm Chelsea, and that little nugget is Nadine."

"Right," I mutter, turning my attention back to Stella with a freaking baby cradled in her arms.

"Cute, right?"

"Uh…" I look between the two of them a couple of times. "Y-yeah, she's cute." It's not a lie; she's got a full head of dark hair just like her mummy, and chubby cheeks.

"It's okay, I'm not about to ask to have one of my own. Jeez."

"S-sorry, I just wasn't expecting—"

"That's what I said," the guy who ran our torture session this morning announces, walking into the room and dropping a kiss to the baby's head, capturing her mum's attention.

"Your London boy did good, Stella."

"Oh yeah?" she asks with something akin to pride in her eyes.

"Yeah. I mean, he's not going to be a real football player anytime soon, but not bad."

"*Real* football?" I ask, more than ready to get into that argument again.

"Food's ready," Harley buts, cutting off any impending debate about the correct shape of a football.

We hang out, eating pancakes and bacon that the girls cooked. It's nice, and it makes me wonder what it might be like back home if the guys ever find themselves serious girlfriends. It'll certainly change our dynamic a little.

We've spent the past few years partying hard, fucking as many girls as we can get our hands on, and generally acting like the fucking assholes that Stella's accusing us of being.

I briefly wonder if things are already changing and I'd not even realised it.

I mean, I flew halfway across the world for a girl without a second thought and inserted myself into her life here.

Only a few months ago, I wouldn't have even considered chasing a girl to the other side of the city.

"Jesus," I mutter to myself, scrubbing my hand down my face.

"You okay?" Stella asks, placing her hand on my thigh, her arms now free from holding the baby.

Warmth floods me from her touch, making my skin come alive... amongst other parts of my body.

"Yeah. I'm just going to go out back and call Theo."

"Okay," she breathes, leaning forward to place a kiss on my lips.

I'm not even out of my chair before she's been dragged back into the conversation.

I stop in the doorway and just watch her for a moment. She looks so happy here. Relaxed. The complete opposite to how she was in London. It makes me realise that the person I met at home isn't really her.

I guess the version of me she met wasn't real, either.

Chelsea notices me watching Stella, a soft smile curling at her lips as she holds my eyes for a beat before

I slip from the room and pull my phone from my pocket.

"What the actual fuck?" It's not until his rough, sleepy voice comes down the line that I ever consider the time difference.

"You should have been up hours ago," I state happily, figuring it's already past lunchtime there.

"You are way too fucking jolly. You got between her legs already, didn't you?"

"Dude, I never kiss and tell, you know that."

"Bull-fucking-shit, bro. You usually delight in telling us every minute detail."

"Yeah, well, maybe times are changing."

Silence crackles down the line for a beat before he sucks in a breath.

"Fuck me. You really have fallen for her, haven't you?"

"No, I... uh..."

"Fucking hell, Seb. She fucking owns you, and you don't even know it."

I think about the time we've spent together since that first fight in Kyle's brother's house, and I can't help the smile that tugs at my lips.

"She's..." I trail off, not knowing how to explain whatever it is that's changed between us. "She's good fun."

"Yeah, man. I know that, I've partied with her."

"And the faster you forget about that night the better."

"But the next morning is fair play for the wank bank?"

A growl rumbles up my throat as that memory hits me, of the heat in my brothers' eyes as they stared at her cunt as I worked her to orgasm.

"Fuck you, Cirillo. Fuck you."

All he does is laugh down the line, making my grip on the phone turn painful.

What the fuck was I thinking?

CHAPTER SEVENTEEN

Stella

"Go and get dressed," Seb whispers in my ear. "I'm taking you out."

Twisting around on the sun lounger I'm resting on with the girls, I find him sitting on his haunches, wearing a pair of ripped jeans and a fitted black shirt. His hair is freshly styled and the scruff on his chin has finally seen a shaver. He looks like he did when we first met.

Hot as fuck.

"Y-yeah, okay. Where are we going?" I ask, although from what he's wearing, I'm guessing it's not anywhere fancy.

"Just go and put something sexy on, Hellion."

The second I'm off of the lounger, he drops onto it.

"So what were we talking about, ladies?" he asks

Harley, Ruby and Poppy. "Stella was telling you all just how insane my dick is, right?"

"Fucking hell," I mutter, walking into the house, not wanting to know if they humor him or tell him the truth about the fact that we were talking about the new cheer routine Ruby is choreographing with Chelsea's help.

The guys' voices rumble down from the den, but I ignore them and make my way up to my room to get ready.

I pull on a pair of skinny jeans and a sweater before applying some mascara and gloss and freshening up my hair.

I stand and look at myself in the full-length mirror before I leave the room.

Not bad for a rush job.

I smile as I think about the fact that he probably wants me in a slutty little dress like last night.

I laugh to myself as I pull the door open.

He thinks he's got away with all his bullshit so easily. Does he really think I'd forget all about his asshole behavior just because he got on a plane and hopped over the Atlantic? Does he not know me at all?

"I'm ready," I call from the sliding doors that lead out to where we were hanging out around the pool.

Seb gets up from the lounger and stalks my way, his annoyingly hot swagger making my mouth water.

Why does he have to be the human version of my kryptonite?

"You look beautiful, Princess," he breathes, running his eyes down my body before zeroing in on my glossy red lips.

"Uh-uh," I say, pressing my hand to the center of his chest when he leans in for a kiss. "Unless you want to go out covered in my gloss."

"As long as it's yours, I couldn't give a fuck, Hellion," he growls, edging closer.

"Seb," I warn when his nose touches mine.

His eyes crinkle with his smile before he ducks to the side and nuzzles my neck instead.

"Fuck. You smell good enough to eat. Maybe we should just stay in."

"Nah, you promised me food. We're going."

"Did I?" he mutters between kisses. "I don't remember promising anything."

"Well in my head you did, so let's go. I'm going to need some sustenance for what I'm sure you're planning."

He chuckles darkly.

"That *I'm* planning?" His hand skims up my body and pinches my hard nipple through my lace bra and thin sweater. "I know you're wet for me, baby, but if you want to pretend that you're not imagining me moving inside you right now, then I guess we can."

Damn him.

He pulls away from me and stares down into my hungry, lust-filled eyes.

"Fuck, you're so easy, Hellion."

My brows lift in offense, but all he does is laugh.

"I've watched you work a room, baby. Don't forget that."

Fair point.

"See you later," I call to the girls, who wave us off.

TRACY LORRAINE

"Gonna tell me where we're going yet?" I ask as Seb leads us toward Harley's car, opening the door for me like the gentleman he most certainly isn't.

"Nope. I thought we could hang, just the two of us."

"And here I was thinking you liked to share your toys."

He's laughing as he walks around the hood and drops into the driver's seat.

"Toys, yeah. You? Never."

This time when his eyes flick down to my mouth, he forgets all about my protests, wraps his hand around the back of my neck and drags me toward him, our lips colliding with his brutal, claiming kiss that I feel all the way down to my toes.

"Mine," he growls before he finally releases me.

We're both gasping for breath when we break apart.

"Sexy," I mutter, reaching up to sweep some of my gloss from his face.

"Thanks." He winks. "I thought I was looking good, too."

"Conceited jerk," I mutter, reaching for my seat belt and clicking it into place before dragging down the visor so I can fix my own face. Seb, however, just rubs at his with the back of his hand and calls it a day.

The sight of the shimmer from my lips that's still smeared up his cheek makes me chuckle. It looks cute on him. Almost.

"Here?" I ask, a little shocked when he pulls up beside Ace's. I'm not arguing, though—I could eat Bill's food every day and die a very happy woman. I'm just surprised.

"Apparently, they have the best burgers in the state."

"Country," I correct.

"Well, there you go then. And," he adds, "I kinda enjoyed our last visit to the beach."

"I bet you did. You're such a dog."

He glances over at me as I reach for the handle. "Takes one to know one."

"Whatever. I'm not having beach sex again. I'm still finding sand in places."

"Maybe you can be convinced, but you're going to need to do better than sand rash."

Rolling my eyes, I climb from the car and allow him to pull me into his body and lead me toward one of my favorite places in the world.

As dates go, it's a pretty fucking epic one.

Bill's milkshakes, burgers, and Seb doing everything he can in an attempt to do what I asked of him and prove that he means what he's saying.

I'm still more than a little skeptical, but I can't deny that he's breaking me down.

The fact that he can't seem to take either his hands or his eyes off me at any one time should freak me out, but I'd be lying if I said I didn't miss both the second Bill lowered a towering burger in front of him.

I don't want to need him. Hell, I don't want to need anyone, but I can feel it happening and I hate it, because when this all turns out to be just another move in whatever game he's playing, it's going to rip my fucking heart out.

"We're going home tomorrow," he informs me once

Bill's cleared our plates and delivered me another chocolate milkshake at Seb's request. I'm starting to wonder if he was just trying to sweeten me up for this conversation.

"Oh, are we?" I spit, moving away from him.

"Baby, don't be like that."

"Like what? Like you're telling me what I have to do?"

He scrubs his hand down his face, his eyes holding mine.

"We need to go home. *You* need to come home."

"Why? So the fucking creep you think is after me can try again?"

The way his face drops at my words clues me in to the fact that he really believes there's a threat waiting for me at home.

"Wouldn't it just be safer for me to stay?" I sulk.

"And wait for him to find you here instead of where I can keep you safe?"

"Because you did such a good job of that the first time."

His jaw tics as he studies me. "I didn't know you had a psycho trailing your ass."

"We don't know that I even do."

His brow lifts.

"Okay, fine. There's a chance I do. The knife thing is weird, I'll admit. But it could just be really freaky coincidence."

"That there's a man running around London with an exact replica of your pink knife and it just so happened to land in your belly? Yeah, I'm sure." He cocks his head to the side and quirks a brow.

"Whatever."

"Argue all you like, Princess. We're leaving tomorrow."

"And you've dragged me away from my friends on my last night here," I complain, knowing full well that I'm going to be getting on that flight tomorrow.

"I won't keep you to myself all night."

"I appreciate it."

"Do you?" he quips.

I suck in a deep breath, ready to come back with some biting remark, but I quickly find I don't have anything.

I love my friends as if they're my sisters, but I've had two weeks with them that I wasn't expecting. As much as I want to be mad about Seb stealing my last night with them, I'm not.

"Take a walk with me?" he asks, his tone much softer than before. Apparently, he can read me better than I was expecting.

Pushing my half-empty milkshake aside, I slide from the booth.

Seb throws enough cash down on the table to cover our meal and then snatches my hand and leads me from the diner.

He walks us all the way along the seafront past all the other stores. We stop and look in a couple of windows as we pass.

"I don't care what anyone says," he mutters. "A football is just not that shape..."

As he talks, something—or someone—catches my attention. Glancing back, I find a man leaning back on the railings, staring down at his cell.

He doesn't look overly suspicious, but something about him gives me pause.

"You okay?" Seb asks when he realizes that I'm not listening to his explanation about why American football isn't really football.

"Y-yeah, I'm good."

Ripping my eyes away from the man, I continue forward when Seb starts walking again.

With my skin still prickling with awareness and my palms starting to sweat, I look back again a few minutes later.

Sure enough, the guy is still there.

Seb's earlier words about some psycho stalker come back to me.

If what he's saying is true and he does exist, surely he wouldn't follow me all the way here. Would he?

"What's wrong?" Seb asks, wrapping his arm around my shoulder and pulling me close, his warm breath coating my skin and tickling down my neck.

"That guy." I nod my head toward the one in question. "I think he's following us," I whisper.

Seb follows my stare and nods at the guy as if he knows him.

"I should fucking hope so. I pay him enough."

I rear back, stepping out of his hold. "I'm sorry, what?"

"Is this really the first time you've seen him?"

"Uh..." I look between Seb and the guy who's now aware we're both talking about him. "Yes, it is."

"He's been watching you since the moment I realized you were here."

My chin drops.

"You had me fucking followed?"

"No, Hellion. I had you protected. There's a very big difference."

Ripping my hand from his, I cross my arms under my breasts.

"Is there?"

"Yes," he hisses, his hard eyes trained on me. "Having you followed would mean I'd be told what you were doing, where you were going, who you were with. I never asked for any of that, no matter how badly I wanted to. I just wanted you safe, Stella."

"So you found me how, if you didn't use your little friend over there? How did you know exactly where I was yesterday morning?"

"I reached out to your friends and begged for their help. It had nothing to do with your protection."

"And if they refused to help, then what? You'd have stalked me using a paid fucking bodyguard?"

His lips part, but no words come out. "I don't know. Okay?" he says, throwing his arms out from his sides. "I don't know what I'd have done next."

"Unbelievable, Seb. Un-fucking-believable."

I stalk off, turning my back on my bodyguard and marching in the direction of the parking lot, more than ready to escape this bullshit.

"Stella, don't do this."

A growl rumbles up my throat, but I don't turn around and bark all the things I want to say at him. I'm too pissed.

"Someone is trying to fucking kill you, baby. What would you rather I did? Sit back and let him get to you?"

Spinning on my heels, I hold his eyes steady.

"It's not your job to protect me, Seb," I bark.

"No? Then whose is it? Because your father has done a fucking shitty job of it, Princess."

Unable to argue with that, I keep my mouth closed for a beat, my fists curling at my sides.

"I can't let anyone hurt you, baby. Not again." He steps toward me, and despite my better judgment, I don't back up. "I thought you were fucking dead. I thought I'd lost you before I'd even really found you."

I swallow, wanting to shout at him again that me being gone is what he wanted from the beginning, but I'm bored of having the same argument over and over.

"Take me home, Seb."

"To Harley's or..."

"To Harley's right now. Then tomorrow, we'll get on that flight out of here."

All the air rushes from his lungs at my words.

"Yeah?"

Stepping up to him, I poke him in the chest. Hard.

"Don't make me fucking regret it, Papatonis."

"Wouldn't dream of it, Doukas."

"I can't believe someone's been following us all this time," I mutter, walking away from him once more. "Oh my God, tell me he wasn't watching us on the beach?"

Images of what we did in my happy place come back to me, and my cheeks heat.

"He's a professional bodyguard, not a creep, Hellion. He knows when to back off."

"I really hope you're right. Enough images of me in compromising positions exist without adding his collection to it."

He hesitates for a second. "You mean the ones I've taken, right?" When I don't respond right away, he tries again. "Right?"

"Maybe." I wink. "Come on, I want to spend some time with my friends before we leave."

Pulling the passenger door of Harley's car open, I drop down and wait for him to join me, already predicting what he's going to ask me the second he does.

"Who else has photos of you, Hellion?"

I shrug. "I wasn't a good girl before I met you, Seb."

He glances over at me as the engine rumbles to life.

"I'm going to need names."

Barking out a laugh, I turn to look out of the window.

"Too many to even remember," I mutter, not even trying to hide my smirk when he growls.

"You're going to be the fucking death of me, Princess. I hope you know that."

"I'm counting on it. You're a pain in my ass alive."

CHAPTER EIGHTEEN

Seb

I sense the second Stella hears the alarm and wakes up because her entire body tenses.

And I know why.

She knows exactly what that alarm means.

Everything is about to change. Again.

Dropping my lips to the top of her head, I breathe her in.

She's not the only one feeling a little anxious over what's to come.

"Come on, baby. We've got a flight to catch," I say, swallowing my unease and dragging my usual mask on.

"Great," she mutters, rolling away from me and sitting on the side of the bed, her shoulders stooped in defeat.

"Not scared, are you?"

Her spine instantly straightens at my question.

Glancing over her shoulder, her eyes lock on mine, making my heart pick up pace in my chest.

"Scared? No, Seb. I'm not scared. I just... this is my home."

"No," I say, reaching for her. "Your home is in London. With me."

"Yeah," she breathes, ripping her eyes from mine. She pushes from the bed and marches toward the bathroom, slamming the door behind her.

My brow creases at her move. I know she's nervous about going back, even if she won't admit it. Why wouldn't she be? Someone in London quite clearly wants to hurt her. I might have got to her in time after his first attempt, but what comes next? What if I—or anyone—doesn't get there? Then what?

Pain like I've never experienced before rips through my chest at the thought of losing her.

No.

It's not going to happen.

We're going to go back, and together we can lure this motherfucker out and end it.

No one is taking her from me, not now. Not after everything it's taken to get here.

The shower turns on, and I'm powerless but to climb from the bed and go to her.

By the time I slip into the bathroom, she's standing under the waterfall with her head tipped back, the water cascading down her mouthwatering body, over her healing scar.

My fists curl as I stare at it, knowing that some sick cunt pushed her own knife into her flawless skin.

I should be the only one who has the power to hurt her, to leave my mark on her body.

She shrieks when I step in front of her, collaring her throat and pushing her back against the tiles.

I stare down into her eyes as her chest begins to heave, hoping she can read everything she won't want to hear right now in my eyes.

"Seb?" she whispers when I don't move.

Grabbing the backs of her thighs, I lift her up the wall, wrapping her legs around my waist as my cock brushes her pussy.

"Nothing has to change, Hellion. We can still be this back in London," I assure her.

"And what if we can't?"

"I won't let it come to that."

A humourless laugh falls from her lips, but I don't bother trying to force her to explain. I already know she won't.

Instead, I set about showing her just how badly I want to continue this truce we've found here when we return.

Slamming my lips down on hers, I kiss her like it's our first and last time all rolled into one, and she returns it with just as much enthusiasm and passion—but I can't help fearing that she's trying to tell me something I don't want to hear.

Goodbye.

Something has shifted with her since we woke up. I

expected it to. I knew going back wasn't going to be easy for her. I just didn't think it would change so quickly.

The two orgasms I gave her in the shower did little for her mood, and having to say goodbye to her friends again only dampened it even more.

By the time we take our seats on the plane, she barely resembles the fun-loving woman I've spent the past few days fooling around on the beach with.

"It's going to be okay, you know?" I ask, resting my hand on her thigh as we sit back ready to take off.

"Yeah, I know," she mutters absently, staring straight ahead at the back of the chair in front of us.

"Have you told your dad you're coming?" I ask, hoping that something will drag her out of herself again.

"No. Have you?" she snaps.

"N-no. I try not to talk to him if I can help it."

She blows out a long breath as the flight attendants begin their safety routine, none of which I pay any attention to. All I can think about is what's going to happen when we touch down.

"You should try to get some sleep," I tell her once we're up in the air.

She's trying to put a brave face on everything, but she's still recovering, and she's still in pain at times. I see it on her face if she moves too fast.

She turns to look at me, her dark, exhausted eyes narrowing on mine.

She might have had a nap before we left Harley's, but it's not going to be enough after a long-haul flight and the jet lag that will come from it.

"Maybe you should keep your opinions to yourself."

Threading my fingers through hers, I lift her knuckles to my lips.

She's still pissed about the bodyguard thing. She told me last night that it was fine, that she understood. But I made a mistake not confessing earlier. I just knew what would happen if I did. She'd have forced me to call him off.

She doesn't think she's in any danger.

I think the opposite. Because I know she is. I also know that the second we touch down, she's basically a walking target.

Galen might have increased security on their house, and Damien might have put security on her, but it's not enough, because I won't be there. Not the whole time.

Turning back away from me, she rests her head against the chair, silently fuming as we continue to rise into the air, leaving her old life behind once more.

I'm glad I came out here. I'm glad we managed to have this time together. But something tells me that the happiness I've found in the last few days might just be about to come to an abrupt end.

Despite not wanting me to tell her what to do, it's not long before Stella falls asleep beside me.

Pulling the blanket from its wrapper, I drape it over her legs to stop her from getting cold and slide my hand back into hers, watching her like a creep.

By the time we touch down on English soil, she's almost entirely shut down.

The happy girl from the beach who held me while I confessed everything I went through with Demi is long gone. Instead, the woman whose hand I'm insisting on holding in mine is the cold, detached one who threw me out of her hospital room.

I'm trying to convince myself that it's just being back here that has her like this, but it's more than that. I know it's me.

We grab our bags and then go in search of my car, which is harder than I was hoping for seeing as I didn't actually make a note of where I left it.

"Did you want to go and get some food or…" I trail off. I'm not ready to let her go yet, especially not when she's in this mood.

She might never admit it, but right now she's vulnerable, and if that fuck is waiting for her…

"Just take me home," she says, her voice hollow, void of any kind of emotion.

"O-okay."

The drive across the city is relatively quick, and long before I'm ready, we're pulling up in front of her house.

Her Porsche is sitting there waiting for her, and her eyes light up when she sees her baby.

I can't help but smile at her excitement. I just wish it had something to do with me, not a fucking car.

She's taken her seat belt off before I've even brought the car to a stop.

"Wait," I say as her fingers wrap around the handle, ready to make a quick escape.

She pauses, but she doesn't look back at me.

"We're done, Seb. Whatever that was in Rosewood... it's over."

"W-what?" I stutter. Part of me saw it coming, but I didn't want to believe it. That she could just cast me aside like the past few days meant nothing.

"You heard me."

"No, wait," I cry, sounding way more pathetic than I was intending as she pushes the door open and climbs from the car.

Before I can get there, she has the boot open and her bags in her hands.

"Let me." I reach for her case—she probably shouldn't be lifting it—but she drags it from my car before I even get a chance to take it from her.

"No," she says firmly, this time holding my eyes to add to her sincerity. "We're done. You've had your fun. You chased me, you got me back. Now, we're over."

A laugh of disbelief bubbles up my throat.

"You don't mean that," I say as she rushes past me toward the front door.

"Don't I?"

She digs around in her bag before pulling a key out and unlocking the door.

She turns back to me. My steps falter a few feet away from her as my heart thunders in my chest and my teeth grind in frustration.

She's lying. I know she is.

Everything these past few days... it wasn't fake. She couldn't have faked all of that. She just couldn't.

"Let me carry your bag in at least."

Anger flashes in her eyes.

"I don't need you to protect me, Seb. I don't need you at all."

My lips part to tell her that she's lying, but before I manage to get a word out, she slams the door in my face.

CHAPTER NINETEEN

Stella

The second I step foot into my bedroom, a wave of exhaustion washes through me. I stare longingly at my bed, kick the door closed and drop my bags at my feet.

Thankfully, the house was empty as I walked through it. The scent of Angie's cooking permeated the air, so I know she's not too far away. And, Calvin's car was parked in the driveway beside my Porsche.

Forgetting about the shower I so desperately need from travelling, I kick my sneakers off my feet, drag my leggings off and slip under the covers.

Despite everything that's spinning around my head, and the fact that my chest is aching, the image of Seb's face when I told him we were done is engraved on my freaking eyeballs. The second I rest my head on my pillow, my jet lag and lingering exhaustion take over and I drift off.

Any hope of a restful sleep is thwarted the second the memories of my time with Seb before I was stabbed blur with those of me running away from some fucked-up psycho wielding my knife and threatening to dismember me when he finally catches up.

"Holy shit," I breathe, sitting upright in bed, my heart pounding a mile a minute and my skin flushed with sweat as if I really was just running away from the devil. "Jesus. Fuck."

I drop my head into my hands and force the fear from my nightmare away.

It's not real. It's just Seb filling my head with stupid assumptions. He has no facts. No one does, or they'd have found who was responsible by now.

Pushing my fingers through the sweat-damp hair, I pull it back and look around my room. I should feel safe, content. But I feel none of those things.

I need to get a grip and set about getting my life back on track. There's a week left of school until the holiday. After that break, hopefully life can resume. Although, I already know that it's going to be a while yet until I'm able to fully get back to gym and cheer.

With a resigned sigh, I throw the covers back and pad through to my bathroom.

I turn the shower on to warm up as I pee and brush my teeth, and then once I shed my remaining clothes, I step under the burning hot torrent of water.

Tipping my face up, I try to let it wash everything away. My regrets, my fears, the pain, the humiliation.

But most of all, that residual pain that seems to have taken up residence in my chest from turning Seb away.

It was the right thing to do, I tell myself over and over in the hope that at some point, I'll start believing it.

I wash my hair, revelling in the scent of my usual shampoo that I was forced to leave behind when I fled the country, and lather my body in my favorite vanilla bath foam.

By the time I turn the dial, cutting off the water, I feel almost like myself once more.

Until I step out of the stall, my eyes catching on something on the other side of the room that makes my stomach drop into my feet.

I don't reach for a towel. Instead, I wrap my arms around myself as I stare at the message on the mirror that the steam filling the room has made visible.

I will find you. And next time, I might be more successful.

Or I might not...

All the air rushes from my lungs, my body trembling with fear.

It's a joke, I tell myself, racing forward and grabbing a washcloth from the sink to wipe the message away.

It was just Seb that night he was here before. He probably did it before the lipstick message to mess with my head.

But you cleaned the mirror, a little voice pipes up in my head. I push it aside.

My chest is heaving by the time the glass is clean and my body is almost dry.

Finally reaching for a towel, I wrap one around my

hair and another around my body before sucking in some confidence and pulling the door open.

My room is empty, exactly as I left it, but I waste no time in rushing to the window and dragging the curtains closed.

If someone is out there…

A shudder rips through me.

Calvin is increasing the house's security. This place is safe.

Despite knowing all this, I feel anything but safe.

I want to believe that it's not the fact that Seb's no longer with me. I refuse to accept that in just a few days, I've fallen into his trap of needing him.

No.

I stand taller and throw my shoulders back.

I'm Stella fucking Doukas, and I'm not afraid of whoever this sick bastard might be. If he even exists.

I'm dressed and sitting at my vanity unit when a loud crash sounds out from somewhere beneath me and I jump from the stool, a terrified shriek ripping from my lips.

"Fucking hell," I mutter to myself a few seconds later when I reason with myself that it was probably just a slamming door.

Knowing that I need to do something before I drive myself completely insane, I dig around my purse for my cell. I turned it on for the first time since I left for Rosewood in the taxi on the way home and watched the thing light up with a stream of messages and missed calls. Ignoring them all, especially the ones from Seb, I open up Calli's last message.

. . .

Calli: I'm so glad you're home. Are you busy later?

I glance at the time it was sent. She knew we were back almost before we landed.

Of course everyone here knew.

Tapping on her name, I hit call and lift my cell to my ear.

"Stella!" she squeals down the line the second it connects.

"Are you home?" I ask, my voice cold and emotionless.

"Y-yeah, I just got in. Are you okay?"

I pause for a minute, fighting my need to just blurt it all out.

"I'm coming over right now, is that okay?"

"Yeah, of course. Wanna order takeout?"

My stomach clenches at the thought of food. I have no idea when I last ate anything, but I also fear that I'm not going to be able to keep anything down anyway.

Another bang from inside the house rattles through the floor, but thankfully, this time I don't react—not loudly, anyway.

"Sounds great. I'll be there in about thirty."

"Okay."

Jabbing my finger into the screen to cut off any chance of her asking if I'm okay again, I place it on the side, making quick work of braiding my still wet hair over my shoulder and rubbing some tinted moisturizer onto my face. That's going to have to do.

Grabbing my purse, I throw it over my shoulder and head to the door to leave. I stop at the last minute, my lingering fear and unease getting the better of me.

Racing over to my sock drawer, I rummage around at the back until my hand lands on Seb's knife.

My finger brushes down the wooden handle. The engraved CP and the wicked-looking skull beneath it make a little more sense now. This was his father's.

Knowing that gives me some weird sense of security.

I might have sent him away, but maybe he can still protect me, even if he has no idea.

Slipping the knife into my hoodie pocket and keeping my hand on it in case I need to use it, I make my way from the house.

"Baby D, you're home," Calvin says from his place on top of a ladder by the front door. There's a tool bag on the floor and a drill in his hand.

I guess that might explain the noise.

Embarrassment washes through me.

If Seb's intentions were to terrify me, then I'm ashamed to admit that they might be somewhat working.

"Hey, how are you doing?"

He raises a brow. "I'm not worried about me."

"I'm fine, honestly. It'll take more than a knife to put me down."

Something like anger passes over his face.

"We need to sit down and discuss a few things, young lady," he says, sounding more like my father than my actual one.

"Sure thing, big man. But I'm going to see a friend. Rain check?"

"Give me your cell," he demands, jumping from the top of the ladder and holding his hand out, his other grabbing some device from his tool bag.

"What the hell?" I ask when he starts swiping the wand thing over my cell.

"Checking that it's not been chipped."

"By who?"

His eyes lift, holding mine for a beat.

"If only we knew, huh?"

"Don't you think this is a little over the top?"

"Stella," he sighs. "Nothing to do with your safety is over the top. Your dad is worried. I'm worried. Hell, even Damien is worried."

"You know Damien?" I ask, although I don't know why I'm surprised.

"For the record, your dad should have told you about all this long before now, but he was convinced he was protecting you."

"Sure," I mutter, snatching my phone back from its inspection. "I assume you've checked my room with that thing?"

"Of course. The house is secure. You don't need to worry about it, baby D."

My lips part to tell him that he's very, very wrong, but for some reason the words don't come.

"Okay, great," I finally mumble, pushing past him. "I'll be back later."

"I've checked your car, too. Stay safe."

I shoot a look over my shoulder. Does he really think that whoever this is would tamper with my car?

The unease races around my body, making my palms sweat and my stomach knot until it hurts. It doesn't lift until I pull through the gates—which open the second I pull up—at Calli's house.

Two seconds later, the front door to her house opens and she comes flying out.

The moment my feet hit the ground, she slams into me, her arms wrapping around me tightly.

"Whoa, I missed you too, Cal."

"I'm so glad you're okay," she whispers, still holding me.

It's nice, and I can't help melting into her—until she abruptly releases me, takes a step back and then slaps my shoulder so hard it stings a little even through my hoodie.

"What the hell was that for?"

"I can't believe you left and didn't tell me."

Guilt swamps me.

"I'm so sorry, I—"

"You don't have to apologise. Not again, at least. I get it. I just... I missed you."

"I missed you too. Come on, before the guys turn up."

My stomach twists. "They're here?"

She looks over her shoulder at the mostly empty

driveway. The answer is obvious really, but it doesn't stop her from answering anyway.

"Not yet. But now you're here, I'm guessing it won't take them long."

"How would they kno—" She glares at me with her brow quirked.

She's right. They *always* know.

"Come on, we've got the house to ourselves."

Calli grabs some drinks from the kitchen before I follow her up the stairs, keeping my eyes downcast as we climb them, not wanting to look at Seb, even if it is a younger version of him.

"So Seb let you out of his sight?" Calli asks when she falls down on her bed, watching me as I walk to her window and look out at her huge backyard.

"He didn't have a lot of choice," I mutter, scanning the treeline as if this person everyone seems to think is following me will just jump out and make himself known.

"I thought you were getting on great in America."

Spinning around, I glare at her. "How'd you know that?"

She shrugs, not looking even slightly guilty as she confesses, "I eavesdropped on a phone call between Nico and Seb."

My chin drops. Not because I'm angry at her for doing it—quite the opposite. I'm proud of her.

"What? I was worried about you. I needed to know he wasn't hurting you."

I raise a brow and place my hand on my hip. "And you didn't believe me when I told you I was okay?"

"I did, I did," she argues. "I just... the guy carved his fucking name into your thigh, Stel, and then proceeded to humiliate you in front of all those arseholes. I just needed to hear it for myself."

"And what did you hear?"

"Nothing exciting. Nico was more interested in telling Seb about some girl he hooked up with the night before." She gags. "In detail."

"Nice," I laugh. "Your brother is a dog."

"Agreed. So what happened with Seb? I had a feeling he was going to attach himself to your hip and never let you out of his sight."

"I'm pretty sure that was his plan," I say, picturing his face as he stood hopelessly in the middle of our driveway this morning. "I gave him a taste of his own medicine," I confess when she waits for more. An evil chuckle falls from my lips. "He thought I'd forgiven him because he gave me a few orgasms. He's a fucking idiot."

"You won't hear any argument from me there. He really let you walk away?"

"I mean, I slammed the door in his face, so he didn't have that much of a choice."

Something drags me back over to the window, and I once again shove my hand into my pocket and curl my fingers around his knife.

"Something tells me you're going to regret that."

My lips twitch. Is it wrong that part of me really hopes I will?

And here I was thinking that Seb was the sadistic asshole.

The movement of a shadow by the treeline makes me tense.

"Are you okay?"

"Yeah... I—"

The need to do something, to take back control of this fucked-up situation races through me.

Turning back to her, I stand at the end of her bed.

"You know that firing range you said you had here?"

"Yeah?" Her brows pinch in confusion.

"We're going there. Now. I'm going to teach you to shoot."

"O-okay." She somewhat hesitantly slides to the edge of the bed. "But not until you tell me why."

Blowing out a breath, I push some stray strands of hair behind my ears.

"Seb—the guys, I'm sure—think that there's someone after me. That the attack wasn't random."

"It wasn't," she states.

"Oh God, not you too."

"He had your knife, Stella. That was not some random attack."

"Yeah, I know. I just... I didn't want to believe it but —" I blow out a breath, refusing to admit that they might just be right.

"My knife was in my bedroom. So for him to have it, it would mean..."

Calli pales despite probably already coming to this conclusion.

"I found something," I whisper.

"What?"

"There was a message written on my bathroom mirror when I got out of the shower this afternoon."

"Holy shit, Stella." She hops up from the bed as if someone just set her ass on fire. "And you're only just telling me this now?"

"It was probably just Seb messing around. He was the one sneaking into my bedroom in the dead of night."

"To screw your brains out, Stel. Not to scare the living shit out of you."

"He's got form, though."

She shakes her head, not believing my argument for a second.

"What did it say?"

I recall the message, much to her horror.

"Please tell me I'm not the first person you've told," she begs, but all I can do is shrug. "Stella, he's been in your house," she argues.

"Which is why I need to go and shoot some shit. Do you know where the guns are kept?

"Yeah, but they're locked up and—"

"Can Nico get to them?"

"Yeah, but—"

"I guess it's time to go and see if he's home then, isn't it?"

I march to her door, ripping it open.

"Stella, I really don't think—"

"Do you want to learn how to protect yourself?"

"Y-yeah but—"

"Pull on your big girl panties, Cal. I'm sure I can convince your brother to do just about anything."

CHAPTER TWENTY

Stella

Calli is hot on my heels as I race down the stairs, her argument thankfully gone until I'm about to crash through the door into Nico's basement.

"Don't you think you should knock?"

"Why? I've already seen him getting sucked off and naked in the same night."

"Fucking hell," she mutters but doesn't say anything else as I swing the door open to announce our arrival and run down the stairs.

"Calli, what the hell?" Nico barks, clearly assuming that my light footsteps are her. "Oh shit, Princess," he gasps when I turn the corner.

"Stella," another familiar voice booms, and before I

can turn to see him, I find myself swept up in my brother's arms.

Yeah, that sounds weird as fuck in my head, and I tense for a beat.

"Toby," I whisper, hugging him back.

"Hands to yourself, bro. You're related and all that now," Nico mutters.

"Fuck you, man," Toby barks, releasing me and running his eyes down my body. But it's not in a sexual way, more of a protective, needing to make sure I'm in one piece kind of way.

Relief floods me that we're going to be able to move past that awkward kiss moment. I hate to have discovered I've got a brother only to lose him again almost as quickly because he couldn't cope with flipping the switch on his feelings on a dime.

I guess me almost dying might have helped with that somewhat.

"So..." I say, turning back to Nico and putting an end to his inappropriate comments. "I need a favor."

An intrigued smile twitches at his lips.

"Go on."

"I need a gun."

He immediately throws his head back and laughs like it's the funniest thing he's ever heard.

"No," he says, suddenly sobering from his amusement.

"It wasn't a question, it was a statement, asshole."

"I'm not giving you a fucking gun, Princess."

Sucking my bottom lip into my mouth, I look up at him through my lashes and take a step forward.

"I promise I know how to use it," I breathe, my voice all raspy.

"I know what you're doing, and it's not going to work."

"Oh no?"

I come to a stop right in front of him and run my fingertips down his chest, feeling his muscles bunch when I hit his abs.

"Princess," he growls. "You're playing with fire."

"I fucking love the burn, Cirillo," I sass.

"Seb will kill me when he finds out," he growls when my fingers stop at his waistband.

"Who says we're going to tell him?"

"Stella, I don't—"

"Trust me," I growl at Calli. Toby, however, is watching me with an amused smirk on his face. He seems more than happy to watch me play his friend.

"As much as I'd love for you to keep going, Princess, I really like my balls attached to my body."

"Oh yeah?" I ask, moving quicker than he can comprehend, and in less than a heartbeat, I've got Seb's knife pressed against the denim covering his beloved cock. "Open the gun cupboard, Cirillo, and I'll leave your tiny cock in one piece."

"You're a fucking piece of work, Doukas."

"Trained by the best. Shame I can't say the same about you."

"Fine," he snaps, throwing his hands up in defeat. "But if you've lied to me about being able to handle one and you shoot anyone you shouldn't, I'll kill you myself."

"Deal. See, now, that wasn't so hard, was it?" I say, tapping his chest patronizingly.

"Seb needs his fucking head checked," he mutters to himself as he takes off toward the stairs.

Calli, Toby, and I all loiter, disbelief covering both their faces.

"I know it's wrong, I know that, but fuck, that kinda turned me on."

"Toby!" Calli squeals.

"What you gonna do, shoot me? Nico needs a woman to knock him down a peg or two. Come on, let's go watch Stella whoop Nico's ass out on the range."

"Hell yes."

The three of us follow Nico toward a side of the house I haven't been to yet before we go down another set of stairs, proving that I was wrong about Nico's basement stretching the entire length of the building.

"Holy shit," I gasp after walking through three secure doors and emerging in a seriously impressive room full of firearms. "It's like porn."

Nico scoffs while Toby chuckles behind me.

Scanning the weapons on display, I reach for a 9mm pistol and inspect it, checking it's loaded before letting it hang at my side.

"You sure mean business with this lot, huh?"

"We've got a lot more enemies than just the nutcase who's after you, Princess."

"Right. Well, I guess it's time to prove that I can look after myself then. Come on, girl," I say, looping my arm through Calli's. "Let's go teach you a lesson or two."

"Oh no, you're not dragging my sister into this."

"Fucking watch me. Grab plenty of ammo on your way out, boys."

The sinking fall sun makes me wince as Calli and I emerge from the house. My previous fear as I looked at the treeline from Calli's bedroom has diminished somewhat now I've got a pistol in one hand and a knife in my pocket.

I'd fucking love for whoever my attacker is to try me right now.

I've got a smile on my face the whole way toward the Cirillos' shooting range.

"You see that house over there?" Calli says, pointing to a roof that I can just make out through the trees.

"Yeah."

"That's Theo's."

"Oh," I say, uncertainty suddenly making an appearance at the thought of Seb showing his face.

I can only imagine what kind of mood he's in after the way we left things earlier. Hoping that he went and got himself so wasted that he can't even stand up, let alone chase me.

"Right then, Princess Doukas. Let's see what you've got," Nico says, coming to stand beside me.

I have no idea what I was expecting to find out here, but I'm impressed.

There's an array of targets sitting in front of a high bank and then the treeline that runs between the two properties, and a small canopy for us to stand under.

Someone's really planned this out. But then I guess

this kind of thing is necessary when you're running a gang.

It's not all that different from the places I've been with both Dad and Calvin over the years, and I feel at home immediately with the weight of the pistol in my hand.

"There's a fine line between confidence and arrogance, Nico. And one is really unattractive."

"Did I say anything about my shot?"

"Your tone said it all," I mutter, stepping up, ready to take my first shot as Toby hangs some fresh target sheets up for us.

The second he's well out of the way, I line up my first shot and fucking kill it.

"What the—" Nico mutters, coming up beside me to get a closer look—not that it's necessary. "Well, fuck me. You're better than the boys."

"Speak for yourself," Toby shouts, walking up and high-fiving me. "Next time I'm in a gunfight, I want Stella right beside me."

"Oh yeah, because caveman Papatonis is going to let her anywhere near that shit."

Turning back to Nico, I place one hand on my hip.

"Seb doesn't *let* me do anything. He. Does. Not. Own. Me."

"You might wanna tell him that, Princess. As far as he's concerned, he might as well have just pissed all over you that first day of school."

"Whatever."

Turning my back on his smug smirk, I lift my arm

again and fire off a few shots, hitting each target right in the center.

"I can't believe you're my sister," Toby mutters behind me.

"Thank fuck she's not mine, because that shit is getting me hard."

I fire off another round, wishing I'd stopped to put some sound-canceling headphones on just to drown those two motherfuckers out.

"Calli, you ready?"

"Uh..." She looks between me and the guys.

"Ignore them, this is about you. Do you want—"

"Yes," she says excitedly, coming closer.

"Now, she's *not* my sister," Toby says, getting his own back as I show Calli how to hold the gun correctly.

"Fucking hell, this was a really bad fucking idea."

I've never taught anyone to shoot before, but even with ignoring the two assholes behind us, I find that I really enjoy working with Calli—especially when her shot actually starts to improve and she doesn't look like she's going to piss her panties every time she fires.

I don't realize that anyone else has joined us until a shadow falls over us and a deep voice announces, "You're showing her wrong."

My eyes widen and my chin drops at the audacity, because I know as sure as the sky is blue that I'm showing Calli exactly how to shoot a gun.

"Excuse me, but I think you'll find..." My voice trails off when I find a weird expression on Daemon's face. The fuck is laughing at me. "You asshole," I hiss, figuring that he's just baiting me.

"Let's see what she's got, then," he says, taking a step back—and this time, I do the same, allowing Calli to take her shot alone.

She misses by a mile and her shoulders sag in defeat.

"I missed," she sighs.

"Not by as much as your brother the first time he tried it," Daemon says, stepping up to her.

"Fuck you, as if you remember that," Nico barks.

"Like it was yesterday, man," Daemon jokes back. "Try it like this."

I stand back and watch as Daemon shows Calli a different trick for hitting her target, and the next time she tries, she just about clips the board.

"I nearly did it," she squeals excitedly.

"Stella, take this," Daemon says, pulling a gun from his waistband and checking the clip.

"You sure?"

"Of course. You seem to know what you're doing. I trust you."

"Huh. Did you hear that, Nico?"

Nico flips me off, clearly hearing every word of it.

"So nice to be trusted without having to threaten any testicles first," I mutter, coming to a stop a few feet from Calli so I can shoot.

Daemon snorts a laugh but backs away to allow us to fire.

I quickly use the bullets that were loaded in Daemon's gun before I stand there watching Calli, impressed by her improvement in such a short space of time.

I drown out the boys' chatter behind us and focus on Calli.

Although I'm not distracted enough to miss the others approaching.

Long before I hear their rumbling voices, I feel him.

My skin tingles with awareness and butterflies erupt in my belly.

I have no idea how he's going to react after what happened earlier. But I guess I'm about to find out.

CHAPTER TWENTY-ONE

Sebastian

"Tell me you've got something?" I demand, sitting in front of the boss's desk.

My intention was to stay with Stella, I'm pretty sure that I'd made that clear, but the second she slammed her door in my face, I got back in the car, this is the address I found falling from my lips.

If I couldn't be there to protect her in person, then I needed to do something.

For all we knew, her attacker was sitting in wait, watching the house, biding his time.

My stomach rolls as I think about him being inside her room to steal her knife.

What if he knew we were coming and waited for her? What if he's already got to her?

"Nothing," Damien sighs.

"This is bullshit," I spit, earning myself a raised brow from the boss. "An eighteen-year-old girl doesn't just get stabbed and the motherfucker gets away with it."

"They do, and you know it."

"But he planned this. He had to have fucked up somewhere."

"Not that we can find. The police records show no fingerprints other than hers and yours—" Something I had to explain in the days after Stella's stabbing. "There's no other evidence that the police, or our contacts can find. But that doesn't mean he won't fuck up."

"I'm not fucking happy about this," I tell him, knowing exactly what he means by that comment.

"Well then, it's probably a good thing that you don't have a choice."

Allowing a long, frustrated breath to pass my lips, I rest back in the chair.

"So what's the plan?"

"Nothing set in stone yet, but she needs to be out. There's no point locking herself up in the house. I need you to make her a target, then we'll catch this motherfucker."

The memory of her limp, lifeless body in my arms hits me once more.

"I'm not sure—"

"Just do your job, Sebastian. We'll catch this motherfucker and put this all to bed. It's time we all moved on."

"Just like that, huh?"

Damien scrubs his hand down his face.

"I know you're still angry, son. But we were in the middle of a war, what happened that day wasn't intentional. Your father was in the crossfire.

"We live dangerous lives. Ultimately, some will pay for that."

I nod, the lump in my throat too huge to even attempt to talk around.

"Galen has done his time. Don't you think that maybe you should cut him a little slack? It seems to me that he brought you something by way of an apology." Damien's brow lifts in amusement.

"This has nothing to do with Stella," I hiss.

"Doesn't it? Correct me if I'm wrong, but only a few weeks ago, that's exactly how you were playing it."

"You knew," I breathe.

"Of course I knew. I also know that she's strong enough to take your bullshit and hand your arse back to you on a platter."

"But—"

"But nothing, Sebastian. Now go and get your girl. Take her out, show her off, and trust that we have your back."

Like you had my father's. The words are on the tip of my tongue, but I bite them back.

Damien's already had his say; bringing it up again is just a surefire way to piss him off. And that bastard is a scary motherfucker when he's happy, let alone anything else.

"Trust us. Trust your brothers," he repeats, as if he can read my mind.

"I'll see what I can do."

Damien chuckles—actually fucking chuckles—as I push to stand. When I glance at Evan, who's sitting over on the sofa with a tablet in his hand and clearly eavesdropping on our entire conversation, I find his lips curled in amusement too.

"In the dog house already, son?"

"Nothing I can't handle."

"That's good."

With a nod, he dismisses me and I make my way back through the security room with my eyes locked on the door at the other end, ready to get the fuck out of here.

The moment I'm in the lift, I fall back against the wall, exhaustion slamming into me like a truck.

My need to go and convince Stella that our time isn't done is going to have to wait.

I shoot a message to Calvin, her security, ensuring that she's actually alive and breathing in the house, and after getting the confirmation I need, along with photographic evidence of her fast asleep in her bed, I call a car to take me back to Theo's to do exactly the same.

I wake up angry. No, not angry. Fucking furious.

My heart pounds, my skin is covered in a layer of sweat, and my chest heaves as I try to catch my breath, my fist curled with my need to hurt someone.

The lingering images of some faceless, hooded figure with his hands on my girl fill my mind.

I was right there, within reaching distance, but fucking dream me couldn't move. My limbs wouldn't work, even as he pushed her pretty pink knife into her body over and over.

I was forced to stand there and watch as her blood began to pool around her feet, as the life drained from her eyes.

"Fuck," I bellow. "Fuck. Fuck."

Only two seconds later, my bedroom door flies open and Theo comes rushing in.

"What's wrong?" he barks, concern written all over his face, but it soon softens when he finds me sitting in bed with the covers pooled at my waist.

"N-nothing. Just..." I trail off, not wanting to admit that I just had that kind of reaction to a fucking dream.

"It's good to have you back, man."

"Yeah?"

He looks around for a beat before his eyes land on my open bathroom door.

"Uh... where is she?"

"Clearly not fucking here," I snap, my grip on the sheets tightening with my frustration over how she ended things between us.

She was lying. I could see it in her eyes. But still, the stubborn bitch pretended like it was nothing. Like what's between us is nothing, that she can't fucking feel it.

"Trouble in paradise?" he asks, dropping his arse to

the chair at the other side of my room as if he intends to stay for a heart to fucking heart.

"Fuck off," I scoff, dragging my knees up and wrapping my arms around them.

I have no idea how long I slept for, but fuck, I feel like hell.

I guess two long haul flights in only a matter of days will do that.

He laughs, much as his father did earlier. "Anyone would think she doesn't want you chasing her."

"Well, that's un-fucking-fortunate for her, because I'm not planning on stopping now."

"You're so fucking whipped, man."

Running my fingers through my hair, I stare at him, wondering for the first time if I'm a completely lost cause where Stella Doukas is concerned.

If being whipped means I get more time with her like this weekend, then maybe, just maybe it's not such a bad state to be in.

"Ho-ly shit," Theo chuckles. "You've fucking fallen for her, haven't you?"

Have I?

And if I have, when exactly did that happen?

"I dunno. All I do know right now is that some motherfucker is out there trying to kill her and she slammed the fucking door in my face."

He laughs. *Again.*

"If you could find this any less amusing, I'd be fucking grateful."

"Bro, you have no fucking idea how amazing this all

is to watch. Sebastian Papatonis falling for the bad-arse mafia princess."

My lips part, ready to spit a biting comeback at him, but I don't get a chance because he continues.

"On that note, you checked your phone yet?"

"N-no. Why?"

"I'll be ready when you are."

With that cryptic comment, he pushes from the chair and finally leaves me alone.

Reaching over the side of the bed, I find the pile of discarded clothes from a few hours ago and rummage around for my phone.

Waking it up, I find a message from Nico.

Unlocking it, I press play on the video.

"Holy fu—" My chin hits the floor as I stare at the footage of Stella shooting out on the range and hitting the target every fucking time.

Fuck protecting her. Maybe she should be the one protecting me.

It comes to an end and I hit play again, my cock already painfully hard.

I watch it five times before I minimise it and look at the message from Nico that accompanied it.

Nico: Your girl sure knows how to shoot a good load. Might see what else she's capable of if you don't show your face sometime soon.

. . .

"Motherfucker."

Throwing off the covers, I jump in the shower, ignoring my aching cock. I already know that my hand isn't going to come anywhere close to what I need after watching that video.

"Let's go," I state, marching through the flat less than ten minutes later.

"What took you so long?" Theo says, hopping up and following me out after tucking his own piece into his waistband. "Gotta say, man," he calls over his shoulder as we march around the side of the main house on our way toward the shooting range between the two properties, "you didn't pick yourself an easy one to deal with."

"When have I ever wanted easy?"

I think about most of the women in our lives. The quiet ones who stay at home, raising the kids while the men do... the shit we do on a daily basis.

I've always known they're not for me. I want someone who challenges me, who calls me out on my bullshit, and tries to make me a better person, because hell knows I could use some help in that department.

It was the danger glittering in her eyes that first night in the graveyard that pulled me in. The lack of fucks she gave about the fact that I was sitting there with a gun. She didn't even bat an eyelid, and instead of running, she got closer.

It should have been obvious that she was the one for me.

She certainly is one of kind, that's for fucking sure.

The sound of gunshots popping off begins to ring

out around us, and as we break through the trees hiding the range from anyone who might be brave enough to venture onto this land, my mouth goes dry.

"I hope you know that everyone wants your girl right now," Theo mutters. "Fuck, man. That's hot as hell."

I keep my eyes locked on her back as we approach, and despite the fact that she doesn't turn around, I know the exact moment she becomes aware of my presence.

Her shoulders bunch a little, her body stilling for a beat before she begins firing off the final rounds in the clip.

"I think that's our cue to leave, Cal," she says loudly, still refusing to turn my way.

Calli hesitantly looks over her shoulder and winces.

Stepping up behind Stella, I wrap my hand around her throat.

"Not so fucking fast, Princess," I growl in her ear, loving the way she trembles in my hold.

"Get off me, Seb." Anger laces her voice, but it does the opposite of making me want to release her. Instead, my semi hardens once more against her arse.

Calli gasps in shock when Stella lifts her arm, bringing the gun in her hand up to my head, resting it beside my temple.

"T-that's empty, r-right?" she stutters, all the blood draining from her face.

"I don't know," Stella says, her voice flat, not giving anything away.

From the number of rounds I saw her fire before she

stopped, I want to say it is. But my girl is a crazy bitch, so I wouldn't put it past her to leave one bullet in the clip just for me.

"Shall we find out?" she asks, slipping from my hold and pointing the barrel right between my brows.

Any normal person would probably panic, try to say anything they can think of to make the other person lower the weapon. But we've both long come to terms with the fact that neither of us is fucking normal.

"Go on then, Princess. Try it. I fucking dare you," I taunt, a smirk pulling at my lips.

"Whoa, Stella, you should probably give me that back now," Daemon says, stepping up beside her.

"Nah, I've got this, thanks."

"Stella," Calli damn near whimpers.

The others' stares burn into me, but I don't take my eyes from Stella's to see what kind of expressions they're wearing.

There's a good chance that Toby is probably egging her on after the shit I've put her through. Can't really argue with that opinion either. I'd like to think that maybe Theo is ready to take her to the ground to put a stop to this.

Her eyes narrow on mine, and I can almost hear her thoughts racing around her head.

"Calli," she says, her voice soft as if she isn't threatening my life right now. "Get my cell from my pocket. I'm gonna need this on camera."

"I'm not filming you killing him."

"Who said anything about killing him?"

"Y-you've got a gun to his head, Stel," Calli

220

whispers, her lack of experience in these kinds of situations shining through. Maybe Stella had a point in bringing her out here for a little training.

"Have I pulled the trigger?" Stella asks, her voice still unwavering. Her confidence is a real fucking turn on, and I can't help but reach down and rearrange myself.

Someone scoffs in amusement, and my smirk widens. "Twisted fucking bastard," Theo mutters.

I shrug.

"So what's it gonna be, Princess? You gonna spill my blood here or what?"

"Calli," she snaps as her friend fumbles with her phone.

Finally, Calli lifts the phone, training the camera on me.

"Smile, *baby*," Stella purrs.

Shaking my head at her, I can't help but do as she says, because fuck if I haven't just fallen even fucking harder for her.

I blow her a kiss and her face hardens with anger.

"Apologize," she demands.

My brothers' laughter fills the air around us.

It's not lost on me that they could get me out of this situation in a heartbeat, but the motherfuckers are enjoying themselves too much to even attempt it.

"For what? Making you see stars all weekend?"

"No," she hisses. "You know exactly what for."

Images of our time together flicker through my mind, none of which help the situation happening south of my waistband.

Her in the graveyard, both times. Nico's basement, her home gym, her bedroom.

"What if I'm not sorry? What if I think you loved all of that as much as I did?"

Her lips purse.

"You carved your fucking initials into my thigh, Seb. That is not fucking okay. Humiliating me in front of these assholes? Not fucking okay."

"Now, I *know* you enjoyed that."

"Not the fucking point," she hisses. "I did nothing to deserve any of that. The only reason you did it was because of my name, and I had fuck all to do with that. As far as I can figure out, my entire existence is one giant mistake, just like the time I've spent with you."

"You don't mean that," I state, my resolve cracking slightly.

"Don't I?" She lifts the gun a little, realising that her aim has slipped.

Silence falls around all of us, anticipation crackling in the air.

Out of the corner of my eye, I notice that Stella's chest is moving faster than before as she tries to keep her shit under control.

I have no idea if she's trying to tamper her anger or her need to give up. I'm also not sure which I want more.

"I'm sorry," I say after the longest silence of my life.

Her eyes narrow as if she doesn't believe a word of it.

"You didn't deserve any of that. None of my issues are to do with you, but I made you the outlet for my hate. I used you. I humiliated you. I. Made. You. Fucking. Mine. Although, I'm less sorry about that last one."

"I'm not yours, Seb," she states. "I don't belong to you or anyone. I'm a fucking person, not a belonging you can shove in the closet until you think they deserve some attention."

"I know," I whisper. "That's not what I want to do with you."

"Just fucking tell her, bro," Theo says, breaking the tension.

"Tell me what?" Stella asks, jumping on his demand. "What do you know?"

"I don't know anything, baby. He's not talking about that."

"Then what the fuck is he talking about?"

"Something I'm not confessing in front of all these motherfuckers."

"I don't think you're in any position to deny me anything right now, do you?"

I shake my head, my eyes begging her not to press this. Not in front of the others. But she's having none of it.

"I want you, okay? And I'm sorry. I'm so fucking sorry I ever hurt you."

Her shoulders sag and her entire body visibly relaxes as my words hit her. For the first time, possibly ever, she believes me.

"You've got a funny way of showing it."

"I'm fucked up, baby. I thought you already knew that."

Her finger twitches on the trigger and my heart jumps into my throat. I might be pretty damn confident that she wouldn't actually shoot me straight between the eyes, but crazier things have happened, I suppose.

"Hellion?" I ask, sensing a shift in her after my confession. "What do you say? Wanna have a go at this without wanting to kill each other?"

Her chest heaves as she stares at me. She might think her expression is blank, but I can see way more than I'm sure she thinks I can.

And she's crumbling faster than she can control.

Just when I think she's going to drop the gun and give me a real answer, her hand twitches to the side, and a loud bang echoes around us as my entire body jolts in shock.

"Holy shit," someone cries, but my attention is still so entirely on Stella to appreciate what just happened.

CHAPTER TWENTY-TWO

Stella

My heart races and everything around me fades to nothing as blood races past my ears, but my eyes never leave Seb as his words repeat over and over in my head.

He wants me?

Like, for real, wants me?

Or was he just saying it because I had him at fucking gunpoint?

I shake my head, at war with myself.

I know the answer. I saw it clear as day in his dark eyes as he said the words.

Unlike all the other times, I saw the raw honesty, heard the sincerity of his apology.

"You're fucking crazy." Calli's words finally break through my haze, but I don't get a chance to respond, or even to turn to look at her, because Seb moves and before I know what's happening, my feet leave the ground and I'm thrown over his shoulder.

"What the—"

"You fucking shot at me, baby?"

"Are you dead?"

His hand smacks across my ass, making me howl as my clenched fists rain hell down on his own ass.

One second we're moving, marching through the trees toward the Cirillo house, then the next he's lowering me to my feet again.

"Thank you," I sass. "Was that really—"

His hands cup my face as his lips crash to mine in an all-consuming kiss that leaves my knees weak and my pussy aching for more.

"Does that hurt your stomach?" he whispers against my lips.

"Does what hurt my—oh," I breathe when I figure out what he's talking about. "N-no, I'm fine. It hardly—whoa, Seb," I scream when he throws me back over his shoulder and continues forward once more. "Put me the fuck down," I cry, looking up just in time to find all the others watching us with amused expressions before we disappear through the trees.

Seb ignores all my pleas to put me back on my feet until we're inside some kind of building. The only thing I know is that it's not the main house, because I saw that briefly before he kicked a door closed behind us.

He jogs up a set of stairs as if he's carrying nothing more than a stuffed toy over his shoulder.

We pass through a living area before another door slams behind me and I'm finally put down against it.

"Thank fuck, my head is—" My back crashes against the door and his body quickly follows, crushing me in the middle as his lips find mine once more.

My lips part on instinct the second he licks across the bottom one. His tongue caresses mine, exploring my mouth as if it's our first kiss.

For two seconds, my head wins out and I pause as he encourages me to give in to him.

"Stella," he growls, his fingers flexing as he grips the side of my neck in a possessive hold.

"I-I—"

"I meant what I said, baby. I want you. I want this."

My heart pounds, threatening to crash right out of my chest.

"What did Theo want you to tell me?" I ask, finding some strength to ask and not just dive headfirst into everything he can offer me.

"He... uh..." His eyes search mine for a beat, and for the first time, the real Seb stares back at me. All his fears, his insecurities are right there for me to see, his pain from everything he's suffered in the past pouring from him.

A lump crawls up my throat. The desire to comfort him, to tell him that everything is going to be okay almost gets the better of me, but I bite down on my bottom lip to allow him to finish what he needs to say.

"He wanted me to tell you that..." I suck in a breath, already knowing that whatever he's about to say is going to make my world tilt on its axis. "I'm falling for you,

Hellion." All the air rushes from my lungs. "Hell, I'm pretty sure I've already fallen. And it started from the moment I looked into your eyes and you told me you were my perfect woman." He leans in, his rough cheek brushing mine. "You were right."

A moan rips from my throat when his lips drop from my ear and kiss down the length of my neck.

"Seb, I—"

"No," he breathes, his voice rough with emotion and desire.

Pressing his fingers to my lips, he ensures I'm not going to continue.

"I don't need to hear anything in return. I know I fucked up. I know I hurt you. And I know I don't deserve this. But fuck, Hellion. I want it. I want it so fucking bad, you have no idea."

I nod, unable to form words even if he did want me to speak.

He lifts me, and I slide up the door until my legs wrap around his waist and he reclaims my mouth.

Nothing more is said. Instead, he puts everything he has into showing me the truth in his words.

"Seb," I moan when he drags my hoodie off. It lands on the floor with a thud, reminding me that I've got his knife in the pocket.

He pulls back to look at me, his brows pinched.

"It's yours."

Lowering me down, he reaches for my hoodie and pulls his knife out.

A smile curls at his lips as something dark flashes through his eyes.

"W-what?"

Twisting his knife around, he takes a step back from me and pulls his own hoodie from his body with only one hand.

The sight of the smooth movement is enough to make my pussy clench, let alone the inches of toned body he reveals. His pants go next along with his sneakers and socks, and all the while I stand there, my breathing ragged as I shamelessly stare at him.

Sitting down on the edge of his bed, he beckons me over, parting his legs so I can stand between them.

Pushing from the door, I walk over, slipping my hand into his free one when I get to him.

"What?" I breathe as he silently stares up at me.

Lifting his knife, he holds it out for me to take.

"I don't—"

He scoots back on the bed and pulls the leg of his boxer briefs up to expose his inner thigh.

"Own me, baby."

All my breath leaves my chest in an explosion of disbelief.

"Y-you want me to..." I trail off. Surely he's not fucking serious?

"Yeah. Make me yours, Hellion."

"Holy shit," I gasp, seeing in his eyes that he really means it.

Most people would probably refuse. The thought of causing their lover pain, seeing them bleed, enough to not even consider it. That's not who I am, though, and Seb damn well knows it.

Taking the knife, I flip the blade out, looking at the sharp tip, my mouth watering for what I'm about to do.

"Sit back," I instruct.

Heat flashes through his eyes as he does as he's told, allowing me enough space to crawl onto the bed as he lies back on his elbows.

I don't pause until I'm between his legs, the tip of his knife only a fraction from his skin.

"I should get a towel," I say in a moment of clarity.

"Just do it, Princess."

I hold his eyes for a beat, waiting for him to back out, to tell me that he's joking, but he never does.

"O-okay," I say, hating that there's a quiver in my voice.

I might have shot someone before, punched a few deserving candidates, but I've never willingly hurt someone. It's entirely different.

Especially someone I care about.

My hand shakes as I press harder, the blade slicing through his soft skin with ease.

"Oh my God," I gasp as the tip of the knife vanishes under a pool of red.

Carving in an 'S' is easier than I expected, and in only seconds he's proudly wearing my first initial on his thigh.

"Fuck, Hellion," he breathes, his chest heaving, his eyes so dark they're almost black and his cock straining against the tight fabric of his boxers.

"Twisted fuck," I mutter, ripping my eyes from him and rubbing my thumb beneath the wound I've created, sweeping away the trail of blood before it seeps into his sheets.

"Princess?"

Lifting my gaze once more, I lock my eyes on his as I lift my thumb to my lips and make a show of licking his blood away.

"Fuck," he barks, watching my tongue as it swirls around my digit. "How do I taste?"

"I prefer your cock."

"Fucking killing me here, baby."

A wicked smirk pulls at my lips and I set to work adding my 'D' to his leg.

The second I'm done, I flip his switchblade closed and place it on his nightstand.

I don't bother sitting up to admire my handiwork. Instead, I dip my head and lick up the trail of blood from his cut.

"Fuck, baby. You were right that night. You're not a fucking angel from above," he groans as I lick around his fresh wounds, the taste of copper filling my mouth.

I kiss around my brand before sitting back slightly to admire it.

The sight of my initials on his skin does something weird to me.

Stilling, I reach out and touch one finger to the 'S,' the strongest sensation of belonging and contentment washing over me.

It's wrong, feeling like this about a person who's only caused you pain.

Has he, though?

Some of our better times—hell, even some of our

worst flicker through my mind. How right it felt every single time we connected settles into me and I push my lingering doubts aside.

"Hellion?"

"Yeah," I say, finding his eyes. "I'm all in."

Confusion flickers through his eyes for the briefest moment before realization hits and a smile twitches at the corners of his mouth.

"I think I like you better with my name on you."

He laughs at my comment, but his humor is cut short when I wrap my fingers around the waistband of his boxers, my knuckles brushing his hips, making them jump from the bed in need.

Lifting his ass from the bed to help me, I drag the fabric down his legs, pulling one free but abandoning them on the other for him to deal with in favor of wrapping my hand around his solid length.

"Fuck. Fuck," he barks when I begin stroking him. "Fuck. I was so mad at you for that little stunt earlier," he groans, his hips bucking in an attempt to make me move faster.

"Oh yeah?" I taunt. "Did you want to punish me for it?"

A growl rips up his throat as my thumb circles his dick, collecting up the bead of precum that's pooled at the tip.

"Fuck, yeah. I-I— fuuuuck," he groans when I lick at him, swirling my tongue around like he's a popsicle. "I just want you safe, baby."

"I can look after myself," I say before kissing and sucking down his shaft.

"I know... fuck... I know." His fingers twist in my hair, holding me against him. Not that I'd be going anywhere. "B-but—argh— two people are better than one."

"Hmm..." I hum against him, making his length jerk. "They sure are."

"Fucking— baby," he cries when I suck him into my mouth, taking him all the way back until he hits my throat. "Fuck."

With my hand wrapped tightly around his base, I work him in and out of my mouth, swirling my tongue around him and grazing his sensitive skin softly with my teeth.

"I'm not gonna last, baby," he warns, his grip on my hair tightening. "Fuck. If you keep this up, I'm gonna— holy shit."

Shifting my position slightly, I take him deeper.

My eyes burn and I fight my need to choke around him as I stare into his dark, hungry eyes.

Every single muscle in his body is pulled tight, his ink rippling as they move beneath his skin.

It's beautiful. So fucking beautiful.

But I soon realize it's nothing compared to the moment he finally breaks.

His cock jerks in my mouth, his jaw falls slack, and his eyes harden for a beat as the pleasure hits him before they soften, showing me that every single word he's said to me tonight is true.

His cock pulses in my mouth, jets of salty cum shooting down my throat, my eyes burning from the size of him along with his painful grip on my hair.

When I finally release him and he lets me up, I've got tears streaming down my cheeks.

"Fuck, you're perfect," he breathes, reaching up to cup my face and wipe my tears. "What did I do to deserve you?"

"Nothing. You don't," I say with a smirk.

"Ain't that the fucking truth."

In a flash, he's flipped us, leaving me laid out on the black bed, gazing up at him.

"Let me make it up to you. Prove to you that I'm not just a cunt who wants to hurt you."

My lips slam shut on instinct, keeping the words I want to say inside.

"What is it?" he asks, peppering kisses to my damp cheeks and licking up what's left of my tears. "Tell me."

"I know," I say on a sigh. "I know that's not just who you are. I see more, Seb. I think maybe I always have."

His lips crash down on mine, his kiss violent as he attacks my mouth, showing me exactly what my words do to him.

His hands roam my body as our kiss deepens, until they come to a stop at the neck of my tank.

"Oh my God," I gasp when the sound of ripping fabric cuts through our kissing and heaving breaths.

"Clothes are overrated, Hellion."

His hand slips behind my back, releasing my bra and freeing my heavy breasts.

"Better. Much fucking better."

This time when he dips his head, it's in favor of my nipples.

Sucking one into his mouth, he rolls his tongue over

the hard peak before making me cry out when his teeth sink into the sensitive flesh.

"You love it when I hurt you though, don't you, Hellion?"

"You know I do," I moan, watching him kiss down my belly, or more specifically over my scar.

"Seb," I moan as his tongue gently laps at my sensitive skin. "I need—"

"I know what you need, baby." He lifts his head, holding my eyes captive. "Trust me?"

For the first time, I nod. "Y-yeah. I do."

His smile is so fucking wide, but I only get the briefest second to admire it before he looks down, getting to work at ridding me of the rest of my clothing.

The second he's ripped my panties from me—literally—and then stuffed them under his pillow to add to his collection, he pushes my legs wide and stares down at my aching pussy.

"I'm fucking addicted, Hellion. I'll never get enough of this."

Dropping to his knees, he trails kisses up the inside of my leg, brushing his lips over my own brand.

"It's healing," he murmurs, although more to himself than me. "Might need to make these more permanent."

"What are you suggesting?"

"I've got a few ideas, baby." His eyes flash with wicked excitement, but I don't get a chance to question him, to find out if he's thinking the same things that I am, because his fingers part me and his mouth locks onto my clit.

"Seb," I scream, my fingers threading through his hair, dragging him closer as he begins lapping at me.

My legs tremble as he slides two fingers inside me, curling them in a way that ensures he hits the spot I'm desperate for.

"Come for me, Hellion," he growls, the vibration of his deep voice doing crazy things to my body.

He pushes another finger inside me, stretching me wide open, and with one almost too hard suck on my clit, I fall into the most delicious pleasure.

My entire body trembles with the strength of it, my eyes squeezing tight as I ride out every wave.

"Oh my God," I pant as he drops a kiss to my clit before pulling out of me and crawling up my body.

"Not God, baby. The devil, remember?" he rumbles, his grin as dark as the devil himself.

"How could I forget?"

His lips claim mine, my own taste filling my mouth. A moan of desire rumbles up my throat as my body heats up, ready for more.

"Wicked princess," Seb growls, settling himself between my legs.

"Yes," I scream like a shameless whore when he pushes inside me, fully hard once again from eating me. My back arches off the bed as he works himself all the way in until we're connected in the most carnal way.

He leans over me, his body lining up perfectly with mine.

My pussy clenches around him, desperate for him to move, but all he does is rest his forearms on either side of my head and stare down into my eyes.

It's weirdly intimate, which is odd considering what's going on below our waists.

"I meant it. You know that, don't you?"

I swallow, the raw honesty in his eyes and voice getting the better of me.

"I do," I whisper, my voice barely audible.

His nose touches mine. It's such a simple move, but it makes my heart tumble in my chest.

"I'm falling in love with you, Hellion."

Oh. My. God.

Tears pool in my eyes, and I hate for the briefest moment that I'm being a total girl about that confession. But the second he sees my reaction, the way his face utterly melts with happiness, I forget all about my show of weakness.

But just like before, he doesn't give me a chance to say anything in return—not that I'm entirely sure what I'd say, because finally, he rolls his hips, and the moan that rips from my throat ensures no words do.

Am I falling in love with him too? Or am I still in the throes of hate?

Sometime soon I might stop lying to myself and admit the truth. Maybe.

Seb's movements remain measured as he carefully watches me.

The need to look away from his eyes is almost too much to deny. I feel ripped open, vulnerable, completely at his fucking mercy, and it terrifies me.

My head might still not quite be on board with this, but my heart? That little bitch is bouncing up and down in excitement, desperate for the rest of me to catch up with her.

"Seb?" I ask softly.

"Yeah, baby." As if he can sense that I'm struggling, he breaks our eye contact and nuzzles his face into my neck, kissing my skin and sending goose bumps racing across my body.

"Are you making love to me?"

He stills for a beat and I can't help but wonder if that's because he wasn't aware or because I'm calling him out on it.

"Yeah, I guess I am. That okay with you?" he asks, amusement laced through his tone.

"Yeah. Just... maybe fuck me after. I'm not sure I can cope with too much softness from you."

He chuckles against me, suddenly thrusting his hips, taking me deeper and making me gasp in shock.

"How about a bit of both?"

"Sounds perfect," I breathe as he does it again and I drag my nails down his back.

I might want him to stop being an asshole, but only in certain ways. I love his wicked side in bed, and he damn well knows it.

Although his movements get a little more demanding, he never ups the pace, just keeps things slow and steady. It drives me fucking crazy, and the second he skims his hands down my body and presses his fingers to my clit, the extra friction makes me explode.

"That's it, baby," he growls. "Milk my cock."

A smile curls at my lips as I thrash about on the bed,

riding out the powerful waves as just a hint of my bad boy slips back.

"Fuck, Hellion. You squeeze me so tight."

Digging my nails into his shoulders once more, I drag them along his soft skin.

"Fuck. Fuck," he chants, the pain mixing with his pleasure and need to hold off, and he falls, his cock jerking inside me, filling me, claiming me.

He collapses on me, his hard, heavy body pressing me into the mattress.

It takes a few seconds for my desire-fogged brain to clear. Seb seems to have the same issue, because it's not until I speak that he shows any sign of life.

"Are those assholes clapping?"

He pushes from my chest, lifting his face from my shoulder and listening.

"I'm going to fucking kill them," he warns, his voice dark and dangerous.

"Or," I start, lifting my hand, cupping his cheek and forcing his eyes back to mine, "you could fuck me again and really show them what they're missing."

"Match made in hell, baby."

CHAPTER TWENTY-THREE

Sebastian

"Don't fall asleep," I say when I look down and notice that Stella's eyes are closed where she's resting on my chest. "We need to get back on London time."

"I'm awake. Just thinking."

"Sounds dangerous," I laugh. "How are you going to try to kill me next?"

"Uh... machete?" she asks lightly.

"I can't believe you nearly shot me," I murmur. Really, I can. It's a total Stella thing to do.

"Oh, don't be a baby. I missed by a mile," she says, pushing up onto her elbow so she can look down at me. Amusement glitters in her blue eyes.

"I felt it fly past my ear. That was not a mile away."

She shrugs. "Guess it was just a good thing you didn't move, huh?"

I shake my head. "It's a damn good job that I—" She sucks in a sharp breath and I catch the words before they fall from my lips. "T-trust you."

Relief floods her face. I might almost be at the point of fully accepting how I feel about her, but she's not quite there yet. I get it. It's not like I deserve any of this, not after all those stunts I pulled before she was stabbed. I don't even want to like me, let alone anything else.

"Can I ask you something?" she asks, her voice suddenly serious.

"Anything. I'll tell you anything you want to know."

She nods, accepting my words for what they are. The truth.

"When you wrote that message on my mirror. Was it the only one you did?"

"What do you mean?" I ask, concern racing through me. My hand on her hip flexes with my need to move, but I force myself to stay put.

"Before you wrote all over it with lipstick, did you... write anything else?"

My brows pinch. "No. Why?"

All the blood drains from Stella's face, and my heart rate immediately picks up.

"I... um... found something earlier."

"Stella," I growl. "If you don't—"

"It was a threat that it wasn't over. I had a shower, and when I came out it was there, in the steam."

"What did it say?" I grit out, fighting like hell not to freak out.

"Something about him being more successful next time."

"Motherfucker," I bark, slipping out from beneath her and planting my fist into the wall. "Fuck. FUCK."

Footsteps thunder in the hallway before the door flies open.

"What the—"

"Fuck, bro. Get the fuck out," I bark as Stella flies under the sheets, covering her naked body up.

"S-sorry. We're waiting for you to kill each other."

"GET THE FUCK OUT."

Thankfully, Theo pushes the others out and closes the door behind him.

"Get dressed," I demand, reaching down for my discarded clothes.

"Seb," she sighs. "Just come back to bed."

"No, Stella. That motherfucker *has* been in your bedroom. He's broken in and—"

"Just like you did," she points out, raising a brow in accusation.

"This is not the fucking same. I snuck in to see you because I couldn't fucking stay away from you no matter how much I wanted to."

"And stole my panties and covered my room in mortifying photos."

I shake my head, needing a second for her words to settle.

"I'm sorry, what? What photos?"

Hesitantly, she sits up, pulling the covers with her.

"The ones you took at Nico's party. All the stuff I couldn't remember. You put them... you put them around my room to hurt me, to make me look like a whore." The truth hits her long before she finishes talking. "T-that wasn't you, was it?"

"No, Stella. It wasn't." My voice is cold and full of fear. "Get fucking dressed."

She nods, this time getting out of bed and following orders.

"What are we doing?" she asks, trailing me down the hallway a few minutes later.

"Let's go," I say to the guys who are all sitting around in the living room.

Alex has appeared—someone probably messaged him so he didn't miss the entertainment of me handing my balls to Stella.

"What's going on?" Theo asks, immediately jumping up.

"Stella's moving in. We're going to get her stuff."

"I'm fucking what?" she screeches as Alex laughs.

"Fuck me, you went from zero to sixty a bit fucking fast, didn't you?" he asks, amusement filling his tone.

"He's been in her room. She's not going back there."

"Seb, you can't just drag me from my home," she says, tugging on my hand that has hers in a vice-like grip.

"Watch me, Princess," I shoot over my shoulder before pulling her from the flat, the others, including Calli, falling into line behind us.

"You should go home," Nico barks at his sister.

"No fucking chance." She steps up to Stella,

243

standing tall beside her. "I'm done with letting you lot walk all over me. I'm a part of this too."

"Callista—" Nico starts, but Stella soon cuts him off.

"No," she spits, violently poking him in the chest. "Stop treating her like a little girl. She's more capable than you give her credit for."

The two of them have a stare-off for a moment, but eventually, Nico backs down.

"Wise move, man," Toby says, slapping him on the shoulder before looking up at me. "Did you know she had a knife to his balls earlier?"

I scrub my hand down my face. "Can't say I'm surprised. They seem to still be in place, so I'm assuming she got her way then, too."

"Hey," Stella complains, slapping me upside the head. "I'm right here, asshole."

"Calli," I say, knowing it'll make Stella happy, "you're with us."

Toby also decides that he's coming with us and climbs into the back of my Aston.

My gaze meets his in the rearview mirror. We've not exactly seen eye to eye recently with all this shit with Stella, but the second I look at him, I see the same fierce determination and need to protect her on his face.

With a nod, I focus on what needs to be done and start the engine.

"Fucking hell," Calli squeaks when I gun the engine and throw her back in the seat as I peel out of the Cirillos' driveway.

Theo's Maserati pulls up right behind us when we

get to Stella's and the eight of us walk up to the front door as a unit.

But our arrival doesn't go unnoticed, because the door opens before we get to it, and Galen stands there, his eyes scanning all of us before landing on his daughter in confusion.

"Stella, it's so good to see—"

"Fucking hell," Theo barks as I launch myself at Galen. "Not again."

"Seb, no," Stella screams, and it's only the sound of her voice that stops me from landing more than one punch this time.

Galen's jaw flexes as he rubs at the place I hit.

He doesn't come back at me. He can't, really, seeing as he's still rocking a sling from the last time.

"What the hell is going on?" the man who's meant to be fucking protecting her booms as he runs out of the house behind Galen.

"It's okay," Stella assures him, and he immediately backs down a little.

"No, it's really fucking not."

"Seb," she hisses. "We need to take this inside."

Glancing over my shoulder at her driveway, I realise that she's right.

Anyone could be listening to this, and the last thing we need is for him to know we're onto him.

My steps falter as I move toward the house, realisation hitting me.

If it weren't for me, Stella would have known about this threat earlier.

How many other things has he done that she just assumed were me playing games?

Guilt threatens to swallow me whole. She could have died because of me and my stupid need for revenge.

I stop and turn back to her.

"What? What's wrong?"

"There's more, isn't there? The photos are just a part of it."

"Y-yeah."

"Fucking hell, Princess," I sigh, pushing my hair back from my brow.

"Let's just get my stuff, then we'll talk."

A smile twitches at my lips. "Oh, happy to move in now, huh?"

She lets out a long breath. "I don't want to be here, Seb. Why do you think I went to Calli's in the first place?"

I nod, reaching for her and pulling her into my body, wrapping my arms around her as tight as I can.

"I'll fix this, baby. I fucking swear to you."

"I know," she whispers, pressing a kiss to the underside of my jaw. "I trust you."

My heart tumbles in my chest. Well, if those words aren't as good as hearing three others, then I don't know what is.

"What's going on?" Galen demands as we close the door behind us.

"He's been here. He's been in her room. I thought you were fixing the security of this place?"

"We are—we have. There's no way he's been here."

246

Anticipation ripples through the air as Galen and I stare at each other.

"I wouldn't put my daughter at risk like that."

"No? Isn't that exactly how we ended up in this fucking mess?"

"Seb, please," Stella begs, her hand landing on my forearm. "He's been here, Dad. More than once. And recently. I found a message on my mirror when I got out of my shower."

"Why didn't you tell me?"

"Oh I don't know," she snaps, finally starting to lose her temper. "Maybe because once again, you weren't here."

"Then you should have told me," Calvin says, hurt covering his face. "If I knew then…"

Stella shakes her. "It's too late. The damage is done. I'm not safe here—"

"You are. I've installed—"

"And even if I were," Stella says, steamrolling over Calvin's argument. "I don't want to be here."

"Where the hell do you want to be instead?" Galen asks, sounding like he's just had the wind knocked out of him.

I don't need to see Stella's eyes flick to me. I feel her attention, even for that brief second. It makes my chest puff out in pride.

Take that, motherfucker. Your own daughter just chose me.

"Him?" Galen spits, his lip curling in disgust. "But you hate him."

"Yeah," Stella says with a laugh. "I do." She steps

up to me and laces her fingers through mine. "It's not going to stop me leaving with him, though."

Galen's mouth opens and closes a couple of times.

"Daddy," she says, her voice softer, "you've brought me up to always go after what I want. To know how to protect myself. Well, that's exactly what I'm doing. I'm not safe here. The entire Cirillo estate is secure. No one will get me there. And this," she says, lifting our hands, "might be completely insane. But it's right." She shrugs. "So it's how it's going to be for now."

Galen clearly knows his daughter well enough not to argue, and all he does is nod and step aside, allowing both of us to move to the stairs.

"Stella," he calls before we take a step up, his voice rough with emotion, "this will always be your home. I hope you know that."

She pauses beside me and sucks in a sharp breath.

"Honestly, Dad, I don't think I've ever actually had a home. Least of all this place, where someone's been inside my room, my space, without any of our knowledge."

Silence ripples around the room before Stella squeezes my hand and leads me up the stairs. The others follow after a beat.

Theo and Alex quickly overtake and climb to the top floor before checking each of the rooms up here.

It's probably overkill. I can't imagine that after all this, he'd be stupid enough to be waiting for us to find him, but I appreciate that they're taking it seriously.

Pushing open Stella's door, I step inside first and look around.

It's exactly the same as the last time I was here, with the curtains shut as if it's the middle of the night.

The realisation that she's done that because someone's been watching her makes me feel physically sick.

"Pack everything you need. We're not coming back here."

"I don't have much. The benefit of moving a lot," she says, her voice empty.

Walking up behind her where she's pulling her underwear from her drawer, I wrap my arms around her waist, resting my chin on her shoulder.

"I'm going to keep you safe, baby."

"I know," she whispers, her voice full of emotion and anger.

I take a step back and let her do her thing when the others enter and join Calli, who's standing by the door.

"All clear," Theo says, not that I was expecting anything else.

"Galen looks pissed," Alex mutters.

"I don't give a fuck," I bark. "He's allowed that sick fuck to get in here. To get to Stella. He doesn't deserve her."

"Seb," Stella's weak voice rings through the room, "stop, please."

I nod, although she can't see me as she continues shoving clothes into a suitcase.

Watching her every movement, the tension in the room gets heavier as the seconds pass.

"Do you want to get the car ready to go?" I ask Theo, my eyes flicking to Alex and Nico too. Daemon is missing; I can only assume he stayed down with Galen and Calvin.

"Sure. You gonna be okay?"

"Of course. Tobes, you staying?"

"Yes," he confirms, his face set as if he's ready to fight for his sister should this all blow up on us.

"We'll be out in a bit."

They nod before disappearing from the room once more.

"This is insane," Calli says quietly as Stella slips into the bathroom to collect up her toiletries.

"Welcome to our world."

A scowl appears on her face before a growl rumbles up her throat and her tiny fists curl.

"It's my world too, dickhead. You've just locked me away from it."

My lips part to say something, but I don't really have a comeback.

"Nico and Theo, they're just trying to—"

"Protect me, I know. It's suffocating."

"Well, stand up to them. I know someone who can teach you how," I say, shooting a look in the direction of my girl.

"Do we need two of them?" Toby asks lightly, trying to insert some humour into our conversation.

"You guys need more than two of us," Calli states confidently.

"Okay, I'm ready," Stella announces, passing me one of the bags she packed while Toby takes the other.

"Let's get the fuck out of here."

Toby goes first, and I gesture for both Calli and Stella to go ahead of me.

Galen and Calvin are standing at the bottom of the stairs when we get there with less than amused looks on their faces.

"Could you give us a minute?" Stella says to me and Calli when we come to a stop.

"N-no, I don't want—"

"I won't hurt my daughter, Sebastian," Galen snaps.

"It's fine," Toby assures me. "Go put these in the car. We'll only be a few minutes."

Taking a step toward Galen, I stare him dead in the eyes, daring him to fucking try anything.

He holds my stare but doesn't say a word.

He can't. He knows I'm right.

CHAPTER TWENTY-FOUR

Stella

I stare at my dad's resigned eyes, my own anger over all of this kicking up a notch once more.

"Why are you letting him do this? Shouldn't you be fighting harder for me?" I ask, needing to know how he can just stand there and let me walk out.

"Because he's right," he says, his voice chock full of emotion. The sound of him falling apart causes a lump to crawl up my throat.

My dad is never emotional. He never shows his feelings. Ever.

"I screwed up. I've tried so hard to protect you from all of this, but clearly it wasn't enough."

"All you had to do was tell me the truth. Tell me who I was, who we are. The things you've done."

His brows crease as I say those final words.

"I know you killed Seb's dad."

He rears back as if I just slapped him.

"N-no. I didn't."

"But he—" I glance to the door where Seb disappeared a few seconds ago before looking at Toby, who just looks confused.

So that wasn't common knowledge then, obviously.

"I took the fall, Stella. But I wasn't the one who pulled that trigger, I swear to you."

"But he thinks—"

"We were never going to come back here. I agreed that we'd move and start our lives over. I'd messed up too badly here, and a fresh start was our only chance."

"Why?" I ask, hoping and praying for some honesty.

"B-because—" He hesitates, his eyes shooting to Toby for the briefest moment.

"Because of my mum. Our mum."

Dad nods once. "I'm so sorry, Stella." His voice cracks and he storms from the hallway, a door slamming so hard that it rattles the house around us.

"What happened with your mom?" I ask Toby, unable to even contemplate calling her my mom yet.

"Let's get you back and we'll talk, yeah?"

I narrow my eyes at him, needing all these fucking secrets to disappear.

"I promise. The whole truth."

"Okay," I breathe, reaching for his hand, because the wrecked look on his face as he even considers telling me whatever it is physically hurts me.

With a glance at Calvin, I take off toward the door, more than ready to get out of here.

"I'm working with Damien's security, baby D. We'll get this motherfucker."

"Yeah," I mutter, not feeling all that confident.

"If you need anything, you know—"

"I'll be fine. Thank you, Calvin."

He sucks in a harsh breath at my cold tone, but I'm so over all of this. I'm past hurting his or my father's feelings. It might not really be their fault. I should have told someone about the notes, the photos. But I thought it was Seb. Never in a million years did I think that someone wanted me dead. So why should Dad and Calvin suspect anything?

Dad kept me locked up in here for weeks—I guess to ensure my safety when I finally emerged—and I can only assume he truly thought everything was okay.

How fucking wrong was he?

When we emerge from the house, we find Theo's car idling, ready to go, but Seb hasn't so much as climbed into his. He's standing there with his eyes focused on us as we walk down a couple of steps, still hand in hand.

He looks fierce. Deadly. But thankfully, since discovering the real connection between Toby and me, I see no jealousy there.

I guess one good thing might have come out of all of this. These two might not kill each other fighting over me. Neanderthals.

"You okay?" Seb asks the second I step up to him.

"Take me home, please."

"Fuck, baby," he groans, slipping his hand around the side of my neck and lowering his brow to mine. "Say it again."

"Take me home."

A wicked smile twitches at his lips before they press against mine for a chaste kiss. Although it might be quick, I feel it all the way down to my toes.

The second he's in the car, he guns the engine and we fly from the driveway behind Theo. Only, he's not quick enough for me not to see my dad standing at the living room window, staring at me as if he's never going to see me again.

Seb notices and reaches over to grab my hand as Calli leans over the chair and squeezes my shoulder.

"Everything's going to be okay. I fucking swear to you."

I nod, choked up all over again. "I know," I squeak, unable to force any more past the lump in my throat.

The journey back to Theo's is quiet. No one says a word, and I'm grateful as it allows me to attempt to process all of this.

Seb and Theo grab my bags from the trunk, and I follow Calli up the stairs where the others have already disappeared.

She slips off toward the couch with the guys while Seb and Toby follow me down to what I assume is Seb's room.

As I step inside, it occurs to me just how many questions I still have about him. About his life, the Family.

They place the suitcases on the end of the bed and both hesitate.

"Toby and I need to talk," I say to Seb. "Do you min—"

"He can stay," Toby says, cutting me off. "I've got a feeling that everything I've been keeping quiet is going to be out soon anyway. Plus, I can hardly expect you to keep it from him after everything."

"Are you sure? If it's personal then—"

"No more secrets, Stella. No more lies."

I nod, already dreading what he's going to tell me. I can tell from the look on his face that it's going to be hella painful.

"Shall I get us a drink?" Seb offers, clearly sensing exactly what I am.

"Yeah. A strong one," Toby says with a humorless laugh.

He falls into the chair in the corner of the room that's covered in Seb's clothes while I drag my suitcases off the bed once more and sit in the middle with my legs crossed, waiting to hear whatever horrifying truths he's been hiding.

Toby is silent, his fingers drumming on the arm of the chair nervously as he waits for Seb to return.

My stomach is in knots as I stare at him. I have no clue what he's about to confess. Whatever it is, it's ripping him apart inside, that much is clear.

The door opening once more startles both of us before Seb slips inside the room and passes Toby both a can of beer and a bottle of vodka.

He ignores the beer and instead downs a good few shots of the vodka before passing it back.

"Thanks," I whisper when he passes me the same.

"You good with beer?" he asks, concern pulling at his brow.

"I'll take whatever I can get right now."

He slides onto the bed with me and wraps his arm around my waist, pressing his lips to my shoulder.

The alcohol burns, but it hits exactly where I need it to.

"Go on then," I encourage Toby, who looks about ready to bolt, his face drained of blood, his eyes haunting.

He looks between the two of us for a beat before focusing on me.

"O-our mum, she's... ill."

I nod, needing a little more than that.

"She's recovering from surgery from having a brain tumor removed."

"What?" Seb breathes, disbelief coating his voice. "How don't we know this?"

"Because my dad is a fucking cunt, that's why."

I look over just in time to see Seb's mouth open and close as he tries to find some words.

"Go on." Seb's grip on my hip tightens, telling me all that I really need to know about his relationship with Toby.

They might have their differences, but what Toby told me that first day we hung out was true. They'd kill for each other. I see that in Seb right now. It might only be Toby and I who share the same blood, but in this family, that doesn't matter.

"She was diagnosed a while back. Dad didn't want to tell anyone, or cause unnecessary drama, because the doctors were hopeful that with some treatment everything would be okay.

"He was right. For quite a few years, things were okay. But then we started noticing changes in her. She'd be more forgetful, go to bed more often with headaches. She waved it off as nothing more than stress. It wasn't until she had a seizure that she went to see a doctor."

"It came back," I whisper.

"Yeah. Well, it never really went away. Was just... controlled. Paused, I guess. Anyway, it had grown, and the doctors decided the only chance was surgery followed by more treatment."

"And you still kept it a secret?" Seb asks, astounded.

"Seb," Toby sighs, scrubbing his hand through his hair. "The man you see and the father I see are very different people."

"What do you—"

"He's abused her for years," Toby confesses quietly. "Us. He's—"

"What?" Seb roars, releasing me and jumping up from the bed, his muscles pulled tight.

But Toby is faster, or just sees it coming and blocks his way as he marches toward the door.

"Don't, Seb. I'm not telling you all of this so you can go over there and put a bullet through his head."

"But—"

"Not yet, okay? Not yet." Seb nods, his shoulders

relaxing a little. "Plus, the day that happens, I'll be the one at the other end of the bullet."

A ripple of tension goes through the room, forcing us all to fall silent.

My head spins and my heart aches for a woman I've never met but feel connected to nonetheless.

Seb remains standing in the middle of the room, looking utterly useless now he can't go and kill someone, and Toby just looks wrecked as he slumps back in the chair. His hair's a mess where he's been running his fingers through it, and his usually light blue eyes are dark and tormented.

"She's why we came back," I state. "My dad came back for her."

"You landed two days before her surgery."

"Fucking hell," I breathe, dropping my head into my hands. "Why didn't he tell me?"

"So you didn't have to go through losing her all over again if the worst happened." I look up just in time to catch the end of Toby's shrug.

"Fuck, I—" Climbing from the bed, I start pacing, unable to sit still with all this anxiety shooting around my body. "Fuck."

Both of their eyes burn into me as I march back and forth, trying to get my thoughts together.

Suddenly, I stop and turn to Toby.

"Is she..." I bite on my bottom lip, feeling so out of my depth with all this it's not even funny. "Is she going to survive this?"

"She's still got to have more radiation, but the surgery was a success. Doctors are hopeful."

"Okay. That's good. That's good. And your dad... does he... know?" Toby's brows pinch. "About me?"

"Stella," he sighs. "There are eleven months between us. I'm pretty sure he'd have noticed."

"Jesus. What the fuck were they playing at? Your mom had a fucking newborn, and a husband, I assume."

Toby nods, confirming my thoughts.

"I don't know what happened. Mum's not in any place to dig up the past right now, and well, I try to speak to my dad as little as possible."

"You said that your dad..."

"He's a controlling cunt. Always has been. Nothing either of us does is good enough. It's—"

"You need to get out of there," I say at the same time Seb says, "He needs to die."

"I know," he snaps. "But it's not that easy. Trust me, if it were, I'd have blown his brains out a long time ago."

The vicious look on Toby's face makes me do a double take. I've always wondered why he was friends with Seb and the others when he seems so different. But right now, with that fierce determination to kill his own father etched into every one of his features, I realize he's not all that different. He just keeps that side of him hidden better than the others.

I'm sure it should probably terrify me, knowing that I'm surrounded by guys who are capable of things like killing their own parents. But with my reality right now, I've never felt safer.

"I can't believe we didn't know all of this. Fuck, man," Seb says, horrified that his friend has been going through all of this and none of them were aware.

"It's okay. None of this is your fault."

Walking over to Toby, I drop down on his lap and pull him into my arms.

"I'm so fucking sorry you've had to go through this alone."

He trembles in my hold and lets out a shaky breath in my ear, but he doesn't utter a word more.

"Can you give us a minute?" I say to Seb without releasing Toby.

"Sure. I need another beer after that."

"Seb," Toby says, lifting his head from the crook of my neck before he opens the door.

"Please don't—"

"I won't say anything, Tobes. I know I'm an asshole, but you can trust me."

Seb's got the door open and is about to slip out when Toby speaks again.

"Galen didn't kill your dad."

Seb stills, his entire body locking up.

"W-what?"

"He just told us before we left Stella's. It wasn't him. I believed him."

"So who was it?" Seb grits out.

"I have no idea. But I think there's more to all of this than we're aware of."

A bitter laugh falls from Seb's lips. "Yeah. There seems to be even more secrets and lies than we all thought."

Without another word, Seb slips from the room, leaving me and Toby alone.

He sucks in another shuddering breath, his arms tightening around me.

"You're not alone anymore, Toby. Whatever you need, you've got me. Them. We figure this shit out together, yeah?"

After a few seconds, he releases me so he can look up, our blue eyes meeting.

"You know, I always thought it would be cool to have a sister."

"Well, it seems like I've made all your dreams come true."

"Well." He clears his throat. "You being my sister wasn't the first thing I thought when I looked at you."

"Well, thank fuck you didn't act on that, huh? Imagine our kids."

"I'd rather not." He laughs, and it's so fucking good to see a smile.

Although my next question wipes that clean off his face.

"How bad is she really, Toby? Is she going to come through this?"

"They're hopeful this will have been successful and give her more time."

"What does that mean?"

He shrugs. "How much time do any of us have?"

Silence stretches between us.

"Fuck. This is so fucking depressing."

"I'm sorry. Why do you think I've not told anyone?"

"How have you carried all this around for this long?" I ask him, genuinely curious and concerned for him.

"How did you start your life over time and time again? We all do what we've got to do. I put up with Dad's shit because it's the only way to ensure Mum gets the treatment she needs."

"Is that why you can't kill him?" I ask.

"She needs the best treatment, Stella. It's her only chance."

"Fucking hell. Has my dad seen her, do you know?"

"I'm not sure. Not that I've seen. Dad has total control of her care. Everyone who comes in the house to look after her has been vetted, signed NDAs. It would take some work to arrange it."

"Why would he come here if he couldn't see her?"

"Just to be close?" Toby says sadly.

"He still loves her," I whisper, more to myself than Toby.

Suddenly, his lack of female company over the years begins to make sense. Has Toby's mum always been it for him?

But why walk away? Why take the fall for Seb's dad's death and take me and run?

"They were protecting you," Toby says, making me wonder if I spoke those questions out loud.

"Have you spoken to your mum about all of this?"

He shakes his head.

"I'm pretty sure the room is bugged. I daren't even mention it. If Dad knew you were here... shit, Stella. I have no idea how he'd react. I don't want you anywhere near him."

A thought hits me out of nowhere.

"Was it him?"

"Was what him?"

"Did he stab me? Has he been stalking me?"

Toby shakes his head. "I can see where you're going there. But that's not my Dad's style. If he wanted you gone, he'd have done it already."

"Shit. It makes sense for it to be him. He must hate me."

"That's not something I'd wish on anyone. I've spent eighteen years on the end of that hate. It's not a fun place to be."

CHAPTER TWENTY-FIVE

Sebastian

Toby's words spin around in my head as I make my way down the hall, the sound of everyone's voices filling my ears.

When I look up, I find everyone looking up at me with concern on their faces.

"How is she?" Theo asks.

I nod, not knowing how to answer that question. "She'll be okay. We can keep her safe here."

"She can stay as long as she needs." As he says the words, it's the first time I realise that I kinda forced this on him.

"Shit, I—"

"It's fine, Seb. It's not like you can take her to yours."

I mutter my agreement.

"Other than the hotel, this is the safest place for her. I've told Dad she's here. He's putting guys outside, just in case."

I nod, appreciating that the boss is on our side with this.

Pulling the fridge open, I grab an armful of beers, I pass one to Daemon, who's sitting at the island on his phone, before lowering them to the coffee table everyone is sitting around and falling down into the empty chair.

"I can't believe Galen allowed that motherfucker into their house," Alex mutters.

"Stella thought it was all me. They had no idea anything was going on until she was stabbed."

"Fuck," Alex says, scrubbing a hand over his face.

"Yeah, well, if you were less of a dick," Calli scoffs.

"Shouldn't you be at home, Baby C?"

"Fuck you, Seb."

"I don't like this," Nico complains, side-eyeing his sister.

"Stella wants me here and you know it. Try and get rid of me and she'll threaten your manhood again."

He shifts, covering his junk.

"You're fucking brave, letting her anywhere near yours," he tells me with a wink. "Bitch is fucking dangerous."

"I know. It's hot." I tug at my jeans, rearranging myself much to Theo and Alex's amusement. All Calli does is roll her eyes at me. "You can leave any time you like, Baby C. I'm sure Nico would love to escort you home."

Her lips twitch into a scowl and a quiet growl rumbles up her throat.

"Ah look, we'll make her into one of us yet."

"Her shot's not bad, you know," Daemon pipes up from behind us.

"No," Nico snaps. "My kid sister isn't getting involved in this shit."

"Excuse me," Calli snaps, rearing back. "Your kid sister will do as she damn well pleases."

I can't help the pride that swells in my chest as I watch the siblings glare at each other.

Nico might be less than impressed, but Stella's influence is doing good things for Calli. It's about time she stood up for herself.

It's another ten minutes before my bedroom door opens and Toby slips out, still looking wrecked from his confession.

My heart aches for him, for what he's going through.

I hate that we had no idea.

I mean, sure, I knew his dad was a bit of a prick. I remember as a young kid him being a total control freak whenever we were around his house. But the naïve, young me just assumed he didn't want his house messed up by kids. I never thought it was anything more. Anything that Toby and his mum, Maria, would have been suffering through all these years.

I let out a breath as I think of her. Whenever I saw her, she was always smiling, always happy. With long blonde hair and bright blue eyes just like Toby's—and Stella's—she always looked stunning. In a non-MILF kind of way. My mum was always in such a state that it was nice to see that others cared.

Their house was the same. Always perfect. I could understand why Jonas, Toby's dad, didn't want us all running wild through it, causing chaos.

"Here," I say, passing him a can as he approaches. "Everything okay?"

He nods, putting on his game face that I now realise we've all been staring at, completely missing everything he's hiding beneath for way too long.

"Yeah. Stella's just having a shower. She'll be out in a bit."

I glance back at the door, my fingers curling around the arm of the chair as my need to go and find her almost gets the better of me.

"She just needs a moment."

I nod in understanding and force myself to stay put.

I can't imagine everything she's going through.

A ripple of silence goes around the room. The weight of why we're all sitting here, why Stella is shut in my bedroom alone presses down on all of us.

"We need to have some fun," Alex announces.

"The Halloween party is coming up," Calli says with excitement.

"He letting you go this year?" Theo asks, nodding at Nico.

"This year, he ain't getting a choice. I'm seventeen. I can shoot a gun now. I'm going."

"Pain in the arse, brat," Nico mutters under his breath.

"Might even find a guy to hook up with," she

presses on, the twinkle in her eye showing that she's just baiting him. Fucking works, too.

"If you could pick someone we're not about to go to war with, that would be ideal."

"How the hell was I meant to know who he was?"

"His name is Antonio Santoro. How did you not know?"

"Maybe, arsehole, because I didn't ask to check his fucking ID before I started dancing with him."

"Well, maybe you should in the future."

"Unbelievable."

"He knew who you were, Calli. It's not possible that he didn't. Why do you think he wanted to dance with you, wanted to spend time with you? The Marianos are making a move, and two of their kids decide to get up close and personal to you and Stella?" My fists curl at the thought of that motherfucker touching her. "Not a fucking coincidence, Cal."

"Ugh, whatever. He was nice."

"He's a fucking Italian. He was sent to you for a reason."

"And what if he wasn't? What if he actually liked me?"

Nico scrubs his hand down his face, taking a moment to figure out his response. The rest of us remain quiet, not wanting to get involved with their sibling spat despite the fact that Nico is obviously right.

"You're unbelievable, Calli. You need to forget all about him. You're just asking for trouble if you keep anything alive there."

"Whatever," she scoffs, neither confirming nor

denying that she's spoken to him again since that afternoon we caught them.

Calli silently fumes while Nico takes a pull on his beer with a smug-as-fuck smirk on his face, knowing that he won that round. Calli can argue all she likes; the hard facts are damning. Antonio was after something, something more than getting into her knickers and getting bragging rights over it. He was planted that night. Both of them were. It's just yet to be seen as to why. Things seem to have quietened down again since the drama that day, or at least no one is telling me anything about it if they haven't.

"I'm heading out," Daemon says after a few seconds. "Calli, do you want a lift home?"

She glances over my shoulder at Daemon before drilling her brother with another deadly look.

"Yes, but not because of this wanker. Because it's a school night."

"Sure," Nico chuckles.

"I just need to say goodbye to Stella and we can go."

Daemon must agree behind me, because she hops through our outstretched legs and heads toward my room.

"Tonight was fucked up, man," Theo offers when Calli has gone.

"You're fucking telling me," I say rubbing at my rough jaw as I shoot a look in Toby's direction. He's distracted, too busy staring down at his can to notice my attention. My heart shatters for him all over again.

"I guess you're feeling pretty smug right now," Alex mutters.

"W-what? Why the fuck would I be feeling that?" I bark back.

"Didn't you see the look on Galen's face when you walked away with the one thing he cares about more than anything? Pretty sure that right there was your sweet fucking revenge."

"Not quite how you planned it, mind you," Theo adds.

Their words roll around my head, but unlike what I expected only a few weeks ago, I don't feel any kind of happiness or joy over the fact that I might just have won.

The reality is that while there's someone out there who clearly wants to get to Stella, then we're both at risk of losing. Because if he gets her again, if he hurts her again, I'm not sure I could cope. Especially if I weren't quick enough next time.

"It wasn't him," I confess, repeating the one bit of information Toby gave me that I can share.

"What? How do you know that?"

"He told Stella and me before we left the house."

"And you believed him?" Theo asks.

"Yeah. I did. After all this, after the way Seb's treated him... If it were him, he'd just confess. He's already lost. It makes little difference at this point."

"I agree with him," I say.

"You do?" Alex asks, looking genuinely confused.

I swallow down the last of my beer and drop my can to the table.

"He's lost. There's no point in covering it up anymore."

"He was a scapegoat," a deep voice says from behind me a beat before Daemon walks around to stand beside us all. "If what you're saying is true, then Damien used him as a scapegoat, knowing he was leaving, to cover up who really did it."

"But why? None of it makes any sense. Why did Galen need to leave at all?"

"To protect Stella," Toby pipes up after a few seconds, earning himself all our attention.

"Go on," Theo encourages.

"I don't know the details. Not yet, anyway. But Mum fell pregnant only weeks after I was born to another man. My dad's not likely to take that lying down. Galen took the fall for Seb's dad's death, knowing that it would be the perfect reason to disappear with his little girl, away from any danger."

"You think your dad would have done something?"

Toby's face turns pale. "I know he would have," he confirms.

"Well, shit," Theo says, leaning forward and resting his elbows on his knees.

The sound of a door opening fills the room, and we all look as Calli slips from my room and looks our way.

She smiles sadly at me before nodding at Daemon. "Let's go."

Nico waits until they've disappeared before announcing that he's heading out too.

"Then why didn't you just take Calli home?" Alex asks, exasperated.

"I ain't getting stuck with her. Plus, I'm not planning on heading home." He winks, a smug-as-fuck smirk playing on his lips. "Enjoy your night listening to those two making up," he announces before shooting me an amused look and disappearing out the door once he's confident Daemon and Calli will be far enough away not to notice him.

"Motherfucker," Alex grunts.

"Feel free to go. You know he's only meeting some skank who'll give him a new STI."

Alex pretends to be offended, but we all know it's a joke. He's hardly any pickier about the women he spends time with than Nico.

"I'm good," he says, reaching for another beer. "I'll chill here. Just promise you'll keep it down, yeah?"

"What? We're capable of doing something other than fucking."

"Yeah, we know. Arguing. Both are equally as loud."

My lips part to disagree, but I soon find I don't really have a comeback.

"I'm not listening to you fucking my sister," Toby chips in.

"Jeez, it's like none of you wants us to have any fun." I roll my eyes dramatically. "You staying, Tobes, or do you need to get back?"

His eyes narrow at me as if I'm about to out him. I'm not. He's more than welcome to keep his secrets. But I'm glad he confessed to Stella. She deserves to know everything about her life.

"I'm good," he says, stretching out his legs. "She's my biggest concern right now." He nods toward my bedroom, and my need for my girl steps up a notch.

"Tell me about it," I mutter.

"No one's getting her here."

"Theo, bro. You've met Stella, right? We can hardly lock her up in a castle. She's not Calli."

He nods, more than aware of the kind of stunts Stella is likely to pull on us if we even consider trying to make her stay put.

"Dad's put security details on her. She won't get to go anywhere without at least two sets of eyes on her at all times."

"Good. But they'd better be the best. I'd put money on her figuring out a way to slip past them."

He laughs, clearly in agreement with me. "They've been warned. Now," he says, pushing up from the sofa in search of more beer, "why the fuck are you still out here with us when she's in there alone?"

"Fuck knows, bro. Night," I call as I take off down the hall for my girl.

Only the glow from my bedside light illuminates the room when I slip inside. I half expect to find her in bed, but it's still made.

"Hey," she breathes, stepping from my en suite.

"Fuck," I bark, lifting my hand to push my hair back at the sight of her standing in just my shirt with her bare legs on show, her braless tits pressing against the fabric. Her makeup-free face allows me to see what all the revelations of today have done to her. She's so fucking beautiful, but she looks exhausted.

"Everything okay?"

"U-uh..." I stutter as my brain short circuits. "Y-yeah. Daemon just took Calli home. Nico left in favour of a hook-up."

"Nice."

"I'm pretty sure you don't need me to tell you he's a fucking dog."

"Because the rest of you are total angels."

"Me?" I ask, pointing toward myself. "I think you'll find I was a virgin until I met you in that graveyard."

"Yeah, all right," she laughs, looking around the room a little awkwardly.

Closing the space between us, I wrap my hand around the side of her neck, threading my fingers into her wet hair.

"What's wrong, baby?"

She blows out a long breath before dragging her eyes up to mine.

"Are we really doing this?" she asks quietly.

"We're doing whatever it takes to keep you safe, Princess. Anything."

She nods sadly.

"Come on, you need to rest."

CHAPTER TWENTY-SIX

Stella

Seb pulls the sheets back and I crawl into bed, watching as he drags his hoodie off and pushes his pants from his hips, climbing in beside me in just his tight black boxer briefs. It's a fine fucking sight, and it sure wakes up my exhausted body somewhat when his bulge in that small scrap of fabric catches my eye.

"Hey," he breathes, his voice deep and full of emotion and hunger. It's an intoxicating mix that hits me in all the right places.

The length of his body presses up against mine before his leg hooks over my hip and his hand snakes around my waist, dragging me even closer.

"Hey," I whisper, staring up into his dark eyes,

quickly becoming obsessed with the depth of them now the anger's diminished.

He doesn't move, just stares into my eyes as if he's as enthralled with mine as I am with his.

"You live here with Theo?" I ask, just one of the many questions burning within me.

"For the most part, yeah."

"But what about—"

"Shh," he breathes, pressing two fingers to my lips. "There have been enough confessions for the day. Tomorrow, I'll tell you everything. I promise."

"Okay," I whisper, trusting that he will.

"Right now, I just want to remind myself that you're here." Kiss. "That you're okay." Kiss. "And that you're mine." Kiss.

My reply gets cut off as he deepens the kiss, sweeping his tongue into my mouth and allowing me to taste the beer he's been drinking.

He kisses me until we're both breathless, our bodies burning up and his cock hard and ready, pressing right against my aching clit.

"Seb," I moan, rolling my hips against him. "I need you."

"You need to rest," he replies, nipping across my jaw.

"I can. After you make me come."

"Fuck, baby. You don't play fair."

"When do *you* ever play fair?" I ask him, knowing full well that he only plays dirty. Every single time.

"One condition."

"Hmm?" I mumble, shamelessly rubbing myself against him, my orgasm already beginning to build from just that alone.

"Fuck, I can feel how wet you are."

"So do something about it."

An accomplished smile pulls at my lips when his hand leaves me in favor of pushing his boxers down to free his cock.

"You're wicked," he moans into our kiss as he rubs the head of his cock through my folds.

"Takes one to know one. Oh shit," I gasp when he teases me by pushing into me ever so slightly. "Please," I beg, my muscles rippling, desperate to feel him stretching me open.

"You need to be quiet. The boys—your brother—are out there just waiting to see if we're gonna fuck or fight first."

I can't help but laugh, which makes my muscles tense and causes a groan of pleasure to rumble up his throat.

"That would have felt even better if I were full of you."

"Fucking wicked."

He captures my lips, obviously taking my teasing as my agreement to be quiet as he slams as deep as he can get in this position.

He hikes my leg up higher over his hip and grinds into me.

It's slow, different to all the other times we've been together.

There's no hate, no pain. Just desperation and promises of something better to come.

"I'm gonna keep you safe, I fucking promise you, baby."

"I know," I whisper, biting back my initial response to tell him that it's not his responsibility. But I figure that if we're gonna really do this, then I need to let go of some of the fights and just let him do what he needs to do.

He never ups the pace. Nor does he break our kiss after I've said those words.

Every single roll of his hips and caress of his tongue brands him straight into my soul.

It's terrifying. Exhilarating.

And fuck, I never want it to stop.

———

When I wake, it's with Seb holding onto me just as tightly as he was when I drifted off.

It only took minutes for sleep to claim me after he came good on my demand and made me come with his slow, measured thrusts, once again backing up all the words he'd told me earlier in the day with his actions and burning touches.

"Morning, baby," his deep voice rumbles from above me.

Lifting my cheek from his bare chest, I look up at him.

He looks wide awake, as if he's been lying there waiting for me to stir for the longest time.

"Hey. You should have woken me," I say, feeling guilty.

"No chance."

Dipping his head, he tries to capture my lips.

"Morning breath," I mumble, trying not to part my lips.

"You're cute." His fingers find my chin and he holds me in place as he takes what he wants. "Now that's what I was waiting for." He drops one more kiss to the tip of my nose and holds me tighter. "Did you sleep okay?"

"Yeah, actually. I did," I confess, nuzzling against his chest.

I shouldn't feel this secure, this content. But I do. And I know that it's all because of him.

"What time is it?"

"Almost eleven."

"Shit. We should be at school."

"Fuck it, we'll go tomorrow."

"You're a bad influence, Sebastian."

"Me? Have you met yourself, Hellion?"

"Pfft." I wave him off.

"You want a coffee?"

"Almost as much as I want you."

"See, you're the fucking devil, baby." He brushes his lips against mine once more before growling, "Don't fucking move. I want you in my bed when I get back."

"I'll see what I can do," I tell him, stealing another kiss before he slips from the bed.

He stretches the second he's on his feet, allowing me to drown in the vision that is his almost naked body.

"Hmm... you sure you only wanted a morning kiss?" I murmur, my eyes glued to his morning wood.

He studies me as he reaches down and rearranges himself, ensuring he flashes me in the process.

"We've got the house to ourselves all day. There's plenty of time. I owe you words before orgasms."

I really want to argue, because the latter sounds like so much more fun, but he's right.

The second he slips from the room, his hard-on still more than obvious, I jump up from the bed and rush to the bathroom in the hope of freshening up before he gets back.

I wasn't sure if I should or not last night, but I unpacked a few of my essentials.

I pee and brush my teeth, but I'm still brushing my hair when his deep voice fills the air around me.

"Hellion?" he booms. "What did I tell you?"

I slip around the door with a shy smile on my lips. The second he sees me, any tension my vanishing act caused vanishes.

"Fuck, I might never let you wear your own clothes again."

Walking up to him, I take the mugs from his hands and place them on the nightstand before running my hands up his chest and linking my fingers behind his neck.

"I'm not going anywhere. I'm not running. Not anymore."

He nods, but I still see uncertainty in his eyes.

"I want this too, Seb. I want to see where this can go."

He leans forward, brushing his lips along my jaw.

"I don't deserve you."

"Nope," I agree happily. "I'm much too good for you, but I'm happy to slum it. For now, anyway."

"Slum it? Baby," he says, pulling back, his burning hand collaring my throat possessively. "There's no slumming it with the Cirillo Family." Something flickers in his eyes as he says the words, reminding me that we've still got a lot of serious things to discuss before we can really embark on whatever this is.

"Get back in bed. I'm not nearly done with seeing you in it yet."

I follow orders and slip back into the warmth we left behind.

He quickly follows, pulling me right up against him as if he can't deal with not touching me at all times.

Looking up into his eyes, I bite down on my bottom lip as I wonder if we've both lost our goddamn minds being here, doing this, after everything that's happened in the past few weeks.

"Theo moved out here when we finished school for the summer, but I was pretty much living at his house anyway. Being out here just gave us more privacy."

I nod at him, not wanting to interrupt seeing as he's decided his confessions are happening right now.

"My house, it's…" He blows out a long, painful breath, and my hand on his waist tightens in support.

"I'm pretty sure nothing else you can say or do will scare me off now, Seb."

"Yeah, you say that, but you don't know just how shitty my life is."

"Try me."

"My mum's a drunk and an addict."

I suck in a breath. I have no idea what I was expecting him to say, but that wasn't it.

"After my dad died, she started losing herself to it. Sophia and Zoe pretty much brought Demi and me up. She was a mess from as early as I remember, although she could mostly function. Then when Demi died... Well, Mum might as well have gone with her.

"Her occasional drug use to supplement the alcohol increased, and she gradually moved onto harder and harder options as each one stopped working, stopped blurring her reality."

"Shit, Seb."

"The person who killed my dad didn't just kill him. They broke my mum. They ruined my family. I've spent all these years hating a faceless person for even daring to point a gun at my father's head. And then one day I was in the house with Theo, and I just happened to walk past Damien's office. He was talking to Evan, Nico's dad, discussing business. I can't remember exactly what they were saying, but hearing my dad's name made me pause before he said the words I'd been waiting for years to hear. 'Galen's been punished for killing Christopher. It's best we just leave it in the past.'

"I knew he was probably right, I should have just left it. But I couldn't. The need to get revenge on the person who ruined my life had been burning within me for years.

"I spent too long imagining all the things I'd do to

that man. I told Theo and Alex, and we started digging a little. Discovered that you existed.

"It was all fantasy. I never thought I'd ever get a chance to look into his eyes and call him exactly what he was, explain exactly what he did to us... but then, there you were. You stood there in that graveyard, not giving a single fuck that I was sitting there with a gun.

"I thought you were my fucking guardian angel that night, until you corrected that, telling me that you couldn't possibly be an angel."

I can't help but laugh at the memory.

"Fuck." He squeezes his eyes tight as if he's bringing back that night. "I never wanted to let you go. You will never appreciate how much you gave me that night when you stood there and challenged me. It was everything I didn't know I needed."

"Then I told you my name," I add for him.

"Yeah. It should have been obvious. No normal girl would have acted the way you did. I should have known we were connected from the very first moment.

"You fucked me up, baby. I wanted you so fucking badly, but I hated you more. Or at least, I thought I did.

"All I could see was revenge. And with you right there, your father's precious daughter that he ran away with to protect, what better way to make my point?"

"That's fucked up, Seb."

"I wanted to hurt you, but not to hurt you. I just wanted to hurt him," he continues, as if he can't stop now he's ripped the Band-Aid off all this ugliness.

"You should hate me, Stella. You certainly shouldn't

284

be lying here with me and putting any kind of trust in me."

"We can all lie here and come up with a long list of things we never should have done, Seb. We've all made bad decisions, mistakes, have regrets."

"But I fucking hurt you." Pain bleeds from his eyes. "I hurt you because of some fucked-up need to hurt the man who didn't even pull that fucking trigger."

His hold on me becomes so tight it borders on painful, but I don't complain. I don't even flinch, because he needs this. He needs me to be his life raft right now, because he's fucking drowning. Right before my eyes, he's drowning under the weight of his reality, his mistakes, his regrets... and it physically hurts me to watch it.

"Seb," I breathe, resting my palm on his scruff-covered cheek. "I get it. I understand."

He blows out a breath, fighting some internal battle.

"You shouldn't, though. What I did—"

"Stop, please," I beg, knowing that he's beating himself up. "It's done, Seb. You can't go back and change anything. You're better off just focusing on how you can make it up to me."

It takes a couple of seconds, but the regret begins to wash away.

"Oh yeah?" he asks, the twinkle of mischief I'm more used to returning to his eyes. "And how should I go about doing that?" His hand slips under his shirt that I'm still wearing, skimming up my side.

"Well," I say, rolling onto my back, allowing his hand to cup my breast. He groans as he squeezes. "You could start by making me scream. Then, I don't know... we're in London. The possibilities are endless."

"Hmm... I'm sure I can come up with something. But first..." He jumps on top of me, pushes his shirt up, exposing my breasts and dipping his head, sucking my nipple into his mouth.

CHAPTER TWENTY-SEVEN

Stella

We're both laughing, hand in hand, when we stumble up the stairs and into Theo's living room later that evening.

Seb took my suggestion of making things up to me seriously. I've had the best day, and I can't wipe the smile off my face. Okay, so we were followed everywhere by two bodyguards that Damien had assigned to me, but after a while I forgot they were there and just lost myself in enjoying everything the city has to offer.

He took me on the Eye, to the aquarium and the dungeons. It was incredible. And he even managed to look almost as excited by it all as me, despite the fact that he's done it all before.

He ended the day with a picnic in Hyde Park. Fall

was almost upon us, the leaves were beginning to turn a beautiful array of orange, and there was a chill in the air —but with the blanket he bought wrapped around us, it was the perfect end to a pretty spectacular day.

It sure beat going back to school this morning and being the subject of everyone's attention. I know it's coming. I can't keep putting it off and doing online learning forever. But today was worth it.

I felt normal again. He allowed me to see a future where all of this bullshit was gone and maybe, just maybe, we could actually find a way to be together.

It's the weirdest thought after everything. But Seb is very quickly turning into my favorite person. Not that I intend on telling him that. His ego is already big enough.

He just... he gets me. He knows how to make me laugh, exactly the right thing to say either to make me happy or to piss me off more than I thought possible. And I kind of love both equally. For as incredible and soft and loving Seb has been, I still can't help craving him wicked.

"You two look like you've had a good day," Theo mutters, looking up from his laptop.

"We sure have. Excuse us," Seb mutters, pulling me toward his room. "I've not nearly eaten enough today."

His dark, hungry eyes hold mine, ensuring I understand exactly what he means by that statement.

"Should I go out?" Theo asks seriously.

"Do whatever the fuck you like, man. We won't notice."

He mumbles something about needing to get laid,

but I barely hear it with the way Seb's eyes bore into mine.

"I need you," he confesses quietly, wrapping his hand around the side of my neck and stroking my jaw with his thumb.

The door closes behind us, and it's just the two of us once again.

The air grows thick with desire around us as he continues rendering me useless with just his possessive touch and his intoxicating stare.

His head dips as if he's going to kiss me, but then he stops himself at the last minute, a thought hitting him.

"Seb?"

"Go sit on the bed. I've got something for you."

"O-okay."

Reluctantly, I step away from him. My heart is racing, my pulse thundering through my veins, all of which seem to collide at my clit, and I rub my thighs together as I take a seat, needing something to lessen the ache.

I watch as he opens his closet and pulls a wrapped box out. A birthday present.

My breath catches as I think back to him outside my hospital room. Was he sitting beside me on my birthday while I was out of it? Probably.

Knowing what I now know about the guy walking toward me, he probably spent the day holding my hand and begging for me to wake up just so I could shout at him.

"You didn't need to—"

"Just open it, please," he says, lowering the box to my lap and sitting down beside me.

"Okay," I breathe, lifting my trembling hands to the bow on the top and pulling it open.

Inside is full of shredded tissue, to the point that I think the entire box is actually empty. But after a few seconds, my fingers find another box.

Too intrigued to question him, I rip the end open and allow the contents to spill out.

"Oh my God, Seb!" I squeal as I stare down at a replica of my pink switchblade.

"It's not the same one, but it's as close as I could get."

Throwing my arms around him, I hold him tight. "Thank you so much."

He chuckles.

"What's so funny?"

"Most girls melt over jewelry. Mine loses her mind over a weapon."

"And this is why you love me."

He stills in my arms and I pull away, needing to look into his eyes.

"One of the reasons, yeah."

"Seb, I—"

"No," he says, once again pressing his fingers to my lips to stop me. "Not yet. Not because of this."

I nod, understanding him. So much so that I wasn't actually going to say what he thinks I was.

"Thank you. It's perfect."

"Turn it over."

Doing as I'm told, I let the knife roll over in my hand and suck in a sharp breath at what I find.

"Welcome to the Family, baby."

"Wow." I stare down at the same engraving as on the one I stole from him. His father's knife.

It's got the exact same skull at the base of the handle, but instead of his father's initials are mine.

"We all get these when we start lower sixth at Knight's Ridge. Kind of a rite of passage. Well, once we've proved our worth a few times over," he chuckles to himself.

"I don't—I haven't proved anything."

Reaching out, he cups my jaw, his thumb brushing over my cheek.

"You have. And Damien seems to think so too, because he okayed this."

My eyes widen. "He..."

"You're as worthy as any of us. Hell, your skills are far superior to some of the soldiers I know, baby."

I flip it over in my hand, loving the weight of it and the feeling of safety it provides me with.

"What is it?" Seb asks, clearly sensing that I have something else to say.

"What do I have to do to get a gun?"

He stares at me for two seconds, his face serious, but then his lips twitch and the most incredible smile appears.

"See," he says, threading his fingers into my hair and pulling me toward him. "This is why I love you."

He captures my lips before I have a chance to respond—not that I would, because he's nowhere near ready to hear anything close to that kind of confession. He's still too busy beating himself up about everything that's gone on before and all the ways he hurt me to even believe me if I were to say the words.

He kisses me deeply, passionately, ensuring I feel every bit of that confession right down to my toes.

When he pulls back, he only goes as far as to rest his brow against mine, our heaving breaths mingling as we fight to get ourselves back under control.

"I'm serious," I tell him. "I want a gun."

"You've got one," he rumbles, dragging up the memory of him trailing it around my body that night he snuck into my bedroom.

"Not one from you. From Damien."

"Fuck, baby."

"So, what do I have to do to get one?"

His lips move to my ear before he whispers. "Make your first kill."

"I'm sure that can be arranged."

"Fuck," he barks, tugging at his pants and making me laugh. "That gets me all kinds of hard, baby."

I look up at him through my lashes. "If you're good, I might even let you watch."

His hands go to his waistband, and faster than I thought possible, he's got his cock in his hand.

"Ride me, baby. I want to see you bouncing on my cock."

"You say the most romantic things to me, Sebastian," I purr, sliding from the bed and dragging my panties down my legs, pulling them off over my boots.

"You love it," he growls as I climb onto his lap, grinding my pussy against him. "Fuck. You're wet."

Slipping my arms over his shoulders, I brush my lips across his cheek.

"So fill me."

He doesn't need any more encouragement. He holds himself up, allowing me to impale myself on him.

"Yes," I cry as he groans in pleasure. I make no attempt at smothering any further ones that rip from my lips, knowing that Theo is only out in the living room.

As far as I'm concerned, he deserves a bit of torture after all the bullshit as well.

Seb rests his palms back on the bed, allowing me control. I circle my hips before using his shoulders for leverage to help me move on his length.

To be fair to him, he lets me have control for longer than I was expecting him to, and it's not until he watches me fall for the first time, using him for exactly what I needed, before he grips my hips and flips us, turning the tables and taking back control.

I can't help but laugh as he slams back inside me, his teeth sinking into the soft skin of my neck.

"What?" he moans as my amusement causes me to clench around him.

"Just can't let go, can you, caveman?"

"Just lie back and take it, Princess. You know you love it."

He thrusts his hips, hitting me so deep that I see fucking stars before a loud hammering starts on the door.

"Fuck off, bro. We're busy."

Theo's laugh fills the room. "Yeah, I fucking heard. Stella, your dad's here."

"Fuck," Seb barks as I sink back into the pillow on a groan.

"Want to keep him entertained? Outside, maybe."

"We'll be right there," I reply, much to Seb's horror.

"You're not fucking serious," he asks, disbelief etching into his expression.

Reaching up, I cup his face and smile innocently up at him.

"Fuck me fast, or finish later."

Dipping down, he sucks my bottom lip into his mouth and nips hard enough to draw blood. "Or both," he growls, rolling his hips once more, making me swallow a moan.

His fingers find my clit and he rubs me with the perfect amount of pressure that has me pulling his pillow over my face in only minutes so I can scream out my release.

He follows me only a minute later, a low growl rumbling in his throat as his cum fills me.

"Okay, now we can go deal with what's going on out there," he tells me, smacking a kiss on my lips and pulling out of me.

Aftershocks shoot around my body as he does so, and I almost reach for him and demand we start all over. But the reality of knowing my father is probably sitting out on the couch stops me.

"What do you think he wants?"

"To apologise again, hopefully," Seb mutters,

tucking himself away. "Want me to go and find out while you clean up?"

"No," I say, shaking my head. "We do this together."

"You're just saying that because you don't want me to hit him again," he calls out to me as I slip into the bathroom.

"Yeah, that too. I don't need you with a broken hand."

"You're less concerned about your dad's face then?" He laughs.

I make quick work of cleaning up the mess we made before finding a clean pair of panties and slipping them up my legs.

"Yeah, I need you fully functioning for a few reasons."

"Huh, and I thought the only reason you wanted me around was for the orgasms."

"That's the main one, yeah."

I pull the door open and step out, dragging him through after me and effectively cutting off whatever response he might have had. Not that I think for a second he really gives a shit about my father's opinion. He did just fuck me with him right out here, after all.

"Stella," Dad breathes when I come into view. His face softens immediately as he looks me over, as if he was expecting me to be hurt.

"Hey," I say awkwardly. It's never been like this between us. Even the few times we've fought over the years, we've always made up almost immediately and cleared the air.

"I'm gonna give you guys some privacy," Theo says,

collecting up his computer and books before disappearing down toward his room.

"You guys want drinks?" Seb asks, being weirdly accommodating. I guess that's the power of a good orgasm.

"Coffee would be great. Thank you, Sebastian."

Seb visibly winces. "It's just Seb."

Huh. He's never told me not to call him that.

I file that little bit of information away for later.

"Baby?" he asks, dragging his eyes from my dad over to me.

"Yeah, coffee would be great, thanks."

Only the sounds of Seb grabbing the mugs and starting the machine can be heard as I stare at my dad, who seems to be lost in his own head.

Snapping himself out of it, his eyes find mine.

"You look good, Stella."

"Uh... what were you expecting?"

His gaze flicks to Seb for the briefest moment.

"He's a good person, Dad." I can't help my internal laugh, because there was a time not so long ago that I never would have dreamed of convincing anyone of that.

"My injuries would suggest otherwise."

"Nothing you didn't deserve," Seb grunts from the kitchen.

"Yeah, well. Why do you think I let you?"

"Let me? Puh-lease, old man." Dad's jaw tics at Seb's teasing.

"He's joking," I assure Dad.

"Am I?" Seb asks, delivering me the first coffee.

Dad shakes his head, trying to focus.

"I'm sorry, Stella. About everything. I was hoping we could sit down and you'd let me explain all the things I should have done a long time ago."

Seb hands him a mug before lowering down beside me on the couch and tucking me into his side.

"Alone, maybe?"

"No," I state, much to Dad's horror. He's about to argue when I continue. "Seb's not going anywhere," I say, and then repeat what I told him in the bedroom. "We do this together."

Dad glances between the two of us, but he must figure that he's going to lose any fight he starts, so instead, he just drops whatever he was going to say and focuses on what he came here for.

"How much has Toby told you?"

"That you and his mother were having an affair. That she's got a brain tumor and is in a bad way. That his dad is a cunt who needs to die and that he probably has one of the shittiest home lives but somehow manages to keep going and plaster a smile on his face."

Dad's chin drops and his eyes widen at my very frank summary of the situation, but it seems that none of what I said is something he can argue with this time.

"Yeah, that about sums it up," he mutters sadly, reaching for his coffee despite the fact that it's so hot it's probably going to take a layer of skin off when he sips it.

He sits back after a second, his eyes glazing over.

"I've been in love with Maria for... forever. But she was never destined to be mine."

Just those two sentences affect me more than

anything he could have said. My heart splinters for the man before me who, up until recently, has done nothing but put me first, make sure I had everything, and given me every possibility for my future.

"We were together as kids. My childhood sweetheart. But life got in the way and we drifted apart when I started working for the Family. It was my fault. My job clouded my judgment and changed my priorities. It's something I'll always regret.

"Jonas and I had always been friends. We all grew up together, much like you and your friends, Seb. But I never expected him to move in on Maria the second we hit rocky ground.

"But, well... he did. And quicker than I could blink, they were getting married and our time together was over.

"I did the right thing. I walked away and allowed them to get on with their lives. Maria was happy. Well, she looked it. I know exactly where Toby's ability to put on a smile and pretend comes from.

"I never questioned it until we were all at an event one night and she literally walked into me as she came out of the bathroom.

"Her eyes were dark. She looked exhausted. She tried to brush it under the rug, tried to convince me that she was ill. But she forgot that I knew her almost better than I knew myself.

"After a little convincing, I managed to get her to agree to meet me the next day while Jonas was working. And, well... one thing led to another."

He drops his head into his hands.

"I'm not proud of my actions, Stella. But I'm not going to sit here and defend them, because it's in the past. And to this day, I'd do anything for the woman who stole my heart all those years ago."

My eyes burn with tears as I stare at him, my hand clamped in Seb's.

I've always wondered about Dad's relationships or lack thereof. But I just assumed he'd never found the one. Never that he'd had her and lost her. That he lived with this kind of heartache every single day.

"We started seeing each other as often as we could. She confided in me just what life was like with Jonas, but by the time she confessed some of his worse treatment, she was already pregnant with Toby."

"Why didn't you do anything? If he was hurting her then you should have—"

"Don't you think I wanted to? Jesus, Seb." Dad scrubs his hand down his face. "This..." he gestures to his injured arm, "I get this more than you can understand. You need to protect Stella to right the wrongs. I get it. I wanted nothing more than to go and put a bullet through his head for ever laying a hand on Maria. But I couldn't—"

"Just like Toby can't now," I interrupt.

"Yeah. He might be an abusive cunt, but he's smart. Too fucking smart. He had things in place to ensure that Maria would be left with nothing, her entire family left with nothing should anything happen to him. I'm sure a similar situation is in place for Toby now. Plus he's got the added concern of Maria's health."

"Jesus Christ, Dad."

"I know."

"Don't you think you should have taken a step back when she was having his baby?"

"I tried."

"Oh yeah, real hard. There are eleven months between us," I point out.

"Yeah." Regret oozes from him as he fidgets with the mug in his hands.

There's a part of me that desperately wants to go and comfort him, but there's another bitter part of me that's still too angry to let any of these secrets go yet.

"Jonas knew. We weren't clever enough. The next nine months were some of the worst of my life.

"We knew she was pregnant again. She assumed you were Jonas's. We were always careful, but Jonas wasn't having any of it and forced her to have a DNA test the moment she could.

"The second you were born, he demanded to know. He was already pissed off because you were a girl, and he wanted to build his own little army of soldiers."

"What a relief I didn't end up stuck there then," I whisper sadly.

"The second we got the results, Maria told me we had to leave. That I had to take you and get the hell away from Jonas."

"But—"

"Trust me, Stella. I went through every possible option. The last thing I wanted to do was take you away from her. I wanted Maria and Toby to flee with us. But she couldn't leave. It was too dangerous."

CHAPTER TWENTY-EIGHT

Sebastian

S tella's hand trembles in mine, but her face is exactly as Galen has described her mum's: a mask of indifference. Seems Toby wasn't the only one to inherit more than the blue eyes.

I brush my thumb over her knuckles, needing her to know that I'm right here.

"So you what? Took me from her arms and never looked back?"

"That was pretty much the plan. Maria was confident that she'd be able to find a way to get away from Jonas, to come and join us and start over."

Part of me hates that she clearly never managed it. It meant Maria and Toby have suffered all this time. But also, if she had, Stella never would have come back here. She never would have found me.

"But she couldn't?"

Galen shakes his head. "And I couldn't come back."

"Because you'd been framed for my father's death?" I add, speaking for the first time in what feels like forever.

Galen gives me a double take.

"Y-yeah. I took the fall for that and a few other things to help the Family out, and we left. They needed a scapegoat, and I needed to protect Stella and Maria."

Silence falls as the weight of Galen's confessions press down on all of us.

"Did you never intend on coming back when it became obvious that she couldn't leave?"

"I always wanted to come back. I wanted you to have your mum. I wanted her to have her incredible daughter. But the risk for all of us was too huge—"

"Until her surgery."

"Maria and I cut ties when I left. But I kept in touch with her sister, and we exchanged what we needed to through her. And when she told me how bad things were getting, I knew we needed to be here.

"I spent that first month putting things into place to ensure your safety and protection. To ensure that Jonas couldn't come for you, or me."

"That's why you locked me up in the house."

"Or tried," Galen says with a knowing look at his daughter.

"Damien assured me that everything was in place, that you weren't at risk, and you started school with the promise that Seb, Theo, and Alex would keep an eye on you."

Stella tenses before glancing over at me.

"You were my fucking babysitters?"

She tries pulling her hand from mine but fails when all I do is tighten my grip on her.

"And what fun we had, Princess."

An angry growl rumbles up her throat.

"Well, I guess that makes a lot of fucking sense. You motherfuckers turned up everywhere."

"All part of the job." I wink at her and her teeth grind. Leaning into her, I brush my lips against her ear. She might be mad, but it doesn't stop a shudder from ripping through her when my breath tickles across her skin. "I'll make it up to you later."

She scoffs but doesn't push me away when I kiss down her neck—much to Galen's delight, if his groan is anything to go by.

"How exactly did you expect them to," she rolls her eyes, "babysit me, and for me not to get close to Toby? If you never stopped us that day... well..."

"I screwed up, Stella. I was trying to keep you safe. I thought... I don't know what I thought. It was wrong. I should have just told you everything."

"Yeah, you should have." She pauses and reaches for her coffee. "I spent all these years wondering if you were gay."

Galen barks out a laugh at Stella's confession.

"No, Stella. I'm not."

"Well, you and Calvin have always spent a lot of time together, so..."

He shakes his head, scrubbing his hand down his

face. "I guess I only have myself to blame. But, for the record, Calvin is straight too."

I narrow my eyes at him, sensing more of a story there as he chuckles at the end.

Stella doesn't miss it either.

"Right," she says, moving the conversation on. "So what happens now? Toby said he doesn't know if you've seen Maria, or what's going on."

"I have. Penny, Maria's sister, has arranged it."

Stella lets out a pained breath. "H-how is she? Really?"

"Better than I was expecting." Leaning forward, he places his mug on the coffee table. "I don't know what Toby told you, but the doctors are hopeful that she can come back from this. She might never beat it, but there's a very good chance of a future."

Stella nods. "Can I... can I meet her?" Finally, her voice cracks as the weight of all of this begins to shatter her hardened resolve.

Galen's smile is so wide I almost find myself doing the same.

"Of course. We just need to wait until the time is right."

"Does she want to see me?" I hate the uncertainty in her tone, but I understand it.

"Stella," Galen sighs. "She's spent eighteen years desperate to be your mum."

"O-okay," she squeaks, her eyes filling with tears. "Then I want to meet her. As soon as we can arrange it. I don't want to put her in danger with Jonas."

"I'll arrange it," he says with a firm nod.

Now everything is out, an awkwardness settles around us.

"Stella, if you want to come ho—"

Panic hits me that she might agree now they've cleared the air, that she might be about to pack up her shit and walk away from me once more.

"No, Dad," she says, her voice unwavering.

All the air I didn't know was stuck in my lungs rushes out at her refusal. She turns to me, a soft, knowing smile playing on her lips.

"I'm staying here. I know Calvin's increased the security, but he was in my room. I just... I can't yet."

Or ever.

"Okay, can't blame me for trying. I wasn't expecting to move here and immediately lose you to someone else."

"You haven't lost me, Dad. But all of this, all the lies and secrets... it's going to take some time to come back from that."

"I know. I—"

"You've lied to me every day of my life."

Galen pales. "I know. But you need to understand that everything I've done has been to try to protect you, no matter how misguided it might seem now."

"Yeah," Stella agrees.

Footsteps thundering up the stairs toward us stop her from saying any more, and two seconds later Alex bursts through the door.

"Yo, you won't believe who I fuc— Oh shit, sorry. Am I interrupting?"

"No, it's okay. I think we were probably about done," Galen says, pushing to stand.

"Okaaay," Alex says awkwardly.

"Theo's in his room," I tell him, allowing him to escape and be able to brag about whatever it was he wanted to tell us when he arrived.

"Great, thanks."

"Is he always so... hyper?" Stella asks quietly as he disappears into Theo's bedroom.

"Pretty much," I say, standing so we can see Galen out.

"I'll let you know when we can go and see your mum," he tells Stella sadly.

"Okay."

"I really am sorry for all this. I know I fucked up, sweetheart."

"Yeah, you did. But I get it. And it's too late to change it all now, right?"

"Right. Well, I guess I'll just..." He thumbs over his shoulder and takes a step back.

"Wait," Stella calls, pushing past me and running at him.

He catches her in his arms and pulls her tight.

"I love you, Dad."

"I love you too, sweetheart." He kisses the top of her head and breathes her in as if he's scared he won't see her again.

They hold each other for long seconds before she pulls her face from his chest.

My heart aches when he reaches to wipe her tears away, because I want to be the one to do that. I want to be the one to pick her up and put her back together.

"I'm sorry about Maria, Dad. I wish things turned out better for you both."

"There's always time. One way or another, we're going to fix this. Jonas is on borrowed time." She nods as my eyes narrow.

There's so much more that he's not telling us. But then, I can hardly expect him to come and expose all the Family's plans and secrets. We're just the kids. We're only trusted with the entry-level shit, like babysitting jobs.

"I hope you're right. Maria and Toby deserve some freedom."

He nods, finally dropping his hands from her upper arms.

His eyes find mine as I step up behind her, replacing him.

"Look after my baby girl, Sebastian. I'm trusting you."

"I know, sir. And for what it's worth, I'm sorry."

"This life isn't for the faint of heart, son. Just remember that things are often more complicated than they appear, and trust those above you. The majority of us have your best interests at heart. Even if we do get it wrong."

He's almost disappeared from our view when I call him back.

"You implied earlier that you were made the scapegoat for more than just my dad's death. This thing with Stella... is it because of one of those?"

"I'd put money on it. Damien, Nico, Charon, and I aren't leaving a stone unturned. We'll find this motherfucker."

I nod, confident that they'll figure it out. I just hope it's sooner rather than later.

The second he's gone, I spin Stella around and pull her into my chest.

She sucks in a shaky breath and squeezes me tight.

We stand there locked in our embrace for the longest time before she looks up, her huge, watery eyes bringing me to my goddamn knees.

"Who's Charon?" she asks quietly.

"Toby's grandfather. Jonas's father. "He's Damien's consig—advisor," I correct when her brow starts to furrow. "He's a good man. There's no way he knows about all this shit with Jonas."

"Then we need to tell him."

I nod. "Yeah. Although I think it probably needs to come from Toby, not us."

"Do you think there's really a way out of this?"

"There's always a way."

"Well, yeah. But if what Dad said was true, then Maria and Toby stand to potentially lose everything."

"We'll figure something out. There will be a way around whatever precautions he's put into place."

A door opening cuts our conversation off.

"Has he gone?" Theo asks, poking his head out of his room.

"Yeah," Stella says with a laugh. "It's safe to come out."

"There's no blood," he says, inspecting his floor.

"No, there isn't. Someone else deserves our wrath right now."

Theo and Alex's gazes narrow on Stella, but she doesn't continue. As much as this might be a part of her story, it's Toby's too, and she wouldn't betray him by spilling his secrets like that.

"Not now," I say for her. "You guys want a drink?"

"Sure," Alex says, falling down onto one of the couches. "I've got laid, I'm good with watching you two manhandle each other. Him, on the other hand…" Alex mutters toward Theo. "He's got friction burns on his hand from jacking off to you two."

"I've barely been here twenty-four hours. We aren't that bad."

"You all know that this is my place, right? I can kick you out whenever I want."

"Yeah, but you won't. Why don't you get the princess to call her friend? She might be willing to help with your little issue," Alex suggests, making Stella's spine straighten.

"My friend? Do not tell me that Theo is crushing on his cousin."

"What?" Alex splutters, spraying the coffee table with beer, much to Theo's disgust. "No. He's pining after the emo chick."

"Emmie?"

"No, I'm fucking not," Theo sulks, getting up to get a cloth, much to Stella's amusement.

"Oh come off it, bro. I saw you eye-fucking her across the common room earlier."

"I was not."

Alex scoffs before looking at the two of us and mouthing, "He was."

"Maybe I should message her. See if she's busy."

"Jesus. Why did I let you stay here? You're just an extension of these fucking idiots," he snaps, throwing his towel down on the table and tipping his own beer to his lips, draining almost all of it in one go.

"I'm not going to take offense by that," Stella says, her tone teasing as she studies Theo. "Because I quite like it here. But if you want me to hook you up, I can give it a go."

"No, I'm—"

"I have no idea what her type is, but..." She studies him, running her eyes down the length of his body as he sits back on the sofa. If it wasn't for the way her fingers squeeze my thigh as she does it, I might be jealous. "You're hot. So give her enough alcohol and she might just go for it."

"Fucking hell," Alex snorts. "I knew I liked you, Princess."

"Dickheads," Theo mutters, draining the rest of his beer.

"Seriously, though. How long's it been? It's probably going to fall off soon."

"Fuck you. You know full well I had a girl here recently."

"Recently? I had Stella coming on my cock recently," I announce, earning myself a slap. "I never heard nor saw anything other than some female clothes that day. And," I add, "it was fucking weeks ago. Alex is right. It's gonna fall off."

Stella smothers a laugh at the incredulous look on Theo's face.

"It's not healthy to just constantly rub one out to the sounds of your friends fucking, bro."

Theo jumps to his feet faster than I thought possible.

"I fucking hate you pricks," he scoffs, storming toward his room and slamming his door like a little bitch.

"Whoops," Stella says, but there's no guilt there, just barely restrained laughter.

"Is he really after Emmie?" she asks after a minute as we all listen to Theo crash around his room, expelling his frustration like a toddler who didn't get his way.

"His cock is, but the rest of him isn't entirely on board."

"Ugh, guys," Stella huffs. "Do you know how hard you make this shit?"

"Us?" Alex asks. "I'll have you know, we make this shit easy. All we want is a quick fuck, no feelings, or lovey-dovey cuddles. Easy."

"Oh yeah?" Stella asks, looking up at me with her brows raised.

"Speak for yourself, bro. I'll take the cuddles," I say, proving my point by pulling Stella onto my lap and nuzzling her neck. Her head falls to the side, giving me better access as her ass rubs against my fast-swelling cock.

"Yeah, well, you've fucking whipped him. I have no interest in restricting myself to one pussy."

"Charming," Stella mutters on a sigh as I lick up her

neck. "Don't worry, Alex. With such endearing sentiments, no woman is going to want to stick around for more than a mediocre roll in the sheets with you."

I snort a laugh against her throat, feeling all kinds of good about myself.

"Mediocre? I'll have you know that—"

"I've kissed you. I know what I'm talking about."

The weirdest sound falls from Alex, making me wish I could see him.

"Fuck," I mutter, threading my fingers into Stella's hair. "I love you."

Slamming my lips down on hers, I push my tongue into her mouth, teasing hers into action.

"Bro," Alex shouts, "they're at it again. Get your baby oil out."

Both of us burst out laughing at his words and break apart.

"You know," Stella says as she falls back on the sofa and places her legs across my lap, helpfully hiding my hard-on from Alex, "you're not so bad."

"Aw, see. We knew you'd soften to us eventually."

"Watch it though. There's still plenty of time for me to threaten your balls with my knife."

Both Alex and I laugh as Theo reappears.

"Oh good, I missed the porno."

He pulls out fresh beers from the fridge and throws them to each of us.

"So, what happens next then?" he asks, ignoring our previous conversation like it never happened.

"Time to go back to school, I guess," Stella answers

on a sigh. "I'm really looking forward to seeing Teagan again."

"She's missed you too, from what I've heard," Alex deadpans.

"I don't doubt it."

The four of us settle into easy conversation about school and life as we drain the beers Theo keeps supplying us with. Stella just fits in like she's always been with the three of us, taking the piss out of the guys and calling us all out on our bullshit.

She really is one of us. It just goes to prove how fucking wrong I was, not seeing it sooner.

CHAPTER TWENTY-NINE

Stella

The next morning comes around all too quickly.

I knew I needed to just rip the Band-Aid off and go back to school, but the thought of getting out of the car and immediately being the object of everyone's attention is enough to make me want to burrow under the covers with Seb and never emerge.

"What's wrong, baby?" he murmurs behind me sleepily, his hand splaying over my stomach and pinning us closer.

"What makes you think anything is wrong?"

"You're tense. I knew the moment you woke up. Your entire body locked up tight."

His lips kiss across my shoulder, making me relax somewhat.

"Just thinking about school."

"You've got nothing to worry about. No one will touch you there. Not now you're one of us. You may or may not have noticed, but almost everyone is scared of us."

"Because the five of you need your egos inflated any more than they already are," I joke.

"Laugh all you like, but you love that you've got five of the baddest, most respected guys in the entire school watching your back."

"Sure, I need more reasons for all the girls to hate me," I laugh lightly as his hand slides lower.

"Since when do you care what anyone thinks of you?" he asks, nudging my thigh with the back of his hand so I can open up for him.

"I-I don't," I gasp when his fingers slide through my folds, lazily circling my clit. "I'm just done with the drama. And I'd rather my car stayed the color I want it to be."

"Yeah, that took a bit of getting off."

I still, his words hitting me.

"The guy thought it was going to need a whole new paint job."

"Wait," I say, rolling onto my back so I can look at him. "*You* got my car fixed?"

A smile curls at one side of his lips. "Yeah, baby. Who did you think sorted it?"

"Um..." I hesitate, heat hitting my cheeks. "I assumed it was my dad."

He kisses along my jaw, his fingers dipping lower and teasing my entrance.

"I stole your key after you kicked me out, called a guy I know. He owed me a favour"

"Seb," I half sigh, half gasp as he pushes deeper in, bending his fingers to find my G-spot. "I can't believe you did that."

"I couldn't leave your beautiful baby like that."

"You think she's beautiful?"

"Yeah, Hellion," he responds with a chuckle. "She is."

By the time we're both dressed in our Knight's Ridge uniforms, we're both much more relaxed and ready to tackle the day. Although, given half a chance, I'd more than happily strip out of it all and crawl back into bed.

Seb slams his fist down on Theo's door as we pass. "Rise and shine, motherfucker. It's a beautiful day."

"Fuck off," he barks in response, making us both laugh.

Seconds later he emerges, looking his usual gorgeous self. It's not fair that he can drink as much as he did last night and still look model-worthy this morning. Asshole.

"I don't like it when you get regular pussy. It makes you too happy," he complains, proving that his mood hasn't improved from the night before.

It's all our fault. We were ribbing him more than probably necessary about his lack of action.

Although the look on his face as we teased him about Emmie was too funny not to continue.

"Rough night?" I ask.

"More like a rough morning," he mutters, raising a

brow at me. "What the fuck are you—" he barks as Seb grabs his right hand.

"Yep," he says, cutting off his complaints. "Alex was right. Friction burn."

I can't help but laugh at Theo's reaction.

"You," he spits at Seb, "are buying me coffee and breakfast. You fucking owe me."

"Hey, it's not my fault I've got a girl and your balls are bluer than fucking Papa Smurf's."

Theo growls at Seb, his hands curling into fists.

"Jesus. I'll buy you both coffee and breakfast, just don't break each other's pretty faces."

"Aw, did you hear that, bro? Your girl thinks I'm pretty." Theo throws his arm around my shoulder and rips me away from Seb's side. "Tell me more, beautiful," he murmurs in my ear, ensuring it's loud enough for Seb to hear.

Christ, these boys and their constant cock measuring contests are exhausting.

"Come on, boyfriend," I call over my shoulder, winking at Theo when he laughs at the expression on Seb's face.

"I'm your boyfriend?" he asks, sounding genuinely curious as the three of us leave the apartment—or coach house, as they call it.

"Don't you want to be?"

"Y-yeah, I... just... uh... I've never been one before."

"No pressure, bro," Theo laughs. "You might wanna do some research, figure out what your job description is."

"Make her scream, make her smile. Think I've got it

nailed. Now, can I have my girlfriend back?" Seb steals me from Theo before we step out into the row of garages beneath the apartment.

"Hey, boyfriend," I whisper up at him, dropping a kiss to his jaw.

"I've got a girlfriend," he whispers as if he needs to convince himself that it's true as he crowds me against Theo's Maserati.

"No sex against, on, or in my car, kids," Theo barks from the other side.

"You know, if I'm staying—"

"You are," Seb interrupts.

"Then my baby deserves a spot in here."

"You want me to move one of my cars out of here, Doukas?" Theo asks, sounding totally affronted by the mere suggestion.

"She's had it rough recently. She deserves some special treatment."

"I'll think about it. Get in before I change my mind."

Seb pecks me on the lips before pulling open the back door and climbing in behind me.

"It's going to be okay," Seb assures me, twisting his fingers with mine after we've all finished the coffees and breakfast wraps that we picked up on the way to school.

"Yeah, I know," I sigh, suddenly feeling utterly exhausted.

So much has changed since the last time I walked out of this place.

I thought my only issue was with the asshole now holding my hand tightly as if he's my lifeline. Little did I know, the rest of my life was even more fucked up than the shit he was giving me.

"I don't care what they think." I'm not sure if I'm saying it for my benefit or Seb's, but I let the words linger in the air nonetheless. "I just... ugh. I hate the drama. I wanted to start here and hide in the shadows, but I'm pretty sure my existence couldn't be further from that if I actually tried."

"Come on, Hellion. Hold your head high and show them what a bad-arse bitch you really are."

Seb leans over, his fingers pinching my chin and twisting my head so that he can capture my lips.

"You've got two minutes before I drag you out by your hair, Papatonis," Theo growls as Seb's tongue brushes across my bottom lip.

Seb flips him off before deepening our kiss, but only for our allotted two minutes. Apparently, Seb is sensing that Theo might be approaching the end of his patience with us this morning.

"Give them hell, baby." He drops one last kiss to the tip of my nose before releasing both our seat belts and climbing out of the car.

"Why thank you, sir," I say in a teasing voice when Theo hands me my purse from the trunk.

"Don't get used to the service, but we're going to be late if you two don't move."

I smile at him. "You're a good friend, Theo," I say, reaching up on my toes and dropping a kiss to his cheek.

"Careful, baby. He might come in his pants, he's so desperate."

I snort a laugh as Theo growls.

"Your boy has a death wish, Princess. Rein him in, yeah?"

I stare at Theo as Seb wraps his arm around my waist, pulling me back to him.

"You think I can control that?" I ask sarcastically.

"That?" Seb snorts.

"Come on, boyfriend. Time to show your empire that they've got a new queen."

Theo smothers a laugh as he falls into step on my other side, the three of us walking toward the entrance as a unit.

I have no idea where they come from, but the second we hit the path that leads to the main doors, the other three join us.

My eyes connect with Toby's for a beat before he steps behind me with Nico and Alex on either side of him.

Knowing they're surrounding me gives me that extra bit of confidence I needed to walk through those doors like I fucking own the place.

The second the six of us step into the common room, all conversation stops and every single set of eyes turns toward us.

Many of the girls glower at me, their lips turning down in disgust as their eyes run the length of my body, judging me. All I do is smile. Jealousy really is a bitch.

Most of the guys are too terrified to openly look at me with my bodyguards standing strong around me.

No one needs to hear their words of warning. Their body language says it all.

Stella is ours, and anyone who's stupid enough to come anywhere near her will die.

A smirk curls at my lips. I've never felt more powerful in my entire life. It really is quite a heady experience.

"Stella!" a soft voice squeals before Calli bounces in front of us excitedly. "I thought you'd changed your mind."

"Nope. Just wanted to make an entrance."

"Well," she says, glancing over her shoulder where most of the room is still solely focused on us. "You certainly achieved that."

"Ah look, it's the princess and her frogs," Emmie says, also completely undeterred by the scary motherfuckers around me as she steps up to Calli's side.

As usual, the two of them are polar opposites with Emmie's dark makeup and shitkicker boots and Calli's almost bare face and cute ballet pumps. The two of them as friends is almost laughable, but it works, and Calli needs some bad influences in her life. I figure that that's exactly what Emmie and I are.

"I'm not sold on the one you chose as your prince, though." She casts a glare in Seb's direction.

"Knight, please," he scoffs.

"Whatever." She waves him off as I elbow Theo in the ribs.

"You can fuck right off, Princess," he mutters before

he and his loyal stooges follow, leaving me alone with my friends.

"Have you actually moved in with him? Tell me Calli is lying," Emmie begs.

"No can do, Em," I say with a wide smile, watching Seb over her shoulder as he moves toward some guys who are also on the football team.

"You should probably readmit yourself to the hospital and get your head checked, you know that, right?"

The bell rings before I get to respond.

"Come on, class is calling," Calli says, looping her arm through mine.

"Yay. It's almost the weekend though, right?" Emmie asks as we make our way out of the common room, putting all the lingering stares and whispers behind us.

"What's your first class?" Calli asks, ignoring Emmie's comment.

"Economics."

"I'm heading that way," Emmie interrupts. "Although I'm sure at least one of your bodyguards is going to deliver you to class." She rolls her eyes.

"There are worse things than being trailed by them," I tell her.

"Really?" she asks as if I've lost my mind.

"What? They're pretty."

"Yeah, if you like that conceited, overinflated ego type."

"They're not so bad," I say, jumping to their

defence—something I never thought I'd do, but hey, here we are.

"Whatever you say. So anyway," she says after we've waved Calli off as she takes a different turn. "Tomorrow night. We should do something."

I swallow somewhat nervously. I hate that I've had to keep both Emmie, and Calli to a point, in the dark about what's really going on with me and the risk I'm still under.

"Maybe. What did you have in mind?"

"I dunno. But I need some fun. I can't cope with all this drama and bullshit."

My steps falter at the sadness in her tone.

"Is everything okay, Em?" I ask, realizing that I've probably been way too wrapped up in my own shit these past few weeks.

"Y-yeah, of course." She plasters a smile on her face, but it doesn't meet her eyes and certainly doesn't make me believe her.

"I'll talk to the guys, see what we can come up with." She gives me a look that says 'really?'. "What? You might like them if you give them a chance."

"Unlikely."

"Okay, well, how about... they're all killer in bed and I'm sure you could make use of that." I wiggle my eyebrows at her and she snorts a laugh.

I have no idea about Emmie's experience in that department—it's not something we've discussed—but for some reason I know she's nowhere near as innocent as Calli.

"That's possibly the only thing they've got going for

them. Although, in my experience, when they need to make that much noise, it's probably because they're overcompensating."

"Well, I can happily report that they are not. Well, not all of them." I inwardly cringe but am equally thankful that I haven't been as up close and personal to Toby as I did the others the night of Nico's birthday.

"Okay, we need to get to class, but I think we need to discuss this in more detail."

"You banging one of the boys?" I ask with a laugh.

"No, the fact that you've clearly been measuring their cocks."

"What?" I gasp, laughing at her. "I have not been doing such things." I bat my eyelashes innocently at her.

"Yeah, yeah. Whatever. Make plans, yeah? We need a night."

"Sure thing," I agree as she slips into her classroom.

I don't look back as I continue forward to where I need to be. He's behind me. I can feel him.

"You need a night for what?" Seb asks, throwing his arm around my shoulders.

"Girls' night. I'm fed up with all the testosterone I've got to put up with on a daily basis."

I can't help but laugh at the look on his face.

"Well, I guess it's a good job we've all got to work on Friday night then."

"Oh? Since when?"

"Since the boss told Theo we were."

"Fair enough."

He comes to a stop next to my classroom door and backs me up against the wall.

"You can have the house to yourself to do all your girly shit," he murmurs, rubbing his nose against mine.

"Girly shit?" I ask, my brows lifting.

"Yeah. Face masks, pillow fights."

"Oh my God," I laugh. "How about you talk to Alex, get us some of that good weed, and I'll get the vodka."

"Hmm... So what you're trying to tell me is that by the time I get home you'll be wasted and high?"

"Good chance."

"And having a pillow fight in your sexy lingerie."

"Less chance of that one."

"Shame."

"You're crazy."

"Guilty. Now, you need to get to class before you end up late." But as he says this, he dips his lips to my neck and starts kissing.

"Yeah, so are you if you don't stop."

"I know a really good storage cupboard," he groans in my ear.

"I'm sure you do," I say with a laugh, pressing my palms against his chest and forcing him to back up.

He looks down at me, his heavy lids lowered and a pout on his lips.

He looks cute. Too stinking cute.

"Class, Sebastian. I'll see you later."

"Last chance," he offers, taking a step back and running his eyes down my body.

"Get to class, boyfriend." The smile he gives me before lifting his hand in a salute makes my knees weak, and my stomach erupts with butterflies.

Dammit, he's turning me into one of those girls.

"Miss Doukas, it's so good to see you back," Miss Phillips, my economics teacher says, coming to a stop in front of me with an amused expression on her face.

"Thanks. It's... uh... good to be back."

"Looks like you're wasting no time in diving back into things," she shoots over her shoulder before slipping into her classroom right as the second bell for the beginning of class rings out around us.

I hurry inside and drop into my seat at the front.

Whispers immediately erupt at my arrival, but I square my shoulders and let their gossip roll off me. It isn't like it's something I'm not used to.

CHAPTER THIRTY

Stella

B eing back at school and being constantly watched by one of five scary members of the mafia at all times made life almost feel normal again.

Wherever I went, one of them seemed to magically appear, and by Friday afternoon, I'd turned it into a little game and tried to do everything I could to evade them, just for my own amusement. Safe to say, I wasn't very good at it.

Since touching down on English soil again and moving into Theo's place with him and Seb, I haven't received any signs that my stalker still exists. But while I might like to think that means he's gone, the guys aren't quite as confident.

Which is why they gave the two security details

standing guard at both the main door to the coach house and the entrance to the garage very stern instructions not to let us out tonight.

All five of them headed off in their hot-as-sin black suits a little over two hours ago to work at the hotel for some event they've got running. I didn't really ask any questions when Theo made it more than clear that he wasn't going to divulge any details about what they're up to. Fine by me, I'm sure I can find a way to get it out of Seb later.

"I need to do something," I complain, placing my empty glass down on the coffee table and looking between Calli and Emmie, who are lounging on the other couch with their own drinks.

The need to break the rules and let loose is burning through my veins. Seb knew it too, hence the extra security.

"The Halloween party is Sunday night," Calli says, apprehension for what I'm about to suggest clear on her face.

"It better be as good as you've promised," Emmie says, giving Calli a side-eye. "If it's lame, you're gonna have a lot to answer for, Cirillo."

"It won't be. The Knight's Ridge sixth form Halloween party is legendary."

"Hmm..." Emmie rumbles. "We'll see."

"It's going to be awesome. Plus it'll be crawling with security, so maybe the guys can actually enjoy it."

"Yeah, it's going to be at an abandoned building full of people in costumes and masks. That's not gonna happen. Seb's already threatened not to go," I say, remembering the very heated discussion we had about it last night.

"No one will do anything."

"You seem very confident," Emmie says, raising a brow at Calli.

"Dad and Uncle Damien have it covered. Nothing is going to happen."

I don't doubt her. I'm starting to think all of this protection just in case this creep tries something else is a little overkill, so I'm just surprised at her confidence. Other than Seb, she's been one of the most paranoid over the past few days, double-checking everything, not letting me into a room at school until she's been in first in case someone is waiting for me. I'm not entirely sure what she thought she'd do if there actually was someone lying in wait, but I can't deny that a part of me wanted him to be just so I could see what would happen.

"What do you want to do?" Emmie asks, ignoring Calli's previous concern.

"Let's go out. I want to go dancing. Just us. No boys allowed."

"Stella," Calli warns.

"What? I can't spend another night locked inside waiting for something to happen. It's suffocating. I want to get out. I want to be normal."

"And you will, when the guys find this twisted fuck."

"Assuming he's not got bored and moved on."

"Or until he gets an opening when you're not protected and does a better job."

"A better job?" I ask, amusement in my tone.

"Ugh, you know what I mean. Anyway, we're unlikely to get past the guys downstairs."

"Oh, I don't know... I think the three of us could be quite persuasive if we want to be."

A wicked smile pulls at Emmie's lips. I still have no idea what's been going on with her. She seems more than happy to push it aside and focus on our lives. I'm hoping that with a little more alcohol and some of Alex's weed that's sitting in my purse, she might just start opening up a little.

"I'm in," she says, sitting forward, her shoulders set in determination. "You got a fake ID, Cal?"

"Uh..."

"Of course you haven't." Emmie rolls her eyes at our innocent friend.

"Why would I even need one? Nico barely lets me out of the house, let alone attend things I'm too young for."

"Right. I got you covered, girl." Emmie grabs her cell from beside her and starts tapping at the screen.

"What are you doing?" Calli asks, sitting up so she can see the screen. "Who the hell is Jonno?"

"Just a guy who can get us anything we need," she says cryptically. "Smile," she says, quickly taking a photo of Calli, much to her horror.

"What the fuck are you doing?"

"Trust me, girl. Jonno will hook you up."

"Wha—I—Stella," she whines, looking at me as if I'm going to jump in and help her.

"What? You need a fake." I wink at Emmie.

"Oh my God," she sighs, falling back on the couch.

"Oh no, you don't. We're going out."

Emmie smiles at me, and together we haul Calli from the couch and drag her to the room I share with Seb.

"For the record, this is a really bad idea," she states, placing her hands on her hips and giving us warning glares.

"Drink this," Emmie says, forcing Calli to take the bottle of vodka she snatched from the kitchen as we passed.

"Then smoke one of these."

"Girl," Emmie squeals. "Have you been hiding the goods from us?"

Putting the joint to my lips, I light it with the Zippo Seb left on the side and take a pull.

"Fuck me," I breathe, releasing the hit. "That's good."

I pass it over to Emmie before I pull up a playlist on my cell and blast it through the entire apartment.

"You've never done it before?" Emmie asks Calli, who holds the blunt between her fingers like it's about to bite her.

I can't help but chuckle at the two of them. They're like light and dark. Angel and Devil.

"Just breathe it in."

Calli shoots me a concerned look.

"You wanted a bad influence in your life, Cirillo. God answered your prayers, because you got two."

"Fuck it," she mutters before taking her first hit and then coughing until I swear she's about to puke all over Theo's fancy cream carpet.

"Oh my God, that's..." She pauses, I assume as the effects hit her. "Actually pretty good."

I throw my head back, laughing when she takes another hit.

"Whoa, virgin. Don't get carried away," Emmie chastises, snatching the joint back as I take a swig of vodka from the bottle before pulling open the closet.

My clothes now take up more than half, something that Seb thankfully wasn't all that bothered by, seeing as he's not properly moved in here either.

"Right, we need something sexy," I announce, rummaging through what I brought for options.

"Do not even attempt to get me in a dress. I'm good as I am," Emmie shouts over the music.

Glancing over my shoulder, I take in her hot pants, fishnets and band tee.

Clearly reading the expression on my face, she holds up her finger, telling me to wait before pulling her shirt off and stealing my pink knife from the nightstand.

In only seconds she's slashed across the neck and ripped the bottom of the shirt off.

She pulls it back on, adjusting it so it hangs low over one shoulder and shows off her slim waist.

"Right, so... just Calli to sort then."

It's over an hour later by the time we emerge from the apartment, much to the horror of the guy guarding the door.

He's older than us, although not by that much, and

clearly not old enough to make any attempt to cover up the fact that he's totally checking each one of us out.

"We're going out," I tell him, my voice slightly slurred but full of confidence as I step toward him with my shoulders thrown back.

"I don't think so. We're under strict instructions to—"

"Do you always do what you're told...?"

"Carl," he finishes for me.

"Do you always do what you're told, Carl?" I damn near purr, my voice dripping with sex appeal.

"If I want to stay alive, yes."

"How about I come up with a way for you to break the rules but still be breathing in the morning?"

"Fucking knew I shouldn't have taken this job," he mutters to himself while blatantly checking out my tits.

Good to know my dress is doing half the work for me tonight.

"Right well, you take us to The Avenue, and I won't send Seb that video of you checking me out," I say nodding to where Emmie is holding her cell. "And I'll convince him that this was all my fault and take your punishment from him." I wink at him and he groans. "Be a good boy and we might even let you dance with us."

"That's a surefire way to end up with a bullet in my head."

Crossing my arms under my breasts, pushing them up that bit higher, I wait for him to make a decision.

"Cass," he calls, and not a second later does the other guy appear from the garage. "We're heading out."

"Uh..." He looks between Carl and me. "You sure about this, man?"

"Nope."

I can't help but laugh as Carl moves toward his car.

"Good choice, Carl. I'd hate to have to get your blood on my pretty new knife." I pull it from where I've got it strapped to my thigh and flick it open.

"Boss was right," Cass mutters. "She is just as bad as the boys."

"Worse," I tell him, pulling open the passenger door of Carl's car and dropping into the seat before Cass has a chance.

"Really?" he mutters, much to my amusement.

"Keep an eye on my girls, Cass." I shoot him a wink and close the door.

I'm playing with fire. The second Seb checks the tracking app he's got connected to my cell, all hell is going to break loose. Excitement races through my veins at the thought.

He's going to be fucking furious, and I might be throwing Carl and Cass under a bus right now, but hell if I'm not desperate for the impending fight we've got coming our way.

I bite down on my bottom lip, my blood already beginning to boil at the thought of his brutal touches and the vicious words he's no doubt going to spit at me for defying orders.

"You're trouble. I hope you know that," Carl informs me, as if it's news.

"I know. But what's the point in life if you can't break a few rules and have a little fun? Right, Em?" I call behind me, knowing full well that she's totally on board with this plan.

"Hell, yes."

The second we pull up outside the club, Emmie slips around the side of the building to meet the guy she was messaging about Calli's fake ID, and only minutes later the three of us and our two shadows are in the line, ready to head inside.

Neither of the bouncers even question Emmie or Calli's IDs, and before we know it, the three of us are in the middle of the dancefloor, rolling our hips in time with the booming music.

"Hell, yes," Calli screams, totally fucking wasted and high as a kite from her first taste of weed. "This was the best idea ever."

Our escorts make themselves useful by supplying us with drinks as the night goes on, but at no point do their eyes leave us, which means I can totally let go and just enjoy my time with the girls.

Sweat covers my skin as we dance, my hair sticking to my bare neck.

Two guys approach Emmie and Calli from behind. They're clearly friends, because they share a look as they begin moving in time with them. Not a second later do I feel someone at my own back.

No words are said as the six of us dance.

It's perfect. Well, almost. The only thing that would be better would be if it were Seb behind me.

The guy, whoever he is, is a perfect gentleman, which shocks the fuck out of me. Although I can't help but wonder if he's clocked our security and is erring on the side of caution.

If he has, then he hasn't warned his friends, who are more than happy to turn the heat up a notch with my girls. Both of them are totally in their element as they shed their inhibitions and grind against the guys.

My cell buzzing in my purse should be my first sign that trouble is brewing, but much like everything else tonight, I push it aside in favor of enjoying myself. It's been entirely too long since it happened.

Carl and Cass's wide eyes as they dart toward me are my second clue, and it's them who make me stop dancing only a second before Calli screams my name a beat before the excitement really begins.

CHAPTER THIRTY-ONE

Sebastian

"This is bullshit," I complain, standing guard at the door of the function room where tonight's hen do is being held.

"Bro, we're in a room full of wasted and horny women," Alex says, his eyes scanning the room, eating up all the skin on show.

"And I could be at home with my own probably wasted and horny woman."

Nico lifts his hand and makes a whipping sound behind him.

They've been trying to get to me all night with comments about me being whipped, but it's not working because I just don't care.

I've handed my balls over to Stella, and I couldn't

be happier with my decision. Well, unless she was physically handling them right now, of course.

"You're just pissed because you can't bang one of the bridesmaids in the toilets like that dog did," Alex says, nodding toward Nico.

"Oh yeah, that's it." I roll my eyes at the pair of them.

Fuck knows why we had to work tonight, leaving Carl and Cass at our place to watch the girls. They could have more than handled this bunch of rowdy women. Hell, they've got to be easier than dealing with Stella and Emmie, that's for sure.

"I'm going to get a drink," I tell no one in particular, pushing from the wall and making my way through the women and half-naked male dancers that are littered around.

"What can I get you, Seb?" Gavin, tonight's bartender, asks.

"Vodka, neat. Fuck the rocks."

His brow lifts. "Not enjoying yourself? The others seem to be. Pretty sure I saw Nico being dragged into the ladies' bathroom not so long ago."

"You saw right," I mutter, pulling my phone from my pocket and unlocking it.

"Amazing what a good woman can do to you, huh?" he asks with a laugh, knowing full well that if it weren't for Stella, I'd be as bad as Nico given half a chance.

"Yeah, I guess," I respond absently as I wait for the tracker to load.

I'm confident that I don't need to bother. She'll be at home with the girls, hopefully getting suitably drunk for when I get back. Hell knows I'm gonna need everything she can offer me after dealing with this lot all night.

Gavin slides a glass toward me and I knock it back while my app continues to search.

"The fuck?" I bark, slamming the glass down so hard it shatters on the bar.

"What's wrong?" Gavin asks, but he's too late. I'm already halfway across the room.

I approach Toby from behind and grab the back of his neck.

"You're with me," I bark, steering him toward the exit.

"What the fuck are you doing?" Theo shouts after us.

"Going to kill Toby's sister," I announce, my voice full of deadly intentions.

"What has she done?" Toby asks on a sigh, not sounding surprised in the slightest.

My grip on his neck tightens.

I might have agreed for her to be out and about in the hope of attracting her stalker so we could put an end to this bullshit, but the agreement was with us—with me—watching her.

"She's going to fucking regret this," I mutter, continuing forward.

"We'll be fine without you," Theo calls sarcastically.

"Was I giving you a choice? Although, if you wanna teach your emo chick a lesson, you might wanna come with." I look back just in time to see him flip me off before Toby and I disappear through the doors.

"Where is she?" Toby asks as we march through the hotel foyer toward the lift that will take us to the underground car park to get my car.

"The fucking Avenue."

"With Emmie and Calli?"

"Something tells me she didn't go alone."

"And what about Carl and Cass?"

"Fucking dead, as far as I'm concerned. They had one job."

Toby bursts out laughing.

"What?" I bark, my patience already long gone.

"You're aware that this is your fault, right?"

"Mine? How the fuck do you figure that?" I ask as the lift doors open and we walk around the people waiting to step inside. The second they look up at us, they take a step back, wisely deciding to wait for the other one.

I hit the button for the basement and the doors close.

"You set her a challenge by telling her to stay there tonight. What did you really expect?"

"For her to do as she's fucking told?"

"You have met your girlfriend, right?"

"Shut the fuck up, Ariti, or you'll end up in an unmarked grave with Carl and Cass."

He laughs as if I'm joking. All I do is crack my knuckles, trying to keep a lid on my temper as the doors open.

The drive to The Avenue only takes fifteen

minutes. The roads are quiet, and by some miracle we manage to park not far down from the entrance.

Ignoring the queue that wraps around the building to get inside, we march straight up to the bouncers who instantly open the rope for us, allowing us inside.

I have no idea what floor they'll be on, but I make an educated guess that they wouldn't have made much effort to go up or down. Something tells me that she wants to ensure I can find her as easily as possible. Why the fuck would she bring her cell, allowing me to track her if she didn't want me to fucking chase her?

The club is packed. I'm not surprised—it's Friday night, after all.

Toby and I stand on the edge of the dancefloor, scanning the crowd. But I don't see her.

My heart thunders so hard in my chest it starts to hurt as my nails dig into my palms with how tightly my fists are clenched.

My eyes are still flicking around all the sweaty, gyrating bodies when Toby's elbow connects with my ribs—a little harder than absolutely necessary, but I forget all about it when I follow his pointed finger.

If I thought I was mad at her little stunt, then it's nothing compared to the sight of her dancing with someone else.

"He's fucking dead," I growl, storming forward through the crowd.

"Seb, no, don't—" Toby's warning fades into nothing as the booming music mixes with the blood racing past my ears, my anger getting the better of me.

Those who don't see me coming get thrown aside in my need to get to her.

She's completely oblivious as I forge forward, her hips rolling against that fuck as she loses herself in the moment.

Enjoy that bliss, baby. It's coming to an abrupt fucking end.

Calli, thankfully, isn't quite so oblivious despite the fact that she's got some cunt's hands all over her. She has to know that this is a Cirillo club. She has to have known that we'd be here.

"Stella," she squeals a second before I get to them, giving my girl the briefest of warning before the guy she was dancing with is thrown across the floor, colliding with other drunk, oblivious people.

"Seb, no," she screams as I step over him, grabbing his shirt to drag him up before my fist slams into his cheek.

The red haze of anger finally consumes me and I lose my grip on what the fuck I'm doing as I take everything out on this fucking chancer.

It's not until hands wrap around my upper arms, physically dragging me back from the passed-out fuck, that I realise just how badly I lost it.

My chest heaves, sweat causes my shirt to stick to my back, and my fists scream in pain. But none of that is enough to stop me from fighting to get free to continue.

"Seb, calm the fuck down," Theo barks in my ear.

My confusion over hearing his voice is what I need to fully bring me back to reality as my feet are dragged across the sticky floor.

People surround the guy I just beat the shit out of, blocking my view of the mess I made of his face.

"We need to get the fuck out of here right now."

"Stella," I shout.

"Toby's got her, you stupid cunt," he growls.

Theo pushes me toward the exit as security guards come rushing up. They know exactly who caused the trouble, but one look at us and they turn a blind eye. Dragging us in isn't worth losing their jobs over.

"You're a lucky motherfucker," Alex adds over my other shoulder as we spill out into the street.

"What the fuck is wrong with you?" Stella screams, getting right in my face the second my feet hit the pavement.

My hand moves faster than my brain can process, and my fingers wrap around her throat, squeezing in warning.

"Me? What the fuck is wrong with me? All you had to do was stay at fucking home," I hiss, my barely controlled anger making my hand shake as I hold her, pushing her back toward where I abandoned my car.

Her lips part to respond, but no words come out.

"Did you want Carl and Cass's deaths on your conscience? Was that it? Because that's all you've fucking done tonight."

"N-no," she finally says as her back collides with my car. "This is on me, not them. They were protecting us. Doing their jobs."

"So why were you pressed up against some cunt who wasn't me when you're meant to be safe at home?"

Her teeth grind, making her jaw pop.

Leaning into her, I run my nose across her jaw, the move at odds with my harsh grip of her throat.

"I shouldn't have to be at work worrying about you, baby."

I sense her intentions before she moves and jump out of the way when her knee lifts.

"I hope you considered the consequences of this little stunt."

Her eyes darken with wicked intent.

"Fucking hellion," I mutter, shoving my hand into my pocket and throwing my keys at Alex, who's standing at my side, watching the show.

"Drive us home, bro. Stella and I need to have a little chat."

A smirk curls at my lips that makes her throat ripple with a swallow.

Oh yeah, she knew too fucking well what she was doing.

Ripping the back door of my Aston open, I growl at her to get in and damn near throw her through the door.

I'm about to follow when a hand lands on my shoulder.

Spinning around, I find Toby staring at me.

My eyes hold his for a beat, hearing his unspoken warning loud and clear.

"You should probably go back with them. You don't need to see this."

His lips part to argue, but I don't give him a chance and climb into the car as Alex drops into the driver's seat.

I don't look back, so I can only assume that Theo, Toby and Nico have Calli and Emmie under control.

Who knows, maybe Theo's night will turn around if Emmie is half as drunk as Stella is.

The engine rumbles beneath us as Alex pulls away from the street.

Stella is still fumbling with her seat belt when I reach over, wrap my hands around her waist and lift her, settling her so she's straddling my lap.

"What the—" Her words cut off the second she looks into my eyes.

Stella's already experienced me at my worst, or so I thought, so the fact that the deadly expression on my face right now renders her speechless really says a lot.

"Bro, don't be a dick," Alex warns, but my only response is to laugh as I drag Stella's bag from across her body and throw it onto the seat beside us.

"Go the long way around," I tell him, keeping my eyes locked on Stella's. "And don't fucking look back," I warn a second before I wrap my fingers around the low-cut of her dress and tug. The thin straps over her shoulders snap as I expose her. "You're going to fucking pay for that stunt, Hellion."

Surging forward, I suck one of her nipples into my mouth and bite until she screams out in pain.

"Fucking hell, Seb," Alex complains.

"Shut up and drive."

"Fuck, Seb. You can't," Stella moans as I soothe the pain with my tongue, lapping at her sensitive flesh.

But in contrast to her words, her hips roll, the

burning heat of her pussy grinding down on my already painfully hard cock.

One look at her in this sinful little dress and I was fucking gone for her, stupid stunt or not.

"Seb," she moans loudly, using my body for her own pleasure.

"Jesus fucking Christ," Alex mutters from the front, but I block him out.

"Oh, no you don't," I say, lifting her slightly so she loses the friction she's so desperate for. "You don't deserve any pleasure after what you've done."

"Seb, please. I need—"

I chuckle darkly. "Oh, baby. I know exactly what you need."

Skimming my hands up her thighs, I push her dress around her waist, exposing her pretty lace thong.

Wrapping my fingers around the sides, I tug. She lets out a wanton moan as the fabric pulls away from her body.

With another mumbled complaint, Alex turns the music up in an attempt to drown her out.

Balling up the scrap of fabric, I stuff it into my pocket.

"Another for your collection?" Stella asks, her voice dripping in sarcasm.

I don't respond. She doesn't need me to.

"Oh shit, Seb," she cries out when I find her swollen pussy and circle my fingertips.

"You knew exactly what you were doing tonight, didn't you, Hellion?"

"P-please," she begs when I move my fingers.

"Answer me."

"Y-yes."

"And you couldn't have just asked nicely? You had to get that innocent guy's face fucked up and two of our guys killed."

"N-no, please don't. This was all on me. They looked after us. Please," she damn near sobs as I apply pressure once more.

Her legs tremble with her need and I push my fingers back, spearing two inside her.

"Yes," she cries.

"You only had to do one thing, Hellion. Stay at fucking home," I mutter, mostly talking to myself as I fuck her greedy cunt, pushing her closer to the release she's so desperate for.

"I-I'm sorry."

"No you're fucking not," I state, ripping my fingers from her and lifting them to her mouth. "Suck."

She doesn't miss a beat as she hungrily sucks my fingers into her mouth, swirling her tongue around them just like she does to my cock before taking me in her throat.

My dick aches, pressing painfully against the fly of my trousers.

"Fuck this," I mutter, ripping my belt open and shoving the fabric down my hips, just enough to free myself.

Stella doesn't release my fingers, but her eyes lock on my cock as I stroke myself a couple of times.

"This what you want?"

She nods eagerly.

"This was what tonight was all about. I fucking love that you missed me, baby, but it was all a little unnecessary when you could have just asked for my cock."

I thrust up into her without warning, fully seating myself in a second.

Her walls ripple around me, making my teeth grind as I try to keep my shit together. She might fucking own me, but right now, she doesn't need to see it. See how she brings me to my knees with just one fucking look, one touch, one wicked comment.

Dragging my fingers from her mouth, I wrap my hand around her throat once more, loving the way her eyes flash with desire the second I do. I roll her nipple with the other, making her gush around my length as I slowly thrust up into her.

"Yes," she cries when I circle my hips, hitting that spot deep inside her that drives her crazy.

"Enjoy it, baby. You're not coming."

"W-what?" she stutters, her eyes widening in shock.

"You heard me. You don't deserve it. You wanted punishing for this little stunt. This is where we begin. Take my cock like a good little girl. You're not getting out of this car until it's with my cum running from your body."

All her breath rushes from her lungs.

There's a bang from the front of the car before I swear I hear Alex mutter, "What the fuck did I do to deserve this?"

"Put on a good show, baby. Alex is really enjoying himself. And we know how you like to please us."

"Cunt. I fucking hate you, Seb."

"No you don't, baby. And that's half the problem, isn't it?"

Her eyes narrow and her lips purse in anger. But the second I buck my hips, her jaw falls slack as pleasure ripples through her.

"Be a good girl and do as you're told, and maybe I'll let you come later."

Her eyes flash with contempt, but all I do is smile in return.

She might have started this game, but I'll play along and make sure I'm the one that finishes it. She can curse me out all she likes, but she knows damn well that it's exactly what she wanted.

I fuck her fast, my hands holding her in place with a bruising grip, but every time she gets even close to coming, I slow my pace and allow it to fade.

"Going to fucking kill you," she grates out when I do it for what must be the fifth or sixth time.

Shooting a look out of the window, I find that Alex has finally had enough as we're only a couple of minutes from home.

This time, I fuck her until I'm the one that explodes, my cock jerking violently inside her, filling her with everything I have.

Her body trembles as she takes it, her own pleasure right in touching distance, but she knows better than to allow herself to fall headfirst into it.

"Good girl," I growl, threading my fingers into her hair and dragging her down so I can kiss her.

"You're a fucking cunt," Alex grunts the second the

car comes to a stop before he jumps out and slams the door behind himself, probably with his cock trying to bust out of his trousers.

Dragging Stella from my lips, her eyes hold mine, amusement sparkling within them, but she doesn't let it out.

"Let's go. I've barely started with you yet."

CHAPTER THIRTY-TWO

Stella

My legs are like jelly as I climb from the back of Seb's car with his cum coating my thighs. My core aches, my muscles clench, desperate to have something to hold onto to recover my lost orgasm.

My throat is dry and my head spins with the lingering effects of the alcohol I've consumed that Seb's brutal touches haven't yet managed to rid me of.

I knew what I was getting myself into tonight. I knew I was playing with fire. But after the past two days at school and having to constantly look over my shoulder, I was more than ready to get burned.

It was reckless and dangerous—and not just for me —but I fucking needed it. And damn if I don't feel better for it already, despite my stolen orgasm.

I need to be me again. I needed to rebel. I needed that rush, that adrenaline. But more than anything, I needed *that* Seb.

He's been so sweet, loving, considerate... and while I appreciate that after everything we've been through in the past few weeks, I needed that boy I first met. The one who didn't handle me like I was made from glass, the one who makes it hurt, who branded himself on my soul before either of us knew he was capable of it.

"You look like a whore," he spits at me the second he's out of the car, his dark, angry and hungry eyes running down the length of me as I stand there holding my ruined dress up, covering my bare breasts.

"And whose fault is that?" I smirk, knowing full well that I looked perfectly acceptable until he got his hands on me.

Stepping up to me, he grips my jaw in his hands, his fingertips digging into my skin in the most delicious way.

The tip of his nose hits mine as our eyes connect.

My chest heaves as I wait for him to kiss me, but he never does.

"Get inside. We're not done."

I should fucking hope not.

"Good," I purr, closing the last bit of space between us and rubbing his semi through his pants.

"Inside. Now."

With his hand on the back of my neck, he pushes me toward the entrance.

Another car pulls in behind us, and when I look back, I watch as Carl and Cass climb out of the black

Range Rover they took us to the club in. I have no idea if they were following us or cleaning up the mess Seb left behind, but also, I don't really care.

"You two had better hope her persuasive skills are good if you want to stay alive," Seb mutters, his deep and dangerous voice sending tingles right through me.

Catching Carl's eye, I wink silently, telling him that I've got their backs before the door slams closed behind us.

No words are said between us as he pushes me up the stairs, his hand burning the back of my neck while the rest of my body aches for his touch.

Everyone's already sitting on the couches with drinks and knowing smirks playing on their faces when we arrive.

"Where's Alex?" I ask, noticing that he's missing.

"Fucker ran straight into the bathroom the second he got up here. What did you do to him?" Theo asks, amusement sparkling in his eyes as he takes in the state of me.

I can't help but burst out laughing.

"If he's imagining you while he's cracking one out, I'll fucking kill him," Seb growls in my ear.

"Rein it in, caveman. He knows I'm yours. He's witnessed it enough."

"Stella, are you okay?" Calli asks me, nervously glancing between my ruined dress and Seb at my back.

"Never better."

"Turn the music up, or go out," Seb grunts, clearly fed up with socializing as he pushes me toward the hall that leads to our room.

Our room.

I might have no idea how permanent my stay here is, but those two words still make butterflies erupt within me.

Seb pauses as we pass the main bathroom and slams his fist down on the door. "Theo bought a new tub of Vaseline, if you need to borrow it," he calls out, much to the amusement of the people behind us.

I snort a laugh when nothing but a grunt comes from the other side of the door.

Seb forges forward, and something tells me that whatever is going to come next isn't going to make Alex's situation any better. He should just go out and get laid.

He gives me a shove when we get to our bedroom and I stumble inside, only coming to a stop when I collide with the bed.

"Hands and knees," he demands, stopping me from flipping over or even turning to look at him when the sound of rustling fabric hits my ears.

I stay there like I've been told as he disappears into the bathroom. Each second he's not touching me feels like a fucking hour, and when he finally comes back, his footsteps getting closer, I damn near moan in anticipation.

My muscles are all locked tight, just waiting to see what he's going to do to punish me next.

Finally, fucking finally, he steps up to me, one hand pushing my dress up over my ass, the fingers of his other hand dipping between my legs, spreading what's left of his cum around me.

"Mine," he growls. As if I really need reminding.

Arching my back, I offer up more of myself to him, desperate to find that mindless pleasure only he can deliver.

But right as I think he's going to give me what I need, his fingers are ripped away before his palm connects with my bare ass cheek, the loud crack echoing around the room a beat before I cry out.

"Yesss," I hiss as he soothes the burn for a couple of seconds before repeating the action, twice more, ensuring I've got a glowing reminder of him right on my ass. As if the brand on my thigh isn't enough.

"Tell me you're mine," he grates out, one hand still soothing the sting while the other dips back to my soaked pussy.

"I'm yours, Seb. All fucking yours."

"Hell, yes."

He lowers down, his breath rushing over my ass, and I still. I'm just about to ask what the hell he's doing when he spits on me.

"Oh God," I whimper, knowing exactly what's coming.

My core clenches with need as he brushes the head of his cock against my backdoor.

His hand slides up my spine, his fingers twisting in my hair.

"I can't promise this isn't going to hurt," he murmurs, opening me up with his fingers for a few moments.

"Seb." His name falls from my lips as nothing more than a needy whimper and only gets louder when he withdraws his fingers and his cock pushes against the tight muscle of my ass.

"Relax, baby," he soothes, his voice suddenly softer, his demanding tone forgotten for a beat.

I do as I'm told, allowing him to push inside.

"Fuck. Fuck, you're tight."

It might be my first experience at this, but fuck if I'm not craving it, the pain, the mindless oblivion that I already know is going to come.

"More," I beg when he stills about halfway to make sure I'm okay. "Fuck me, Seb. Take what you need. I need it too."

"Fuck, you're perfect, baby."

He surges forward, his restraint snapping at my words.

Pain renders me useless for a few seconds, but it quickly eases when he pulls out, sending shockwaves around my body as his grip on my hair tightens.

"Fuck," he barks again as he pushes back in, loud enough to be heard over the music filtering down from the living room.

I arch back, forcing him deeper now the pain has subsided and my lost orgasm makes itself known.

"That it's, baby," he encourages, slipping his hand beneath me to find my clit.

I moan loudly as he plays me perfectly as his hips thrust into me at the most teasing yet delicious speed, allowing me to feel every single movement.

"I'm not gonna last, Hellion," he tells me after a minute or two of me drowning in him.

"Then come," I demand. "I want to feel you coming in my ass."

"Fuck."

He ups his speed, his fingers dipping into my pussy while his thumb continues circling my clit.

"Oh shit, baby," he grunts as my muscles clamp down with my impending release. "Come for me, Princess."

I fucking shatter, screaming out as my body convulses around him, my limbs giving up and forcing me to fall onto the bed.

He's right behind me, though, and he crashes on top of me as the sounds of our increased breaths fill the room, our bodies slick with sweat sticking to each other as we come down from our incredible highs.

He brushes my hair from my ear, his hot lips tickling against the shell as he says words that make my heart flutter wildly in my chest.

"I fucking love you, Hellion. Never, ever stop pushing me to be the worst version of myself."

"Deal," I breathe, already losing myself to my exhaustion from the night.

Oh my God.

Every single inch of my body aches when I roll over the next morning. My muscles pull, my butt cheek hurts, and a brass fucking band has taken up residence in my head.

I groan, shoving my face into my pillow, praying

that sleep will take its hold once again and make it all go away.

I don't remember much after Seb pinned me to the bed once he came in my ass, but as I lie there, little flashbacks begin to flicker on the edge of my consciousness.

How cold the bathroom counter was as Seb ate me like a starved man. The shower wall. The bed. Again.

Fuck. No wonder everything hurts.

My need for the bathroom stops me from even attempting to go back to sleep.

Throwing the covers off, I gingerly swing my legs over the side and sit up, praying that my stomach doesn't roll and force me to bolt for the bathroom.

Thankfully, it seems to stay settled, and aside from the continued pounding in my head, the only thing I notice is the state of my thighs.

"Fucking hell," I mutter, running my fingertip gently over the bruises Seb left behind.

Finding a glass of water and pills on the nightstand, I eagerly swallow them down and drain the water before walking to the bathroom and risking a look in the mirror.

"Christ." I look like I've been mauled by a bear. Or a bad boy with an anger problem.

I can't help but smile as I think of the previous night.

It was stupid of me to play him like that. But damn, it was so fucking worth it. And if anything, I just proved that I can leave the house without some headcase trying to kill me. Bodyguards, brutal beatings and car sex in front of Alex aside, it was a fairly normal night out.

I laugh at myself and shake my head.

Normal.

What the hell do any of us know about normal?

I pee, brush my teeth and clear my face of last night's makeup before finding one of Seb's shirts and pulling on a clean pair of panties and slipping from the room in search of my guy.

Deep voices rumble from the living room, and when I round the corner, I find Seb, Theo and Toby sitting on the sofas, all with coffees and chilling in sweatpants. Both Seb and Theo are shirtless with their ink and abs fully on display. It's quite a sight for first thing in the morning.

"Hey," I say, not really feeling bad about interrupting whatever they're talking about as I drop myself into Seb's lap.

"Hey, baby. I was going to come and get you in a bit. Toby brought coffee and breakfast."

"My hero," I breathe, kissing Seb on the cheek and reaching for the takeout cup that I assume is mine on the coffee table.

"Thought you might need it," Toby mutters, his cheeks heating with embarrassment.

"Where are the other two idiots?" I ask, attempting to change the subject. I really don't need to sit here and have a conversation with my newly discovered brother about one of his best mates fucking me until I passed out last night.

"They went out after you... disappeared," Theo says, finishing his breakfast wrap.

"Apparently Theo's tub of Vaseline wasn't good enough for Alex," Seb announces happily before Theo balls up the paper bag in his hand and launches it at his head. "Hey. It was a fact, not a jibe."

Rolling his eyes, Theo mutters, "He better not have stuck his fingers in my Vaseline," making us all howl with laughter.

"So what are we doing today?" I ask once my giggles have subsided.

"We usually spend Saturday mornings training, but we were waiting for you."

"Training? Like, in a gym?"

"Yeah, you wanna join us, Hellion?"

"Watch you three, sorry two," I say with a wince in Toby's direction, "get all hot and sweaty in the gym? Uh... hell yes!"

Seb grabs my jaw, turning my face toward his, his eyes narrowing at me.

"Calm down, caveman. Everyone here knows who I belong to."

"Good. So they fucking should. Eat up and then we'll go. Theo's gonna need to go and get a shirt on."

"Fuck you, bro. Ain't my fault your girl would rather watch me flex my muscles."

I groan at them, but equally, I can't wipe the smile off my face. I can't help but poke at them into bickering like old women. It's turning into my favorite hobby.

We spend almost all day in the Cirillo gym at the end of Theo's garden. Alex and Nico eventually appeared, looking worse for wear after their impromptu night out. Clearly, Alex didn't drink enough to forget about what he was forced to experience the night before, because the second he walked into the building, he stepped right upto the punching bag I was taking all my aggression out on and asked me how my ride was.

Safe to say, I moved faster than he was anticipating, evidenced by the black eye that he's now sporting, much to the amusement of the rest of the guys.

I trained with each of them, much to Seb's irritation and concern, but it was great to have a range of sparring partners of varying skills. It turns out that my very own brother is pretty hot shit in the ring, and unlike Nico and Theo, who were scared to go full throttle on me despite my insistence that I was fine, he didn't actually hold back. Even Seb relaxed a little from his position beside the ring, watching my every move and rocking a very obvious erection behind his sweatpants.

Knowing what I was doing to him in my sports bra and leggings only spurred me on, even if my body was still screaming at me from everything he put it through the night before.

After showering, someone took the initiative to order a fuck load of Chinese, and Nico reluctantly went and collected Calli. We all spent the night hanging out. It was nice, and no one had to have a pit stop in the bathroom with Theo's Vaseline for company.

Well, not that I know of, anyway.

CHAPTER THIRTY-THREE

Stella

"I don't like this," Seb complains from his spot lazing on the bed as I pack a bag ready for the night.

"It's going to be fine. You said yourself that Damien and Evan have personally overseen the security. We know everyone on the guest list, and no one else is getting inside the party."

"I know but—"

"Seb," I say, cutting him off. "You're acting like a pussy. Nothing is going to happen to me."

"I know," he says, pushing to sit on the edge of the bed. "I just... I can't do that again."

"Me either. But it's not going to come to that. We're not going to lock ourselves in here and hide from that motherfucker. If we're lucky, he'll try and crash and we can catch him, end Halloween by putting a bullet through someone's skull."

He stands, walks over to me and wraps his arms around my waist. "Now that sounds like a perfect way to end the day. We will get him," he assures me for the millionth time.

"I know. But we're not going to halt our lives in the meantime. I want to see how you Brits celebrate."

Seb shakes his head, knowing that I'm not going to concede on this before ducking down and capturing my lips.

"Uh-uh," I say, pulling away. "You're not going to distract me with sex this time."

"I'm sure I could." He drops his face to my neck, sending shivers of desire racing through my body.

"Nope. I need to get over to Calli's. She'll be waiting."

"At least tell me what your costume is." He pouts.

"I don't know. Calli has kept it a secret." It's something that doesn't sit quite right with me for fear that she's going to dress me up like some princess Barbie or something. I shudder at the thought, but I can't deny that I would quite like to witness her attempt to wrestle Emmie into a sparkly, frilly dress.

"You do know something, don't you?" Seb growls, assuming my smirk is because I'm lying.

"No, I really don't. It'll be a surprise to both of us. You got your fangs ready?"

"All ready to drink your blood, baby."

Okay, that statement shouldn't do the things to me that it does.

Fifteen minutes later, Calli is practically dragging me from Seb's clutches so we can go and get ready for whatever tonight holds. She's been telling me for days about how awesome their Halloween party is, but until I see it, I'm going to reserve judgment. It doesn't take a genius to work out that the Brits don't celebrate the holiday to quite the extremes that the Americans do. I swear I could count on one hand how many pumpkins I've seen. It's just not right.

"Come on, Em's waiting. I told her she can't see the costumes until you're here."

I follow her through the house and up the stairs as Seb heads in the opposite direction to meet the guys in Nico's basement.

"Finally. We didn't think he was going to let you out of his sight," Emmie says, a bottle of some pink premixed drink in her hand.

"He wasn't thrilled about it."

She sighs. "It can't go as badly as the other night. What's his issue?"

"I dunno, Friday night was pretty damn awesome."

"So we heard," she deadpans.

"Everyone survived. No one got arrested. Don't see the issue."

"Only one of us got laid," she mutters.

"I told you they've got skills, girl. Shoulda just jumped one of them when you had the chance. Didn't Theo take you home?"

"Yeah, the rude fuck barely even uttered a word to me."

"I never said you had to have a conversation with him, Em." I wink.

"Calli's right. You are a bad influence."

"On you, I highly doubt it."

"Right, enough. I want to show you our costumes," Calli says excitedly.

"Oh, I can't wait," Emmie sings, mocking Calli's enthusiasm and clapping her hands like an idiot.

"You can be uninvited, you know," Calli tells her, her tone deadly serious.

Emmie rolls her eyes.

"Let's see what we're dealing with."

A wide smile lights up Calli's face as she turns to the dress bags hanging on her closet doors.

I glance at Emmie, dread settling in my stomach.

"Oh, hell no," Emmie announces. "Not a fucking chance."

Turning back, I can't help but burst out laughing at Calli's costume choice for the three of us.

"Wait," she says, lifting the hanger, "it gets better."

"Better?" Emmie asks in pure disbelief.

She turns the bubblegum pink jacket around, and instead of 'Pink Ladies' like I'd expect to see, we've all got 'Princess' in sparkly diamantes.

"Fuck right off, Calli Cirillo. There's no chance I'm walking out of this house wearing that."

"But the skirt will look so cute on you," I say, eying the black sixties style skirt with a pink dog on it.

"I don't do skirts. No way. No fucking way."

"Aw come on, don't be a spoilsport. I thought it would be funny."

"It kinda is," I say, walking over to the jacket and running my finger over the word. "We are all princesses, after all." I wink at Emmie.

"Yeah, and I'd rather *they*," she says, referring to the guys, "didn't know about my connections."

"Dude," Calli says, exasperated, "your surname is Ramsey and you ride a freaking motorcycle. They're gonna figure it out if they haven't already."

"Whoa, someone's been doing their research."

"I know nothing about my life, I may as well learn something about yours. Your uncle is hot, by the way."

"Cruz? Seriously, Cal. He's way too old for you."

"Yeah, I know. Still hot, though."

"Just like your dad," I add. "Now drink that pink shit and let's get ready."

"I'm not wearing the skirt," Emmie sulks, obviously deciding that's a fight she might win.

"I had a feeling you'd say that, so I got these for you two."

She throws a bag at each of us and we pull out wet-look leggings and crop tops.

"Well, it's better than a skirt, I guess."

"Stop your bitching and get your ass into them. They might even help end your drought."

Emmie's lips part to argue, but she quickly shuts them again, knowing that she doesn't have a comeback.

By the time we're dressed and our hair and makeup are on point, we've finished off the cocktails and made our way through the bottle of vodka Emmie had in her purse.

I'm feeling more than a little lightheaded as we

make our way down the stairs to meet our vampire escorts.

"Whoa," I breathe when we find the five of them waiting at the bottom of the stairs for us.

"Holy shit," Emmie gasps beside me, but her reaction is swallowed by the guys' laughter at our outfits.

Both Emmie and I are rocking the leggings, her with biker boots and me with killer heels, whereas Calli has gone all girly with her skirt and Mary Janes.

"Fuck, you look unbelievable," Seb says, dragging me into his body and leaning in to kiss me. The contacts in his eyes make them even more mesmerizing than usual, and I utterly drown in them.

"Uh-uh, no ruining the lipstick. Suck my neck, baby." I wink, and he groans as if he's in pain.

"Let's get this show on the road, kids," Nico announces, sounding bored out of his mind.

"What's up with him? And where's his shirt?"

"Fuck knows. Come on." Seb threads his finger through mine and we make our way out to the cars.

The drive to the abandoned building is shorter than I was expecting, but the second we pull off the main road and head down the dark lane with low, overhanging trees, shivers begin to run down my spine.

"You okay?" Seb whispers in my ear, sensing my reaction.

"Yeah, of course." I smile widely at him, telling myself that it's just the anticipation of what this night full of horror might hold.

Calli has promised the scare house of all scare

houses, so I guess we're soon to find out if she's about to eat her words. Although, if my reaction is anything to go by, then I don't think she will be.

"Oh wow," I breathe as what I can only assume is the location of the party comes into view.

The old building looks creepy enough as it is without the zombies that seem to be surrounding it, greeting everyone as they arrive.

Smoke fills the dark sky and low lights flicker in the windows. None of it does much for the unease that's trickling through my veins.

"You sure you're okay?" Seb asks again.

"Yeah, I'm excited."

"Damn, I hoped you'd be terrified and have to cling onto me all night." He winks and I laugh at him, loving his goofiness.

The cars come to a stop and we pile out, meeting the others who join us.

"See, I told you," Calli says excitedly, bouncing on her feet.

"It's... really something."

Glancing over at Emmie, I find her also looking up at the old building with something like awe on her face.

Feeling my stare, she looks back at me.

"Maybe this night isn't going to suck after all."

"I've got something you can suck," Alex offers, already off his head on something.

"Christ. I take it back."

She turns toward the entrance where zombies, who I assume are Damien's security, are checking everyone off their guest list and allowing them inside.

"Evening," Theo says to the two guys, and on closer inspection, I recognize them as my accomplices from Friday night.

"In you go," Carl says as Cass counts us all in.

"Good to see you're still alive," I say as I pass. I hadn't seen them since that night, and I must say the thought had crossed my mind that they'd already been disposed of somewhere.

"Thanks for not offing them," I whisper-shout to Seb as we make our way into the party.

He laughs at my comment. "I'm not a total monster, Princess."

"You sure?" He shakes his head and grabs two glasses from the tray of blood-red drinks that we're offered by another zombie.

"I'm impressed," I say, staring down at the floating eyeball.

"Drink up, baby. I've got wicked plans for you tonight."

"When don't you?"

As a group, we move deeper into the building.

The place is off the hook. The decorations are impressive, and there are even animatronic zombies and mummies in dark corners which scare the ever-loving shit out of most of the guests—something we all spend way too long laughing at as we drink more fake blood than I'm sure is healthy before we find the huge makeshift dancefloor.

"Now this is how you're meant to dance, Hellion," Seb breathes in my ear, his hands clamped on my hips, my ass grinding against his semi. "These leggings are driving me insane," he admits.

"Wishing I chose the skirt so you could slip a hand up, huh?"

"You know me so well," he mutters, kissing down my neck.

Each song blurs into the next as the drinks we've consumed begin to really take effect. The room starts to spin a little as my body heats.

Turning in Seb's arms, I capture his lips, kissing him with everything I have and showing him just how I feel about him.

I haven't found the words yet, or at least not the confidence to confess them to him. He's all in with this, but there's still just a tiny bit of doubt right at the back of my mind, the memories of what we were at the beginning still just a little too fresh to be able to fully forget.

But I will. It fades that little bit more with every touch and every whispered promise he gives me.

Needing to catch my breath, I rest my head on his shoulder and just move with him, loving the feeling of his arms around me.

He tenses, something catching his eye, and when I look over, I find Theo and Alex trying to get his attention from the doorway.

"Sorry, baby. I'll be right back, okay? You good with Calli and Em?"

"Of course. Don't be too long," I say, not even caring that I sound like a love-sick fool.

He drops one more kiss on my lips before slipping from my hold.

Turning to my friends, I grab the last drink from a tray a zombie is carrying past me and knock it back in one before passing him the glass back. He nods before disappearing into the crowd.

"How freaking awesome is this party?" Calli shouts over the music. She's wasted, her eyes wild and her dancing completely out of time to the music filling the space around us.

"Yeah, you were right. This is pretty sweet."

I grab both of their hands and we dance together, not needing guys to enjoy ourselves.

As we move, my body begins burning up to the point that I have to stop moving and fan my face.

"You okay?" Emmie shouts.

"Yeah. I'm just going to get some air. I'll be back."

"You want us to come?" I glance at Calli with her head thrown back and her eyes closed.

"No, you stay with her," I say with a laugh.

As I push through the crowd, my need for some cool air begins to get the better of me.

My head spins, my legs start taking on a life of their own, and I find myself leaning against the wall.

Holy shit. What was in that drink?

Realization makes my eyes widen.

No. Surely no one would have...

I stumble through a door, hungrily sucking in some cool evening air as I rummage in my purse for my cell.

My vision swims as I stare at the screen. I think I find Seb's contact and hit call, but right as I put my cell to my ear, a figure appears around the corner of the building.

I don't know how I know. But I do instantly.

"Better run while you can, Estella Doukas."

Fear rips through me, and I do something I would never do if I were sober and not suffering from the effects of whatever that fucking drink had been spiked with.

I run.

"Stella? Stella?" A voice rings through the darkness as my feet lead me into the trees that surround the abandoned building. "Stella? Where are you, baby?"

Seb.

It's just Seb.

"I-I'm in the trees. He's here. He's here, Seb." I think I whisper it, but I'm quickly losing my grip on reality.

Footsteps get louder behind me, a twig snaps, and I scream like a little bitch.

"We're coming, baby. We're coming."

I collide with a tree and stumble back, falling on my ass, and when I look up, I find a dark figure looming over me and a gun pointed right at my head.

"You won't win this," I warn him, wishing like hell I had a fucking gun of my own strapped to me right now.

Think, Stella. Fucking think.

But my brain is mush.

"They're coming. And they're going to kill you, you motherfucker."

A gunshot rings out, making me flinch, and for a

second I wait for the pain to come, but it never does. And when I look up, he's gone.

I blink a few times as my guys—I assume—run deeper into the trees.

Echoed shouts filter down to me as I fight with my unwilling body to get to my feet.

Two more gunshots pierce the air, and my body jolts at the sound.

"NO," I hear someone scream. A voice I recognize.

The fear within it is the push I need, and my legs start moving. My lungs burn, my head spins, but I don't stop until I stumble through the trees and discover the outcome of those gunshots.

"No," I cry, seeing two bodies on the floor and recognizing instantly that neither are that of my stalker... but two of the most important people in my life.

Stella and Seb's story concludes in WICKED EMPIRE
ONE-CLICK NOW!

Wondering where Calli went while Stella and the guys were dealing with the stalker?
Read her steamy short story
DARK HALLOWEEN KNIGHT for FREE NOW!

THORN

CHAPTER ONE
Amalie

"I think you'll really enjoy your time here," Principal Hartmann says. He tries to sound cheerful about it, but he's got sympathy oozing from his wrinkled, tired eyes.

This shouldn't have been part of my life. I should be in London starting university, yet here I am at the beginning of what is apparently my junior year at an American high school I have no idea about aside from its name and the fact my mum attended many years ago. A lump climbs up my throat as thoughts of my parents hit me without warning.

"I know things are going to be different and you might feel that you're going backward, but I can assure you it's the right thing to do. It will give you the time you need to... adjust and to put some serious thought into what you want to do once you graduate."

Time to adjust. I'm not sure any amount of time will be enough to learn to live without my parents and being shipped across the Pacific to start a new life in America.

"I'm sure it'll be great." Plastering a fake smile on my face, I take the timetable from the principal's hand and stare down at it. The butterflies that were already fluttering around in my stomach erupt to the point I might just throw up over his chipped Formica desk.

Math, English lit, biology, gym, my hands tremble until I see something that instantly relaxes me, *art and film studies.* At least I got my own way with something.

"I've arranged for someone to show you around. Chelsea is the captain of the cheer squad, what she doesn't know about the school isn't worth knowing. If you need anything, Amalie, my door is always open."

Nodding at him, I rise from my chair just as a soft knock sounds out and a cheery brunette bounces into the room. My knowledge of American high schools comes courtesy of the hours of films I used to spend my evenings watching, and she fits the stereotype of captain to a tee.

"You wanted something, Mr. Hartmann?" she sings so sweetly it makes even my teeth shiver.

"Chelsea, this is Amalie. It's her first day starting junior year. I trust you'll be able to show her around. Here's a copy of her schedule."

"Consider it done, sir."

"I assured Amalie that she's in safe hands."

I want to say it's my imagination but when she turns her big chocolate eyes on me, the light in them diminishes a little.

"Lead the way." My voice is lacking any kind of enthusiasm and from the narrowing of her eyes, I don't think she misses it.

I follow her out of the room with a little less bounce in my step. Once we're in the hallway, she turns her eyes on me. She's really quite pretty with thick brown hair, large eyes, and full lips. She's shorter than me, but then at five foot eight, you'll be hard pushed to find many other teenage girls who can look me in the eye.

Tilting her head so she can look at me, I fight my smile. "Let's make this quick. It's my first day of senior year and I've got shit to be doing."

Spinning on her heels, she takes off and I rush to catch up with her. "Cafeteria, library." She points then looks down at her copy of my timetable. "Looks like your locker is down there." She waves her hand down a hallway full of students who are all staring our way, before gesturing in the general direction of my different subjects.

"Okay, that should do it. Have a great day." Her smile is faker than mine's been all morning, which really is saying something. She goes to walk away, but at the last minute turns back to me. "Oh, I forgot. That over there." I follow her finger as she points to a large group of people outside the open double doors sitting around a bunch of tables. "That's *my* group. I should probably warn you now that you won't fit in there."

I hear her warning loud and clear, but it didn't really need saying. I've no intention of befriending the cheerleaders, that kind of thing's not really my scene. I'm much happier hiding behind my camera and slinking into the background.

Chelsea flounces off and I can't help my eyes from following her out toward *her* group. I can see from here that it consists of her squad and the football team. I can also see the longing in other student's eyes as they walk past them. They either want to be them or want to be part of their stupid little gang.

Jesus, this place is even more stereotypical than I was expecting.

Unfortunately, my first class of the day is in the direction Chelsea just went. I pull my bag up higher on my shoulder and hold the couple of books I have tighter to my chest as I walk out of the doors.

I've not taken two steps out of the building when my skin tingles with awareness. I tell myself to keep my head down. I've no interest in being their entertainment but my eyes defy me, and I find myself looking up as Chelsea points at me and laughs. I knew my sudden arrival in the town wasn't a secret. My mum's legacy is still strong, so when they heard the news, I'm sure it was hot gossip.

Heat spreads from my cheeks and down my neck. I go to look away when a pair of blue eyes catch my attention. While everyone else's look intrigued, like they've got a new pet to play with, his are haunted and angry. Our stare holds, his eyes narrow as if he's trying to warn me of something before he menacingly shakes his head.

Confused by his actions, I manage to rip my eyes from his and turn toward where I think I should be going.

I only manage three steps at the most before I crash into something—or somebody.

"Shit, I'm sorry. Are you okay?" a deep voice asks. When I look into the kind green eyes of the guy in front of me, I almost sigh with relief. I was starting to wonder if I'd find anyone who wasn't just going to glare at me. I know I'm the new girl but shit. They must experience new kids on a weekly basis, I can't be that unusual.

"I'm fine, thank you."

"You're the new British girl. Emily, right?"

"It's Amalie, and yeah... that's me."

"I'm so sorry about your parents. Mom said she was friends with yours." Tears burn my eyes. Today is hard enough without the constant reminder of everything I've lost. "Shit, I'm sorry. I shouldn't have—"

"It's fine," I lie.

"What's your first class?"

Handing over my timetable, he quickly runs his eyes over it. "English lit, I'm heading that way. Can I walk you?"

"Yes." His smile grows at my eagerness and for the first time today my returning one is almost sincere.

"I'm Shane, by the way." I look over and smile at

him, thankfully the hallway is too noisy for us to continue any kind of conversation.

He seems like a sweet guy but my head's spinning and just the thought of trying to hold a serious conversation right now is exhausting.

Student's stares follow my every move. My skin prickles as more and more notice me as I walk beside Shane. Some give me smiles but most just nod in my direction, pointing me out to their friends. Some are just downright rude and physically point at me like I'm some fucking zoo animal awoken from its slumber.

In reality, I'm just an eighteen-year-old girl who's starting somewhere new, and desperate to blend into the crowd. I know that with who I am—or more who my parents were—that it's not going to be all that easy, but I'd at least like a chance to try to be normal. Although I fear I might have lost that the day I lost my parents.

"This is you." Shane's voice breaks through my thoughts and when I drag my head up from avoiding everyone else around me, I see he's holding the door open.

Thankfully the classroom's only half full, but still, every single set of eyes turn to me.

Ignoring their attention, I keep my head down and find an empty desk toward the back of the room.

Once I'm settled, I risk looking up. My breath catches when I find Shane still standing in the doorway, forcing the students entering to squeeze past him. He nods his head. I know it's his way of asking if I'm okay. Forcing a smile onto my lips, I nod in return and after a few seconds, he turns to leave.

THORN and the rest of the ROSEWOOD series are now LIVE.

DOWNLOAD TO CONTINUE READING

ABOUT THE AUTHOR

Tracy Lorraine is a *USA Today* and *Wall Street Journal* bestselling new adult and contemporary romance author. Tracy has recently turned thirty and lives in a cute Cotswold village in England with her husband, baby girl and lovable but slightly crazy dog. Having always been a bookaholic with her head stuck in her Kindle, Tracy decided to try her hand at a story idea she dreamt up and hasn't looked back since.

Be the first to find out about new releases and offers. Sign up to my newsletter here.

If you want to know what I'm up to and see teasers and snippets of what I'm working on, then you need to be in my Facebook group. Join Tracy's Angels here.

Keep up to date with Tracy's books at
www.tracylorraine.com

ALSO BY TRACY LORRAINE

Falling Series

Forbidden Series

Rebel Ink Series

Knight's Ridge Empire Series

Wicked Summer Knight: Prequel (Stella & Seb)

Wicked Knight #1 (Stella & Seb)

Wicked Princess #2 (Stella & Seb)

Wicked Empire #3 (Stella & Seb)

Deviant Knight #4 (Emmie & Theo)

Deviant Princess #5 (Emmie & Theo

Deviant Reign #6 (Emmie & Theo)

One Reckless Knight (Jodie & Toby)

Reckless Knight #7 (Jodie & Toby)

Reckless Princess #8 (Jodie & Toby)

Reckless Dynasty #9 (Jodie & Toby)

Dark Halloween Knight (Calli & Batman)

Dark Knight #10 (Calli & Batman)

Dark Princess #11 (Calli & Batman)

Dark Legacy #12 (Calli & Batman)

Corrupt Valentine Knight (Nico & Siren)

Ruined Series

Ruined Plans #1

Ruined by Lies #2

Ruined Promises #3

Never Forget Series

Never Forget Him #1

Never Forget Us #2

Everywhere & Nowhere #3

Chasing Series

Chasing Logan

The Cocktail Girls

His Manhattan

Her Kensington

Printed in Great Britain
by Amazon

38896487R00223